"A harmless man is not a good man. A good man is a very dangerous man who has that under voluntary control."

- Dr. Jordan Peterson

Dear Reader,

This is the first of many one-off side stories I wish to tell from the same world as Clint and his family. You see, I know we all want to know what happens next with Clint and the BDL and Logan and what antics Les and Arnie will be up to, but I feel it's important to remember that this event is hitting everywhere, not just in Boerne and San Antonio. I wanted the opportunity to introduce you to some other characters from this world and show you how they are handling things and how they may or may not be making it. This also gives me the chance to show other survival techniques that may work better in different geographies or scenarios that just wouldn't make sense for Clint and his group to end up in. I hope you enjoy this expanded view of the Crown Acres Universe.

- Caelen

Chapter 1

Mid-November

"Hey, gather up!" the guard yelled through the bullhorn from the relative safety of his tower.

The inmates gathered in the yard, looking at one another suspiciously. The breeze swirled small dust clouds across the ground and the bright sun was deceptive as it warmed the skin and dark areas of clothing, but the cool west Texas air bit at the ones that were foolish enough not to wear their hoodies and watchcaps. It was odd that about half of the inmates from inside had been herded out into the yard at the same time, regardless of their cell block. They'd all noticed that there wasn't any power in the building anymore, and the food they were being served was getting lighter and lighter at each meal. The commissary was closed and nobody got visitors, so they were writing letters to protest the conditions, but the guards weren't even doing a mail call anymore. Nobody knew what was going on, but they knew it was something.

"When I call your name, you step through that gate into Yard E," the guard announced.

The yard between the main prison wall and the tower was split by a fence that ran from the building out, separating A-Yard from E-Yard, and allowing one tower to easily cover both yards. Almost two dozen guards came pouring out of a door in the wall of the prison, forming a 3 rowed phalanx with full riot gear on, with shields and batons at the ready. The first two rows were clearly there to handle any disobedience, but the rear row of five was largely covered from view.

"Able, F., Able, R., Aristal, Ayous, Azzelle, Baldor, Banks, C., Banks, D., Banks, R., Bengar..." the guard began to read off.

One by one the men walked out of the crowd and through the doorway in the fence. There seemed to be no other pattern than alphabetical order that anyone could trace, as various prison gangs and ethnicities were mixed together on the other side.

"...Callen, Carter, F., Carter, G., Camber, Cash — KNOCK IT OFF ASSHOLES!!" the voice screamed as a small scuffle began between two inmates.

Apparently they were both after the inmate named Camber, and when he began to cross the yard they had each planned to attack him. A single, well aimed shot rang out from the tower, and put a hole in the ground directly in front of them. The round hadn't been rubber like they expected, and there was no tear gas either. As the packed clay of the west Texas dirt let a small curl of smoke up around the men's knees, every inmate in the yard seemed to realize all at once that this was not a standard drill.

"Keep fucking around, see what happens," the guard announced over the bullhorn, and after a brief pause he continued on, "Carter, M., Cazwell..."

Alexander Conary waited patiently for his name. He didn't know if having it called was a good thing or a bad one, but he wasn't the kind of man who liked to be kept waiting. He had no doubt that he would be safe crossing the yard if his name was called, he had kept his head down for the entire five-year stretch at FCI Big Spring, Medium-Security Federal. He had twenty-seven years left on his sentence, and hoped he would be on parole before his dick was limp and his head was full of jello.

Alex wasn't the kind of man most inmates wanted to cross. He was in his prime at 34 and stood six foot ten inches tall and tipped the scales at around 350 pounds of hard, steel-like muscle. He usually kept his thick, black hair pulled back in a ponytail, but whenever he found out he was going into Gen Pop he would leave it loose around his face. It looked more intimidating this way since it hid his eyes and had the added benefit of being harder for someone to grab ahold of if a fight broke out. His hands were large enough to palm a man's head, and seemed strong enough to crush it like a watermelon under a truck tire.

He had combined his intimidating appearance and reclusive nature to create the reputation of someone who liked to be left alone. He would meditate and read in his cell, walk during yard time and only entertain audiences with absolute <u>shot callers</u>, holy men and <u>drillers</u>. Most of the time politely but firmly rejecting the shot callers' offers, listening to the musings of the holy men, and employing the drillers for some new work or coverups.

He had never caused trouble for the guards, choosing to keep them at bay as well, but he was often addressed with a small amount of respect rather than open derision. He had no doubt they could, and would, make his life hell, but it seemed they were just as content to not go down that path as he was. Whenever they asked him a question of any kind, he responded with a "yes sir" or a "no sir" and only elaborated further by saying, "trying to do my time and get out."

Sure, there had been multiple attempts at recruiting him to one gang or another during his tenure. The Arian Brotherhood being the most persistent by far, but it really didn't matter that he was white and had a decidedly Greek/Irish name, everyone wanted him in their corner. His sheer size would give them an advantage in the yard, if only they could sway the behemoth to side with them. The Blacks, the Latin Kings, MS13... They all wanted him, but he had decided against alliances the day he arrived. He'd tried that before and wasn't going down that road again.

"...Celtor, Cemper, CeMal..." the guard continued on.

5

The whole reason he was in here was because of an alliance. He had been part of The Rebels Motorcycle Club before he came in, but after what happened he wasn't part of them anymore. He'd have to answer for that someday, but since the club didn't have anyone else in here and he was looking at no less than 25 years before he was eligible for parole, he had decided to worry about that later.

"Cifuentes, Cinamon, Ciprianno, Cisneros, D., Cisneros, F., Cisneros, L., Cisne -- ah screw it, if your last name is Cisneros, get over to E-Yard, Clay, Clayton…" the guard continued.

Alex was growing impatient. His last name started with a damn C, how was it taking so long to get to him? He looked around and of the 900 or so inmates the prison could hold it seemed like there were only about 300 standing in the yard. He didn't see any trustees or any of the short timers he knew of, but he didn't know many since he had chosen voluntary solitude over community.

The only other prisoner he'd ever even been close to was Alberto Ramirez, the trustee that brought him his books from the library and would occasionally sit with him during meals. The thin, lanky Mexican resembled John Leguizamo, but had a more calm, fatherly reproach than the actor's usual characters. He had a salt and pepper goatee that he would stroke when he thought about answers to questions Alex would ask. He'd been in for possession with intent to distribute and was rounding out his 7 years with only six months left to go, but Alex hadn't seen him in almost a week.

"Coleman, Comal, F., Comal, S., Conary, Conley…"

Alex slowly stepped forward. He was cautious not to get too excited since he wasn't sure whether he had won or lost quite yet. As the list ran on everyone seemed to relax a bit as

6

they were all called except around two dozen inmates. After the final name on the list was called the phalanx of guards moved over and closed the open gate between the yards, then turned back towards the remaining prisoners.

"You, back to your cells!" the amplified voice called from the tower.

At first the men began to challenge the decision, yelling, screaming at the guards, one pulling a weapon from his pocket. Alex couldn't tell if it was a shank or a shiv but it didn't really matter. The inmate was quickly dropped with a single round from the tower. He fell into a pile as the bullet exited his skull in a sticky gray explosion and everyone froze. The guards had done a lot of things. They'd gassed them, tased them, clubbed them with batons, but they'd never shot them. This was definitely *not* just another day inside.

The guards in the phalanx began pushing forward and the remaining inmates decided it wasn't worth fighting anymore. They turned and filtered back into the prison, the door closing behind them, their fallen companion bleeding into a pool on the ground as his body began to cool in the morning air. The guards turned and walked back over to the gate to E-Yard, filing in under the cover of the rifle in the tower.

"As you can see, if you act like animals, we will put you down like him," the megaphone barked as the guard on the tower catwalk pointed to the body on the ground.

The silence was deafening as the man walked back into the tower and a few minutes later emerged from the heavy metal door at the bottom. He was average sized, around five-foot-seven and built like a former athlete, with sandy blonde hair close cropped under a straw hat. Unlike most of the guards he wore a white button down shirt under his open prison jacket and, rather than a nametag, simply wore a patch that read "WARDEN."

The guards in riot gear moved to either side of him, and for the first time the shotguns being held by the men at the back of the formation were brought up to the front and clearly seen. They were black with wooden stocks and fore grips, not the bright orange plastic the inmates were used to seeing on the "less-lethal" models.

"Listen up! There's still three rifles up there pointed at y'all, and these shotguns aren't loaded with rubber rounds, so keep it civil or your lottery winnings here will be cut short," he boomed in a voice that belied his stature. "I'll start with the bad news. The power has been out for about two weeks and nobody knows why. Our generators ran out about a week and a half ago and we are on the last of our rations. We have been unable to get in contact with anyone and we have no guidance on what to do with any of you."

The men began to mumble and squirm a bit, unsure of what was about to happen. Some of them tried to move to the back of the gaggle of bodies, but Alex just stood still. His back was to the fence that separated them from A-Yard and he knew with his size there was no hiding if lead started to fly. He really would have given anything for a cigarette before being lined up for the firing squad.

"I only had a year left, man! You can't kill me!" one of the inmates yelled from the center.

"Shut up Gomez!" the warden yelled, "You keep it together and nobody gets shot. Like I said, y'all won the lottery. We've reviewed each of your files and decided that you are either short enough or low enough risk that you are going to be released with a few conditions."

Everyone gathered quieted immediately. If this was a joke it was another level of sickness, even for the most sadistic of the guards. Some of it was obviously true though, the power being out, the rations being thinned down... how much else was true?

"Condition 1: you will act in a civil manner, like human-fucking-beings as we process you out. If you start shit with one another or my guards, you will be put down. No second chance. Condition 2: you don't have to leave Big Spring, but if you do not have family in the area, you aren't going to be pushing anyone out of a home. You need to figure out how you're going to make a living," he paused and took a deep breath before continuing, "and finally, condition 3: you will be branded on both forearms with the initials 'BSPR' for 'Big Spring Prison Release.' This is not optional. If anyone in the area has a run-in with you, you are going to be put down. You will not be tried, you will not be given an appeal. If you are causing trouble and acting a fool, you are done. If you accept these conditions you can move over to this corner of the yard, if not, head back to A-Yard and we'll take you back inside," the warden gestured with his hand to the corner of E-Yard that was empty.

Some of the prisoners began to mutter among themselves, but a few of them took the opportunity and immediately walked over to the open corner. The brands would only add to their tattoos and the promise of getting out was enough for them to take the leap. Alex had been counting and he knew there were just under 250 inmates in the yard and only about two dozen had jumped at the offer. He pulled himself off the fence and raised a monstrous hand slowly over his head.

"Warden, can I ask a question?" he asked cautiously, not wanting to challenge the man who was offering him freedom.

"Go ahead, Conary," the warden answered with exasperation. He hadn't planned on fielding questions but the big man had always been respectful and maybe it would help move the others along.

"Actually, have a couple of questions, warden, but I think they go together. Where are the rest of the prisoners and trustees? What happens if we say no to the branding? How do we get out of Big Spring if we want?" the big man asked loudly.

"Good questions, and the only ones I'll be taking," the warden answered, "the trustees left last week. They were all given brands as well, but theirs had a 'T' instead of the 'P' and they have a slightly different deal where they were given jobs and shelter out the gate. If you say no to the branding, you're going back inside," he said frankly, "and believe me when I tell you, you don't want that. Finally, if you want out, we are going to take you out to one of the four corners of the city on a highway and drop you off there."

"What happens to those inside?" someone yelled from the crowd.

"They have been found irredeemable, their new sentence will be carried out tomorrow," the warden answered sadly.

It was clear he took no joy in knowing that he was ordering the execution of hundreds of men, but it was a fact. Some of the guards shifted nervously at the plan being said out loud, as though they'd been able to hide it from God until that moment, but it was now laid bare. The prisoners that were not being turned loose on society couldn't be left to starve, that was far too inhumane, but the alternative was to put the blood on their hands… literally.

"Seems like a pretty clear choice then," Alex said loudly as he walked over to the corner of the yard and joined the other men.

He was followed by a steady stream of inmates that grew until there was no one left on the other side of the yard. The warden nodded thankfully, glad that there were no more souls being added to the roster of who had to be taken care of inside. He held his hands out to his sides and gestured to the guards holding shotguns.

"You are not in the clear yet. Like I said, you will act like human beings. You mess with my guards or start any beef with one another and you will be put down. Period," he said. "We are going to move you into E-Block to stay warm while we start the outprocessing. You'll be called in order again, branded, and then given your personal possessions. After that, we have water bottles and a small rations package we'll give you, sort you into groups of who is going to leave from where and then move you out. Don't blow this opportunity, keep your heads on straight. I fear that you'll do better in the world we are releasing you into than you would have in the old one."

The men walked back into the building, laughing and shouting as they celebrated the early release they had only dreamed about before their yard experience. A few lamented that they had friends or allies who weren't in the yard and therefore were going to be put down, but most were simply happy that they were in the group they were in.

The guards put them all in a common area, calling the first ten inmates alphabetically to follow them to outprocessing. The men seemed nervous, knowing that the first step was to have searing hot metal pressed into their skin, but it seemed a small price to pay for their freedom. Alex had no idea where he was going to go since he wasn't from the area and had no family to return to.

He wished there was a way to get his bike back and ride until he couldn't find gas anymore, but he knew that would never happen. The first edition 1990 Fat Boy was long gone. He'd never see that beautiful chrome or the 22 different shades of green in the ghost flames that stretched over the fenders and tank. The bastards in the Rebels had made sure of that. He subconsciously brought his left hand up to his upper right arm and rubbed the Rebels tattoo he had never gotten around to covering up. It already felt like a searing hot brand anyway.

When his turn was called Alex followed the guard outside where they walked through the various yards that were now open from one to the next. As they entered E-Yard Alex saw the pool of blood in A-Yard where the prisoner had fallen, but the body was gone. They proceeded to follow the guard through the yards in reverse alphabetical order, D then C. He could smell the fire before he saw it, but it didn't take long to figure out why it was there. The coals of whatever they were burning were glowing almost white, with four long metal handles sticking out of the fire. The soon to be former inmates were separated into two lines of five, one on either side of the fire.

"Any volunteers to go first? It's better if you don't psych yourself up too much," one of the guards by the fire said honestly.

"Let's get it done," Alex said in his deep baritone of a voice.

The guard took a deep breath, obviously not liking this part of his job, and gestured to a wooden sawhorse with two leather duty belts running over it. Alex walked over and threaded his massive arms through the loops and the guard used his entire body weight to tighten them down. The belts barely stretched far enough to get one hole into the buckle between the thickness of the wood and the massive wrists combined. Once Alex was cinched down, the guard turned and grabbed one of the pokers from the fire, locking eyes with Alex.

"This is gonna hurt like Hell," he said softly.

"I know," the massive man replied, and without any countdown or warning, the guard plunged the branding iron into the inside of Alex's left forearm.

A lightning bolt of pain shot from his arm up into his shoulder then spread through his entire body. His jaw and fists clenched tightly, as though his teeth would shatter and his fingernails would tear into his own palm. His knees began to buckle and he felt his toes curl inside his boots. His eyelids were sealed tightly and just as the pain was beginning to subside he felt the hot lightning strike inside his right forearm as well. Apparently the guard had switched pokers in the middle of Alex's pain induced lack of focus and struck the other arm. Oddly enough it still felt like the poker was on his left arm as well. This time the pain did take the large man to his knees.

"Breathe," the guard said firmly, "breathe through it."

Alex focused on his breathing, willing the pain to pass. He saw the stars in his vision clear and slowly opened his eyes, becoming aware of the screaming coming from the opposite side of the fire from him. Another inmate was receiving his second brand and was already a blubbering puddle on the ground, nothing holding still except the area from his elbows down. Apparently the horses had originally been designed to go around the upper forearm on an average man.

"Conary, you good? Don't screw things up when I take these restraints off," the guard cautioned.

"I'm good, Sir," Alex said firmly.

He wanted to rip this man limb from limb. To beat him to a pulp. To see his olive skin fade to a hundred shades of green, purple and black as he pounded him over and over. He wanted to, but he knew this man was only doing him a kindness. The first step in releasing him rather than killing him.

As the restraints came off, Alex stood again and once he was cleared that the brand was deep enough to hold, he was brought inside and a prison doctor put A&D ointment on the burns and wrapped what appeared to be strips of a bed sheet over his wounds. The doctor asked his name, then pulled his file and reviewed it quickly. He confirmed that Alex didn't have any communicable diseases and wasn't on any medications necessary for survival, then gave him directions down the hall as the next branded inmate walked in.

Alex walked the hall, feeling oddly alone as there was no guard to escort him. The gates and doors to rooms were all open and he simply continued through them like he was in some twisted, sadistic highschool hallway. The only light in the halls came from the occasional window in one of the rooms to his left, which seemed to be why the doors were all open.

He wasn't entirely sure where he was supposed to be going, but then heard someone yell "turn around" from one of the open doors he had passed by. He turned and looked into the room to see a man on the other side of a large half-wall with a cage on top.

"Name?" he asked formally.

"Conary, Alexander," Alex replied.

"Hang on," the guard turned around and walked back into rows of shelves and boxes, returning with a bin and setting it on the counter. He pulled a slip out of a clear plastic pocket on the top and began to read down the list of items. "Denim jeans - one, black leather boots - one pair with laces…" he continued down the list as Alex opened the bin and looked through his only possessions in this world, "you can change in that room," he said as he jutted his pen towards one of the doors on the side of the room.

After he'd fought his way around in the 4 foot squared room and changed his clothes Alex came back out to the now empty counter and left his inmate jumpsuit, jacket and other articles in a pile on the countertop. He was surprised that the lighter and pocket knife were already being returned to him, having half expected them to have disappeared in the shuffle. He was trying to figure out where he was supposed to go next, when the guard returned with a mesh laundry bag containing some sheets, a couple of blankets and the few personal possessions he'd had in his cell.

"Nope, you get to hold onto any of this stuff you want. I'd recommend the carhart and watch cap at least. It's not getting any warmer out. We grabbed some extra socks and underwear, some other stuff we could find in your size, but for you there wasn't much," the guard said kindly, "but we threw in a little extra food and stuff so you can try to trade for something."

"Thanks," Alex replied, not even opening the bag. He grabbed everything from the pile he'd put on the counter and stuffed it into a laundry bag, leaving only the prison coveralls on the counter. He had been tempted to toss the leather and denim vest with the huge "Rebels" club patch onto the counter and leave it there, but the fact that they were giving so much made him think it might be worth holding onto.

"You'll take a right out of here, go five gates down and there will be someone there to load you on the bus you want to go on," the guard finished, "good luck."

Alex threw his laundry bag over his shoulder and took a right in the hallway, walking through five gates. He could occasionally hear other inmates behind him, either screaming from the branding or protesting something or another. It was amazing how the sounds echoed down the halls without the buzzing and clattering of lights and electronic gates covering them. When he arrived at the end of the hallway there was another guard, one of the newer guys, with a clipboard. He was at least a foot shorter and probably two hundred pounds lighter than Alex, and would have likely been eaten alive by the inmates if the circumstances hadn't changed.

"Uh, n-name?" the young guard asked as the large man in full biker regalia approached him.

"Conary, Alexander," Alex answered him.

"And, uhm, where are you going Conary?" the guard continued through his script.

"I'd like to request whichever direction has the fewest other inmates going that way. I don't have anywhere to go, but I don't want to go where the rest of them are headed," Alex replied.

"East it is. So far most of the inma—er—released men have been talking about Midland, Lubbock or San Angelo. If that changes, we'll let you know," the guard jotted down on his clipboard.

"Sounds good. Where should I wait?" Alex looked around as he asked.

"Everyone is gathering in the chow hall until we outprocess y'all. You can wait there," the guard replied as he pointed to the door to his left.

Alex walked in and sat at a corner table, keeping his distance from the group. The population in the chow hall was growing and people were still breaking off into old cliques. It reinforced to him that he wanted to go where there were as few of these folks as possible, because as soon as they were on the outside, dumb shit was bound to happen. Alex was minding his own business, trying to avoid the glances in his direction, when he saw the warden headed his way.

"Conary, where are you headed?" the warden asked him.

"Wherever as few of these folks are as possible," Alex replied. The warden simply smiled and nodded his head as though he already knew that would be the answer.

"I read your file, you know," he continued, "if you hadn't been in a club and hadn't actually killed those men you probably would have just gotten probation."

"So I've heard," Alex replied dryly. He had no interest in rehashing his case with the warden.

"I'm only bringing this up, because I think you're actually a decent guy. You kept your head down, never started trouble, treated us with respect. I'm curious because if you don't have anywhere to go, I might have an option for you," the warden said as he sat down across from the large man.

"Yeah? What's that?" Alex asked. He wasn't sure he wanted to hear the offer, but he knew it was a start.

"You and a couple of the others like you, well, my family has a farm on the outskirts of town towards Coahoma, near Moss Lake. It's not much, but it does produce. I need strong men who are willing to help work it though," the warden carefully proposed his plan.

"So you're telling me this, thinking that if I was to say yes, great, but if I wasn't interested I wouldn't come looking for trouble?" Alex asked.

"Something like that. Plus Ramirez vouched for you. He's out there now with another trustee," the warden answered.

"Let me think about it for a bit, warden," Alex replied. It really wasn't a bad deal, and knowing Ramirez was there would at least put a familiar face on the deal.

"Fair enough. I'll check with you before we load up. If you're game I'll take you straight there with the others," the warden said as he stood, "you'd be a huge help, and there's not much else out there other than bad stuff."

"I said I'll think it over," Alex replied definitively.

He knew the warden was right of course, it was always going to be tough to get out. Where most inmates would just go back to their old ways and old friends, Alex had burned every bridge that he had. There was nothing out there for him anyway, and he'd always imagined he would just kind of ride off into the sunset on a stolen Harley until the Rebels found him.

But if the world really was coming unglued out there, it wouldn't even be that easy. He was trying to figure out the warden's angle and how this was all supposed to play out as he watched the warden walk away, approaching a large Hispanic man that was also sitting by himself.

Alex kicked the idea around for the next couple of hours. The pros were easy to see, food, a bed, some form of security while he figured out what was going on in the world. The cons were tougher to see though. He was so used to trying to find the angle on everything, who would benefit, who was going to try to screw him, how would he get out if it turned sour... but this didn't fit the mold. The warden was stacking the deck against himself by bringing out multiple convicts and simply asking for labor and security. Was he really going to give them tools? Weapons? How the Hell was he going to maintain control if they wanted to leave? As the chow hall filled in, the warden found his way back over.

"Time's getting short, Conary, you made a decision yet?" he asked.

"What happens if I decide I want to leave after I've been there?" Alex pushed back.

"You walk away. This isn't a work detail or a probationary release program. This is just a chance to land on your feet and maybe help some others out," came the honest reply.

"This doesn't make sense, warden," Alex continued, "you claim there's no power, no computers, the world is going to shit and people are getting illegal and your solution is to bring home criminals?"

"Well when you say it like that it sounds really stupid," the warden grinned back.

"That's because it is," Alex replied, failing to see the humor in the matter.

"Look, everything will be explained better when it comes time, but for right now, I just need you to decide if you're in or not," the warden answered, more seriously now.

"Alright, I'm in, but you'd better not be bullshitting me, warden, or I'll kill you," he said finally.

"Wouldn't dream of it," the warden smiled back, "and call me Todd. You just stay here, I'll send the others over to you and after the buses leave we'll get you out to the farm."

Alex tried to relax as the warden, "Todd," walked away to gather the other men he'd gotten sign off from. Todd... the name didn't fit. About a month after he'd arrived Alex had seen the warden jump into a brawl where a guard was on the ground. He had a club in each hand and was clearing men left and right. He'd been busted up a bit himself, but at the end of the day the prisoners definitely got the worst of it.

Todd...

Huh...

A group of three men came walking over, led by a large Hispanic man with tattoos up and down his arms, a bandana tied around his bald head and a Cottonmouth Kings shirt on under a flannel button down and a pair of cholo shorts, with his socks pulled up underneath, past the bottom hem.

"Jefe says to wait with you," he said as he sat heavily in the chair across from Alex and extended a hand, "names Guillermo DelRio, most folks just call me Guille."

"Alex," he replied as he took the offered hand and shook it.

He noticed the Latin Kings tattoos on the man's arms. The crown covering a hand with thumb, index and pinkie fingers extended, the ALKN and 5 point star on his hands. His brands were also covered with thin strips of cloth, the A&D ointment beginning to seep through a bit. There was a good chance that Guille was used to being the biggest guy in the room, but he was still smaller than Alex by a good 4 inches and around fifty pounds.

The two other men sat down in chairs near them as well, introducing themselves as Oscar and Grady. Neither of them would ever qualify as heavyweights, but they weren't small either. Grady was a clean cut black man who wore a button-down shirt and slacks over dress shoes and looked as though he'd never been in a fight in his life despite having been locked up.

The Hispanic man named Oscar spoke with a different accent than most of the Mexican inmates. Still obviously from Central America, but not using the same inflection or emphasizing the same syllables as the Mexican inmates. He wore his prison issued Carhartt over a wifebeater shirt and black denim jeans. He was wiry with the type of musculature that some boxers had, indicating his hits might not hurt on their own, but he'd throw so many, so fast, that he was dangerous in a fight. He was truly covered in tattoos, from the tips of his fingers, up his arms and chest, his throat, even his face and shaved head.

Seeing Oscar covered in MS13 tattoos sitting next to Guille with his tattoos from a rival gang laughing and clowning on one another certainly set Alex at ease a bit. If these two gang members that should have been bitter rivals were willing to grill up their beef and eat it, then maybe this wasn't such a bad idea.

"So, you really think this is on the up-and-up?" Grady asked. He had a worried look on his face, as though he hadn't really trusted the warden either.

"I don't know, but I'll say this, if all four of us decide we aren't going to play nice, he'd better have some heavy artillery. There's gotta be over eleven hundred pounds of ex-con here, not something most people wanna piss off," Oscar replied through his toothy, gold-plated grin and face full of ink.

Alex did some quick math and figured Oscar was probably right. It didn't take much to see the two smaller men at 250 pounds a piece, and he and Guille easily covered the remaining 600. It was an interesting crew for sure, a Latin King, a flashy MS13 banger, the mulatto complexion of Grady and the large white biker. The four of them would have never been caught dead at the same table before today, and it was hard to ignore the looks they were still getting from others assembled in the chow hall. Maybe these four really were different.

They went on to hash out a little about themselves. Oscar and Guille were both in for boosting cars and possession of narcotics, Grady was in for a DWI where he'd hit a couple coming home from a dinner out. They didn't die, but they were in really bad shape after the accident. All Alex told them was that he was in for three counts of third-degree murder. They all got quiet when he said it, and he just let it hang in the air.

The silence was deafening as other inmates were called out and filed out to their waiting buses, loaded on like school children headed home at the end of the day. Heavily inked and pierced school children with bags of bedding and food and a dicey disposition. Finally, the warden came walking over and broke the awkward silence.

"Alright guys, let's load up in the van out there and we'll head out," he said.

"Thank God," Grady muttered as the men gathered their supplies and walked out into the sunlight of the vehicle yard.

The buses had already left with the other released inmates and the warden climbed into the front of the ancient Ford Econoline van. They were getting situated in the creaking old seats that clearly dated back to the mid-70's when they heard a series of shots ring out.

"What the fuck was that?" Oscar asked abruptly as he tried to spin in his seat and see what was going on.

"We felt it was a waste of resources to wait until tomorrow," was all the warden said as he put the vehicle in drive and pulled out the front gate.

Chapter 2

The group was shocked to see vehicles all over the road as they drove through Big Spring. Although none of them were actually from the area, they couldn't help but notice that they were passing brand new vehicles stranded on the sides of the road and people were traveling on bicycles, horseback and walking instead. There were faces peeking out through windows of houses at the sound of the vehicle driving by and one man even drew a rifle until he saw the writing on the side of the van.

"What the hell is going on here man?" Oscar asked in astonishment.

"We don't really know to be honest. It was Halloween night, everything was fine. Kids were trick-or-treating and people were gathering at some of the local spots to party. The football team was up 14-6 and everyone was expecting to see the teens out 'dragging Gregg Street' like they always do on weekends. The world was normal. Then, out of nowhere, everything went down. No power anywhere in town. Vehicles stopped working, the computers went down, the water stopped flowing. It was bad," Todd said, his mind seeming to drift off. "The first couple of hours were okay, even into Saturday morning. That's when it got really bad…" He didn't seem to have anything else to say on the matter, and changed the subject.

Todd the warden went on to inform them that they had to take FM 700 to the south of the city because I-20 to the North was the route that people on foot were allowed to take around the city but not stop, and 4th street through the center of town was crowded with stalled out cars that hadn't been moved yet and the remnants of the rioting that took place a couple days after everything went dark.

He said that the hospital at Scenic Mountain was still up and running on some back-up power that they were using sparingly. The leadership at Howard College was trying to coordinate the city and organize people to work together but it was proving to simply be too large. Crime was running rampant, people stealing from one another, assault, rape, even murder.

The men in the van sat in stunned silence. Being told that the world had caught up to them at the bottom of society, that everything was falling apart and people were devolving to their level was shocking.

"Dios mio," Guille sighed, "how far does this go?"

"Don't know. We've heard it's everywhere, from Panama up to Canada, but we aren't sure," Todd replied.

"I mean, my abuelita in Las Guaras didn't even have power to her house, so I doubt many of them even know it happened, but this place... and what about the cities?" Oscar asked.

"As far as anyone knows they are a total shitshow. We tried to warn those who wanted to head to bigger cities about what was going on, but they insisted on going. I guess if my family was in Lubbock or Abilene I might try too, but I can only imagine what's going on in San Antonio, Dallas, El Paso, and beyond," Todd replied as he slowed in front of a large roadblock. He rolled down the window as a man with a bulletproof vest and rifle approached the driver's side door.

"Morning Deputy," Todd said out the window, "what do you know?"

"Nothing' worth telling'. This more of your releases?" the man outside the window drawled.

"Yes sir, headed out towards Coahoma," Todd replied as the deputy walked around the front of the vehicle and opened the large sliding door.

The cool wind pushed in through the large opening and chilled the inside of the vehicle as the deputy stood there looking over the four large men that each had a seat to themselves in the back. He sniffed hard and coughed up flem into his mouth before spitting a loogie on the ground.

"I advised against cuttin' y'all loose. I said we should just lock the gates and let you eat one another, but I was overridden. The sheriff and the warden here seem to think there's something redeemable about y'all. Do not let me see anyone with one of those branding scars running around starting trouble. I will shoot you in the gut and let you bleed out. Got me?" the angry deputy spat the words at the recently freed men in the back seat.

"Gee, you must be a load of fun at parties," Oscar said sarcastically.

"What did you say?" the deputy growled as he started to climb into the vehicle, reaching for his baton on his belt.

"Well, can't waste fuel resources chatting, deputy, we'll have to catch up later!" Todd yelled as he hit the gas and the vehicle lurched forward, spilling the deputy out into the highway.

He kept his footing and glared at the passing van as Alex pulled the sliding door closed and all five men inside burst out laughing. Grady looked out the back window and saw the deputy stewing in the street before he marched off towards the roadblock, likely to scold them for letting the vehicle through before he had given explicit permission.

"Deputy Orville Carver, a real shithead," Todd said from the front of the vehicle, "he's ruthless. He proposed that we basically turn you into slaves. Put you to work as field hands and laborers, even trade you off to other communities for resources. When that didn't fly he wanted to just open the interior of the prison, lock the gates outside and let you starve."

"So when he said he wanted to let us eat each other, he meant literally?" Guille asked.

"How is what he wanted to do any different from what you're doing, warden? Aren't we just labor for you?" Alex interrupted before Todd could answer.

"Yeah, unfortunately he was serious," Todd answered, "and look guys, nobody really knows what I'm doing with y'all except my family, a few neighbors out there and you. This isn't slave labor by any means, but don't think for a minute that it's a free ride either. I told you you're going to work and I damn well meant it, but now you can see how most people are looking at things."

"Shiiiiit, give me a leaf blower El Jefe! I'll have your yard looking amazing muy rápido!" Oscar joked from the back seat.

"You're not even Mexican pendejo!" Guille laughed.

"I'm whatever he wants me to be to not have to eat people," Oscar said seriously.

"Hell, *I'll* be Mexican if that's what it takes," Grady chuckled.

The men in the vehicle couldn't help but laugh as Oscar rattled off various ideas for beautifying a farm he'd never seen before. He was going to paint the fences, turn the fields, pick the oranges and peppers, shoe the horses, and more when they finally turned off FM700 and onto the eastern tail of I-20. They passed another checkpoint, but since they were headed out of town they weren't even slowed down.

They continued down the highway to Exit 184 for Moss Lake Rd and turned off, traveling the gridded roads back to Old Colorado City Highway, which they followed for a bit before turning off onto the dusty packed caliche driveway, turning over the cattle guard that ran from one side of the drive to the other between large metal fence posts.

The farm was little more than a few buildings and one large live oak. The driveway came back about two hundred yards from the road where it turned into a pin head around the ancient tree with a very Rockwellian tire swing hanging from a large branch. The house was a classic farmhouse design that had been built God only knows when. The white wooden siding and dark asphalt shingles gave it a quaint appearance. There was a wrap-around porch on the first level, complete with porch swing and white, turned-spoke railing.

The van slowed to a stop and the large men climbed out as it shifted, rocked and groaned with the release of over a half ton of weight. As they looked around the land they could see and smell the freshly turned lome in the fields, and the only other buildings on the farm were the large barn, what seemed to be a freshly built outhouse and one other building that Alex couldn't quite identify. Todd walked around the front of the van and cleared his throat.

"Well, this is it gents. We sit on about five acres of land here, but the neighbors are friendly and want to come together, so we have around forty acres total we can farm. Some of it will be handling goats and cattle, some of it will be fields planted with potatoes, carrots, greens, and anything else we can get to grow without crazy amounts of water. There's a few spots around here we can draw water from with the tractors, but there's only so much we can use between rains," Todd said as he gestured around the farm.

"Now, if you want to leave, the road is right behind you. You can walk out whenever, head back to the highway, Big

Spring is to the West where the sun sets, Coahoma to the East where it rises. You're free men here," he continued, "you'll be sleeping in the barn there, there's a bunk house on the back side, already has two trustees staying in it. Ramirez and Walton if you knew either of them."

"Yo, Ramirez was cool as shit man! He used to bring me hooch, I mean, Gatorades," Oscar tried to recover since the hooch was contraband and he didn't want to get either of them in trouble.

"Yeah, I know," Todd grinned at him, "he's actually in the process of trying to make something that's tolerable now so we can start trading it off."

"Sweet, he makes a good hooch," Oscar grinned.

"Well, hopefully it will be even better since it doesn't have to be hidden anymore, but it's not for us to drink, it's for trading," Todd said as he stared directly at Oscar.

"*No comprende Ingles...*" Oscar replied in his thickest, best Speedy Gonzales impression, holding his hands out as though he was truly confused.

"Es para intercambiar, no de beber," Todd grinned back.

"Que mierda..." Oscar grumbled as he kicked a rock and everyone around him, even Alex, started laughing.

"Alright, get your stuff in the bunkhouse guys, we'll have dinner tonight and talk about what you can do and answer any questions, introduce you to the family and friends and such," Todd said. "Tonight starts guard duty, Alex, I'd like you to take a shift with me."

Alex nodded as the others grabbed their laundry bags and headed towards the bunkhouse door on the back side of the barn. He picked up his stuff and walked towards Todd who was standing under the large live-oak in front of the house, looking over his shoulder.

"Hey warden, I've got a suggestion," he said.

"You can call me Todd, and what's that?" he asked.

"If you go back to the prison, there's a whole section in the library about animal husbandry, crops, planting, even a few survival books. Guys used to check them out until they realized it was just what plants to eat and how to start a fire and not stuff that would help them break out, but there was some other good stuff in them too," Alex offered.

"Yeah, um, I'll look into it when I go back tomorrow," Todd replied as he nervously looked over his shoulder.

Alex looked back through the window of the house and saw two young kids looking back. One of them waved at him through the gauzy linens on the window before the arm of an unseen adult whisked them both away. He looked back down into the eyes of the man in front of him and saw him nervous for the first time.

"You've got kids in there," Alex said. It wasn't a question by any means, he'd seen them and Todd knew it.

"My sons and a daughter, yes. They're three and five, she's eight and they don't understand what's going on. That's why I needed you and the others. I needed big guys to keep us safe. You'll see tonight, but most of the folks out here are older, they aren't going to be able to fight if it comes to it, but we can work the fields and have trade goods and be safe if we have guards like you guys," he answered.

"This was a stupid idea, warden. What happens when one of the guys you picked turns on you? You want us walking guard duty then you'll need to arm us with something. I'm guessing the arm that just pulled them back from the window was your wife? What happens when one of us animals gets hungry and she's the only thing around to eat? What about your kids?" Alex was truly shocked. For some reason when the warden had said "his family" he expected it to be a true family plot with parents and siblings and the rest, but not little kids like that.

"I know Conary, that's why I invited you here. I saw your file. I know why you were in and I don't think you'd tolerate that. Guille and Oscar were gangbangers, but they aren't the kind that would hurt kids. They took beat downs inside because they had refused to target kids when they were outside and Grady made a stupid choice, but never even meant to hurt anyone. He was a highschool teacher for crying out loud!" Todd replied, "I only offered to the four of you because I didn't think you'd do that, but there were others that were released, others that even wanted to come East that would. I can't defend them all, all the time. We needed guards, but you, we needed someone like you. You were willing to kill your own club members to—"

"I know what I did, warden. I know why I did it too, and it's damn stupid of you to assume you can count on me to do it again," Alex grumbled, "I'm going to the bunkhouse- get the books from the prison so we can start learning."

Alex turned and walked to the barn, leaving the warden behind him hanging his head and questioning if he had made the right choice or if he had just endangered his entire family because he made an assumption about the large man. Even though the mercury would have said it was a warm day the wind cut across the opening between the barn and the house and made it feel particularly chilly as the large man walked to the back of the barn to join his compatriots.

The large, old barn might have been a sight to see in its day, but that day was long since past. The siding was pale and weather-worn wood, with the paint having long ago faded and chipped away, the occasional piece of vertical clapboard siding broken off in some random place. It had to be 200 feet long and fifty feet wide, with the huge swinging doors in the front sagging on their ancient hinges. The 2-story front portion still housed livestock and equipment of various types, but at some point in the building's history someone had added a bunkhouse to the back. There was a clear line where the newer siding picked up and covered the addition on the first level, complete with windows and an individual door that opened into the living area.

As Alex opened the door he heard Oscar and Guille yelling at one another in <u>Spanglish</u> as they argued about something to do with bunk arrangements. There seemed to be only two lower bunks left and Alex was not in the mood to argue the point. The large man walked over to one of the remaining bunks and tossed his bags on the bed.

"Is this a problem?" he growled as he looked around the room.

"Nah hermano, we knew you'd need that one, but this little gusano thinks he's going to take one too and he can be a top bunky," Guille replied.

"C'mon man! I roll out of bed and if you put me on top I'mma roll out and–" *SMACK* Oscar slapped his hands together loudly, "caiga de culo!"

"If you get on the bottom bunk I'll bust your ass for you!" Guille laughed back.

"Pinche mojado..." Oscar pouted as he tossed his gear up on a top bunk.

"Awww... pobrecito," Guille chided him, "do you need a hug?" Oscar flipped him the bird as he grabbed his shave kit and stomped to the bathroom area that also contained two showers.

"Short shower! We don't know how much water they have," Grady yelled after him.

The rest of the group unpacked their minimal gear, rolling out their sheets and blankets. They were well matched to the standard, prison issue mattresses and pillows that the warden had apparently snagged for them. The place was actually starting to feel like home with the familiar drapings, sights, sounds and smells. Just as Grady was hanging a picture of his family on the wall next to his top bunk there was a loud scream from the bathroom. Oscar came running out, naked as the day he was born with water running down his back.

"Aye chingow! There's no hot water!" he screamed.

"Who's the mojado now!?" Guille crowed as he and the rest of the room burst out laughing at Oscar's expense.

"Cállate!" he screamed at them before walking back into the shower area.

"Guess it'll be easy to keep showers short," Grady chuckled.

Oscar's shower was going to be done much faster than he had originally planned, but he was going to do his best to get cleaned up for the first time in a week. When he came walking out again, this time fully dressed, the rest of the group was sitting at the large dining table dealing cards around and playing "War." They were debating starting a game of "Spades" when the door opened and Ramirez walked in.

"Qué paso, boys?" the thin former-trustee announced with a huge smile as he walked in. He was in his late forties and although he was by no means old, he had a certain worldliness to himself. While his hair and beard were mainly thick and black there was more than a little salt sprinkled through the pepper as well. He was the shortest man there at only five and a half feet tall and any one of the inmates in the room could have snapped his thin frame like a toothpick if they chose, but none had a reason to.

"Hey! Ramirez!" Oscar yelled as he shook hands with him and threw an arm over his shoulder.

"How are you Alberto?" Alex asked him as he stood and shook his hand.

"Life is good man, life is good," he answered.

The group said their pleasantries and discussed how messed up the situation was, how great it was to be out, and so on. When Walton came in from his duties Ramirez made it a point to introduce him as well and everyone got situated for dinner. They were to sit at the bunkhouse table and dinner would be brought out to them by Todd and some neighbors. They were just getting back to discussing the possibility of a round of Spades when there was a knock at the door.

Walton had always seemed a little off to Alex, but he couldn't put his finger on why. He wasn't a bad guy, and seemed to just be socially awkward and unaware of how what he did made him seem to others. He was just over five-feet tall but round in the middle, causing him to have a slight waddle when he walked. Even with the reduction in food it seemed like Walton was still maintaining his girthy appearance.

"Evening gents, who's ready for some grub?" Todd asked as he stepped in through the door.

He carried a plate of pork chops with a half-dozen thick slabs of bone-in meat on it, followed by another man who had a large bowl of mashed potatoes, and a woman who carried a tray of carrots that had been grilled. The feast was laid out in front of the ex cons as an older woman set a jug of milk on the table and then went to a cupboard and took some plates and glasses down.

"Now this is <u>raw milk</u>, so don't drink too much right away or it'll turn your stomach," she said cheerfully.

"I didn't know you had to cook milk? I've been drinking it raw for years," Oscar said seriously.

"It's called pasteurization, and they did it before it was sent to the store," Alex informed him.

Oscar took his turn pouring a glass and sniffed the milk, then took a small taste. He didn't exactly turn his nose up but it was clear that it was different than he had been expecting. The dishes were passed around and the men each took a scoop of the food before passing it on, all under the watchful eye of the warden.

"This isn't prison anymore guys, take some food. You're going to need it," Todd urged.

"We brought out your share. Think of it as your wages since money isn't good for much more than toilet paper anymore," the older man said.

It had been a long time since the four newcomers at the table had tasted food like this. The pork had fat on it and the bone had added flavor they never could have dreamed of inside. The carrots were fresh and sweet and popped in their mouths and the potatoes had actual butter on them, melting down the sides and exploding in creamy morsels on their tongues.

"And who are these folks?" Alex asked as he scanned the room and chewed on a chunk of pork.

"Oh, sorry, forgot to do introductions," Todd apologized, "this is my wife, Jessica, my mother Donna and my step-father

Gordon. They live on the farm next to us and have around 20 head of cattle. Later you'll meet some other folks around here that have some chickens, goats, and pigs and such."

Gordon held himself like a former cop or guard. There was no doubt that he had worked in the system at some point the way his hard eyes passed over each man at the table. It was an attempt at dominance, just a reminder that he wasn't afraid of them.

Unlike her husband, Donna maintained a pleasant and caring demeanor the entire time. She was a short, round woman that had thin hair that was difficult to distinguish in color. It would fade from blonde to silver and back, and showed signs of where it used to be well maintained but had fallen into disarray since the world had changed.

Jessica was an olive skinned, dark-haired stunner. In another world she could have been a movie star or a model, but she had apparently chosen the life of a prison guard's wife instead. She was in a conservative blue dress with her dark hair pulled back into a ponytail. She glided around the table, focusing on the meal and never meeting the eyes of her guests.

"More of our tasks?" Alex continued, he'd moved on to mixing the carrots and potatoes together and scooped a large portion into his mouth.

"Well, yes, there's about five farms out here in our little co-op, and we need help all the way around. None of the livestock herds are very big and most don't require much tending other than what they did before, the main concern we have is rustlers and thieves. It's getting pretty common that we chase someone off almost every day or night, sometimes multiple people," Todd continued.

"So we're gonna be like the Regulators from that old cowboy movie?" Oscar chimed in with a mouthful of mashed potatoes.

"Young Guns isn't an *old* movie, you're just a youngin," Ramirez grinned at him as he waved his fork accusingly.

"I'm with him on this one, that's an old movie," Guille piped in.

"I nominate the two youngins to shovel pig shit," Gordon laughed.

Everyone at the table chuckled and the two younger men quickly changed their tunes and started praising the cinematic masterpiece and timelessness of the classic film "Young Guns." There were brief introductions of the ex cons and, to set the minds of the others at ease, a brief discussion of what each had done to get where they were. The last in line was Alex, who sat quietly as the heads all turned to him.

"I was in for three counts of third-degree murder," he said, then picked up the bone on his plate and started chewing on the meat that remained, offering nothing more.

"That's all we get?" Guille asked, "c'mon man, tell us what happened."

"I told them to stop what they were doing. They didn't, so I made them," Alex wanted desperately to put an end to this.

He made a habit of reliving the event in his head multiple times a day during meditation and reflection in his cell, but he hadn't said what had happened out loud since his hearing. He didn't need anyone telling him what he did right or wrong or could have done differently. It was done, and it had cost him everything.

"Alex, we'd really like to know the kind of person you are if you are going to be living here, but I understand if you aren't ready to trust us yet," Jessica said as she crossed the room and took Todd's hand, "my husband has seen your file, he says you are trustworthy, and I trust him."

The room got quiet and everyone looked to Alex, waiting for him to take the moment to relay his story. He chewed on his bone like a dog that had been cornered, long black hair hanging down over his face making it hard for anyone to see exactly where his eyes were looking.

"Thanks," he finally replied.

It was as if someone had pricked a balloon with a pin and let all of the air and tension out of the room. There was clear disappointment in some of their faces, but they would have to wait. He wasn't looking to be pressured and he damn sure wasn't going to stick around if this became a regular thing.

"Alright, you guys enjoy, we'll leave you to it," Todd said as he started to usher his family out, "Alex, can you meet me on the porch of the house at sundown?" Alex simply grunted his acknowledgement and nodded his head in reply.

The four family members walked out and left the men gathered around the table. It was quiet until Guille started talking about the bones and wanting to boil them down for a broth. That sparked a discussion over how best to season a bone broth and whose grandmother had done it how and with what. Alex let them talk. His grandmother had been the only sweet woman in his life and he took the opportunity to let his mind drift back.

He'd always been a bit of a wild child, but the six years he'd lived with his grandmother in HIllsboro Georgia had been the best years of his life. His mom got locked up when he was eight. It was hard to remember what for, she'd been in and out most of her life. His dad was military and Alex was the result of a one-night party before his dad deployed to Panama. It would be just his luck that of only 23 Americans killed during Operation Just Cause one of them would be his dad.

When his mom got locked up again he was sent to live with his dad's mother, the only Grandma he'd ever known. From eight to fourteen he ran around the hills of the Piedmont National Wildlife Refuge, camping, fishing, and trapping. The family had almost nothing, but lived on some land in an old, one room trapper-style cabin. It was just him and his grandmother, but it was the most love he'd ever felt.

He'd set traps for rabbits and squirrels and other critters or wet a line for catfish, crappie and occasionally bass then bring his haul back to her and she'd cook it up with something from her vegetable garden or some wild concoction when there was something particularly tasty in season. In the fall they would take a deer or two and cure the meat, eat their fill for days on end. It was the highlight of his life.

Although most people would have only seen a simple mountain woman when they looked at her, they would have been sorely mistaken. She was brilliant. Before giving up on the modern hustle and bustle of the world she had received a degree in modern educational philosophy from UCLA. Her prized possessions were a complete set of encyclopedias and mountains of books.

She had Plato, Nietzche, Descartes, Voltaire and more. She made sure that Alex had a well balanced education in that backwoods shack, learning math from Descartes, Newton and Russel, geography from Bel and al-Biruni, science from Aristotle, Plato, and Einstein. He loved that, unlike the teachers he'd had before, she never told him what to think, but asked him what he thought and then made him defend it. She was loving, but tough, fair, but challenging. Like almost all of his memories though, it would go from a wonderful, pleasant musing to a bitter trauma before long.

One morning he left with the old lady still asleep. He took some cornbread from the night before and some homemade blackberry jam, grabbed his poles and went out to gather dinner. He spent the day fishing, setting traps, and running through the woods. He was only 14 and still loved to climb trees and explore the random caves he would find in hillsides. At the end of the day he returned home with a game sack stuffed to the top with catfish and rabbit and was ready to celebrate in style with a feast for dinner. He opened the door to the small cabin and found her lying on the floor. He ran to her side and rolled her on her back, finding she wasn't breathing.

It took almost an hour because the sun was going down, but he eventually made it to town and alerted the fire department. They sent out a team to recover her body and brought the young man in to stay at the firehouse for the night. The next day the sheriff took him back out to the cabin and asked him to collect his belongings because he was going to be put in foster care. Alex wasn't interested.

He gathered up some clothes, his father's pocket knife and zippo lighter that his grandma had always kept in a box by the bed, one of her bracelets and a copy of "Locke's Important Works" from her bedside. As they walked through the woods back to the road he took a route he knew would be slick with morning dew and as soon as the sheriff went down, he took off.

That was the last time he saw his home in the mountains or any of his grandmother's books. He lived in the woods for a long while, fishing and trapping like he had before, reading from Locke and defending his understanding of the works to the trees and birds and mountains. After over six months of living in solitude he found his way into a town where he planned to trade pelts for money and try to get a small .22 rifle to hunt with and maybe a heavy sleeping bag. He'd been keeping himself alive, but living off the land had left him thin and lean and the cold nights were coming soon.

There was some type of motorcycle gathering going on and the entire town was roaring with motorcycle exhaust and seemed to be soaked in beer, liquor, vomit and blood as bikers stumbled from building to building and drank and fought in the streets. He couldn't help but stare in awe at the bikes that were lined up on both sides of the street, grumbling and rumbling with pure power.

After arguing for an hour with the people at the feed store he finally made his trades and was headed to the gun store to try and get a rifle when he was approached by a set of bikers. They started to shake the kid down, trying to get money from him, thinking he was much older than his 15 years because of his size and hardened appearance from so long alone in the wilds. He had been treated like garbage by the people at the feed store and now these people. If this was what the world was, it was time to head back to the woods for sure. They weren't expecting him to fight back, but at that point he was almost more beast than man and wasn't accustomed to being told what to do by anyone.

The conflict didn't go quite the way they wanted it to, and he beat the two men to a bloody pulp. He was scared to death that the rest of the bikers would attack him, and he ran to the back of an alley and hid behind a dumpster. The wretched stench of rotting food and molded papers was enough to choke him and he couldn't wait for long. As he cautiously made his way back out of the alley, he saw the two men stumbling along, but now accompanied by four more men. One of the beaten bikers lifted a shaky hand and pointed to him as he turned and ran back down the alleyway.

It wasn't long and a large man wearing a denim vest blocked his exit from the alley. He spoke softly, but firmly, calling Alex out to face him. There was a familiar click of revolver's hammer being pulled back and the man told Alex that if he didn't come out and face him, he'd be shot. Alex decided it was better to die on his feet as he'd always imagined his father had, and the boy crawled from behind the dumpster and stood as tall and wide as he could. At only 15 years old, he was already the size of the man blocking his path, and in a straight fight with no weapons, it might have even gone his way.

He'd never find out though. The man in front of him instantly recognized that this wasn't a grown man, but a grown man sized child, and lowered the pistol. He approached Alex and spoke to him gently, kindly. The first person since he'd come out of the woods to talk to him like he was a human. The man offered to buy him a meal and brought him out of the alleyway promising that no one would hurt him. True to his word, the man who wore the name tape "<u>Fragnet</u>" on his vest escorted him to a huge grill by some trucks and motorcycles and got him two burgers, a pile of fried potatoes and a soda.

He sat at a table with Fragnet and learned that the club he rode with were called the "Sin Eaters" and were composed of almost entirely combat veterans. Fragnet was their <u>Sergeant at Arms</u> and was in charge of making sure that all of the rules of the club were obeyed. He apologized for the way the two other men, he called them "<u>Prospects</u>," behaved and assured Alex they would be reprimanded for what they tried to do to him.

Alex and Fragnet spoke for a long while. He found out that Fragnet was an Army Ranger and had been sent to Afghanistan after the 9/11 attacks. He got the nickname Fragnet, or Frag-Magnet, after he had taken multiple pieces of fragmentation from multiple explosions. He got out of the Army and now he rode with this group. They usually did charity work, helped other veterans and went to festivals like this. When Fragnet asked him about his life, he told him the truth. He told him about his dad, about his grandma, living in the woods, everything. Fragnet didn't try to capture him or put him in foster care, he just offered to let him use his tent until he wanted to go back into the woods.

Alex decided to take him up on his offer, in no hurry to get back to his life of solitude after tasting the grilled beef and fatty oils that dripped off of the fries and explosions of sugar in the soda. He stayed the first night in Fragnet's tent while the vet stretched out in a hammock between two trees. The next day he was informed he'd need to earn his keep if he wanted to stick around and was handed a bucket of hot water and stacks of dishes. He felt it was only fair and washed the dishes, expecting to be told to piss off after he was done, but instead he was welcomed back to the table for the next meal.

This went on for four days. He would eat, clean, gather firewood for the campfire, run small errands for the club, and pick up the empty cans that littered the campsite each morning. Alex sat mesmerized as any kid would be by the war stories and tales of riding motorcycles through the mountains, across deserts, and drinking by fires. At the end of the week he had no desire to go back to the life of a hermit he had lived for the last year. He wasn't sure how he was going to make the change, but he knew he needed to do something. As they packed up, Fragnet handed the kid a $50 and told him that if he ever found himself in Columbia, South Carolina to look the club up and swing by.

That was all Alex needed. After the festival was over he was able to find bags and clothes that had been discarded and left behind. He even managed to find a warm jacket tossed in a dumpster. He used the money he had from Fragnet and the sale of his pelts and bought a regional map at a gas station and plotted his route. It was about 200 miles to Columbia and he'd need to sleep and find food along the way.

He didn't want to go through Augusta on the way because his survival skills weren't well suited for the city life, so he chose instead to aim for US-378. Smaller towns, easier to get through, more places to hide out and gather food when needed.

He gathered his wits and checked his pockets. He had almost $100 in cash, the most money he'd ever had, and figured that would get him there pretty easily.

He was wrong, of course, but he managed to stretch it quite a ways. Luckily it was late September and the days were in his favor to be warm but not miserably hot and the nights were bearable and didn't get too cold. He walked from slightly before sunrise to after sunset and after five days he was on the outskirts of Columbia. It wasn't until he was looking down on the city that it occurred to him that he had no idea *where* in Columbia to find the clubhouse, or how, or even the idea that the offer might have been hollow and maybe Fragnet didn't actually want him there. It was too late to turn around, so he bedded down for the night and the next morning he walked into the city and started trying to find the Sin Eater clubhouse.

He finally found a Harley Davidson dealership and decided that if anyone would know, it had to be someone there. A mechanic in the back happened to be a member and welcomed him in with a cold coke while he called Fragnet. The mechanic went by the name "Kong," which Alex would later find out was because he loved dogs but they always seemed to think he was a chew toy and he'd been attacked a dozen times or more. Kong loaded Alex into his truck after he got off work and took him to the clubhouse where Fragnet was waiting.

He welcomed Alex in with a large hug and brought him into the building, bragging to everyone that he had told them the tough kid would make it and he was already man enough to be a Sin Eater. Fragnet pleaded his case before the leadership of the club and they said they'd let Alex stay at the clubhouse in one of the bedrooms for a while. He was supposed to help cleanup and take care of things. He learned to work on bikes, fix plumbing and electrical works and become somewhat of a jack of all trades. At 17 the club gifted him a '72 Sportster to fixup himself and learn to ride on. He turned the wrenches and fixed the old ironhead up and it was Fragnet that taught him to ride. Once he was 18 he approached the club leadership and said he wanted to prospect, and that's where the memories turned sour again.

Alex was enraged when they told him he wasn't eligible. They only took honorably discharged combat veterans and if he wanted to join he'd need to enlist, deploy, and come back. He could continue to be a hangaround but he would never be allowed to prospect until he had served. Even Fragnet couldn't save him from what he did next. He snapped, as many young men do, and screamed at them. He cursed them. He stormed out and jumped on his bike and tore out of the clubhouse lot. He left his possessions behind. The tools he had collected, the Harley hoodie Fragnet had given him for his birthday, his grandmother's bracelet, her copy of Locke's works, were all gone.

The only place he could think to go was across town to the worst hole in Columbia. He pulled into the Rebels' clubhouse and parked his bike. He knew how they operated and right now it was all he wanted. Two members came towards him to tell him to pound salt. He grabbed their heads and knocked them together like he was crashing cymbals in a band. He kicked the doors open and demanded to see the Sergeant at Arms.

Unlike Fragnet, this man instantly drew back to swing on the huge biker that had breached his clubhouse and apparently taken out two guards. He was big, but by this point Alex was bigger. He stepped out of the way of the large fist and crushed the Sergeant at Arm's jaw in a single strike. As he crumpled to the floor, Alex bellowed that he swore off the Sin Eaters forever and wanted to prospect. This was the true unforgivable sin. It didn't matter now if he served, if he deployed, or if he won the Congressional Medal of Honor, he would never be welcome back. The bridge was burned by his own hand.

The next three years of prospecting for the Rebels saw humiliation and degradation of new levels. He was treated as lower than dirt, made to do horrible, vile things in order to prove his loyalty. He would occasionally see Sin Eaters at various functions and shops around town and they always turned their back on him. He was dead to them, and every time it happened his rage grew. He hated them almost as much as he hated his own club, but even more than the Rebels, he hated himself.

It was three years later in the summer that he became a full member. There was a large gathering at Columbia Bike Week and every club in 500 miles was there. The Sin Eaters had set up a charity auction, raffling a variety of prizes and a brand new bike to raise money for homeless veterans. They were causing quite the stir when they started auctioning off bikes that were being donated by members. Their own personal bikes were being auctioned off to raise even more money.

The president of the Rebels came over to Alex and announced that he was going to be given his colors. Full membership, no more scraping out spittoons or cleaning up puke, no more tuning bikes or patching up members who got their asses whooped. One final test and he was a full member. He gathered the club and all of their brothers from other cities and laid out Alex's final challenge. Alex was to deliver an epic beatdown to a man of the president's choosing. After Alex agreed to take on the challenge, he waited patiently, looking around the crowd to see who the Rebel president would choose.

His heart sank as the man's finger pointed at the large, grinning Sin Eater standing on top of the picnic table, calling up the next bike to be donated, the man wearing the vest that read "Fragnet." He couldn't believe it. The cruelty, the pure *evil* in the president's heart. He knew who that was, knew who he was to Alex, knew what he'd done for him. He knew *exactly* what he was demanding.

Alex had no choice. He was between a rock and a hard place. If he didn't beat Fragnet down the Rebels would kill him when they got back to the clubhouse. He couldn't run, his Sportster wouldn't outrun their bikes and they'd just wait for him to run out of gas or shoot him in the back as he tried to get away. He had one choice, and could only hope that someday Fragnet would know the truth and would forgive him.

He walked over to the table where Fragnet stood on top and had just announced that the next bike to be auctioned off would be his personal, first year release 1990 Fat Boy with custom paint. As the bike pulled up in front of the table, Fragnet saw the huge form parting the sea of people that had gathered to bid on the rare motorcycle. He called all of his people to turn their backs.

Alex yelled at him, calling him out, challenging him in front of everyone. When there was no response but a wall of Sin Eater vests facing him, he charged and grabbed Fragnet by the collar, throwing him to the ground. The surrounding Sin Eaters attempted to pull him off, but the other Rebels jumped in and started the brawl. All Alex could see was Fragnet laying on the ground, bruising and bleeding as strike after strike landed on his face. He didn't try to fight back, he didn't even try to block them, he just took the strikes.

After a dozen or more blows, Alex noticed the splotches of water mixed in with the crimson stains. It took him a moment to realize that he was crying and the tears were falling, mixing with Fragnet's blood. Alex stopped hitting him, and saw him raise a hand slowly, clapping it down on his shoulder. Fragnet whispered that he understood, and tucked the keys to his bike in Alex's vest pocket.

Alex jumped up and turned towards the bike. He began throwing people left and right, Sin Eaters and Rebels and other bikers alike. He threw a leg over the Fat Boy and took off. He couldn't get his head straight. The fight, the mercy, the forgiveness, the keys. Why? Why didn't he fight back? Why did he give him the keys? What would happen next?

After riding for hours Alex went to the only place he knew he could, and pulled into the parking lot of the Rebel clubhouse to cheers and celebration. He was presented his full colors and toasted to all night. He had beaten down that smug Sin Eater bastard and even stolen his bike! He'd gone above and beyond and brought them mountains of the twisted form of honor that the Rebels recognized.

Three days later he was standing in the lot of the clubhouse with two other Rebels when twenty Sin Eaters came riding up. One got off his bike and stood in the street, calling him out. Alex walked into the street to meet the man and was shocked when he was handed an envelope with the title to the Harley Fat Boy and a picture of him and Fragnet that had been taken at the campout where they first met. He was told that Fragnet would live, but the brain damage was too severe, he'd never ride again. Alex gave it a week, then claimed it was too dangerous for him to stay in the area and left for the Dallas chapter. That's where everything really went south.

"Hey, Alex, you better get going. Todd is going to need you for patrols tonight," Ramirez said.

Alex jolted as though he'd been shocked and realized that everyone else had finished their meals and cleaned up and he was still sitting at the table with a half-empty plate of food.

"Where'd you go?" Ramirez asked him.

"Nowhere pleasant, Alberto," Alex answered as he shoveled the food into his mouth and took his plate to the sink area where a still soapy tub of water waited for him.

"You go hermano, I'll take care of it for tonight," Ramirez told him, "it's important Todd has someone with him."

"Thanks Alberto, I'll watch his back," he replied as he headed to the door.

"And Alex," Alberto called to him as he walked out, "this life will be hard enough, there is no need to pay penance for ghosts that are long dead."

Alex just nodded and sighed as he walked out the door.

Chapter 3

Alex walked up the drive to the porch and saw Todd standing at the top of the stairs. He took a sip from a flask and tucked it into his back pocket. He had a duty belt wrapped around his waist and a bolt action rifle leaned against the wall. His Carhartt jacket was similar to the ones they were issued in prison, but the collar was sherling and it had a hood, while his knit cap was definitely a prison issue that he'd grabbed, identical to the one that was holding Alex's hair up under it that night.

"Going to get cold tonight, Conary," Todd said as Alex approached.

"How do you know?" Alex asked him.

"Gordon's knee is hurting," Todd laughed back.

"You know, if you look at the tree out front and see how the birds are all clustered together instead of spread out on their own branches," Alex said as he pointed into the tree then turned to the field of cattle, "or look out at the cows and the way they are gathered up, that's a better indicator than an old man's knee."

"Good to know," Todd replied. "Here."

Todd reached inside the front door and pulled out a double barreled shotgun. He handed it to Alex, the long gun looking like a kid's popgun in his massive hands. Alex looked it over, rolling the gun back and forth in his hands before opening the breach and seeing two empty chambers. He closed it and looked up at Todd.

"I'm crazy, yes, but I'm not stupid. Let's take things slow," Todd said as he held up two 12 gauge shotgun shells. "Way I figure it, if you want me, you're just gonna club me, strangle me, and take my guns anyway, but I'd feel better if you had a gun on you in case anything happens. We haven't been ambushed yet, we usually sneak up on people poking around where they shouldn't be, so you should have time to load it if you need to."

Todd tossed the shells to Alex who put them in his pocket. The two men walked down the drive to the road, the sound of the gravel on the caliche crunching under their feet. Alex had his hands wadded in his pockets since he didn't have gloves big enough for his hands, the shotgun hanging from the crook of his arm like a toothpick in a turkey wing.

"You don't have gloves?" Todd asked him.

"Big hands, warden. The prison didn't have any that'd fit and I didn't have anyone on the outside to hunt any down," Alex replied.

"We'll get that handled. My mother is a hell of a knitter, I'm sure she'd be happy to make you a set," Todd mused with a grin.

Alex came to a halt in the middle of the road and exhaled heavily. This man had the nerve to bring him here, introduce him to his family, feed him, and now he was going to ask his mother to waste time, energy, and resources on making him gloves? Really? He turned and faced the smaller man who had a mix of confusion and caution on his face.

"Warden, you really need to stop treating me like I'm some buddy of yours that's here to help you move a damn couch. I'm not your buddy. You seem to think that there's some redeemable quality in me, something like a poem by Russell, but it's not there. I am a monster, held at bay only by the fact that my monstrous side hasn't realized it's out of the cage," Alex rumbled in the growing darkness.

"You're wrong, Alex. Do you know how I know you're wrong?" Todd asked.

"Please, do tell," he sneered in reply, staring down at the silhouette in front of him.

"Because monsters don't talk like that. 'A poem by Russell?' What poem? 'Held at bay?' Hell, I don't think ninety percent of the men in that prison know what it means to be held at bay! You are far smarter than you pretend to be, and there's way more to you," Todd said with a sudden flash of bravery. "How many men in that prison, guards included, do you think understand that birds huddled in a tree or cows in a field means anything?

"You can walk around and play the bullshit inmate games of who's scarier and who's more deadly. Fine. Just know that I see through it," he continued, "Oh, you're deadly, for sure, but you killed those men *for a reason*. Not just for fun, and not just because you wanted to. *They* were monsters, you were doing the right thing and got screwed by the system."

Alex felt like he could be knocked over with a feather in that moment. He'd spent years, decades convincing himself that the books he'd read and the things he understood were just a vision of his grandmother trying to break through. Sure, he had picked up some stuff here and there, but that he was smart? That he was good? He could feel his blood starting to boil.

"You don't fucking know me, warden," he growled.

"I've worked in the prison system since I was 18 years old, Conary. 900 men in that prison, constant in processing and discharges, best I can figure I've seen around 20,000 prisoners over my 22 years in that shithole," Todd replied, "I might not know you, but I know inmates. If it looks like a duck, walks like a duck, and quacks like a duck, it's a duck. You, my *friend*, are not a fucking duck."

The standoff was cut short by a sudden running of cattle at Todd's parents' farm. Todd simply looked at Alex and said, "And call me Todd," as they ran off in that direction. The two men approached from the roadside slowly, trying to mute their steps on the dirt. Alex waved a hand down low and got Todd's attention in the waning light. He pointed towards the grass as he gently stepped off the pavement and walked slowly towards the fence that divided the property from the road.

Todd followed suit on the opposite side of the drive and the two men walked rapidly on the grass. They circled in opposite directions around the house and in the backyard almost scared Gordon to death. He was standing on his back deck in a pair of boxer shorts and a bathrobe that hung open in the front. He had a rifle in hand and luckily had just enough light left to recognize Todd as he came around the house and not shoot him.

The three men met at the bottom of the four step staircase that led from the deck to the lawn and Gordon informed them that there were at least two men in the cow pen trying to single out one animal but the cows weren't really having it. As Gordon went inside to get dressed Alex and Todd made their way past the barbed wire fence and towards the cows. There wasn't much cover, but they split-up so that hopefully they wouldn't both be seen at once.

"Freeze!" Todd yelled as the two would-be rustlers came into view.

"Who the hell are you!?" the shocked rustler yelled back.

"I'm the guy who's cattle you're trying to rustle you rat bastard!" Todd yelled back.

"I told you they knew we were here!" one rustler hissed to the other.

"Oh shut-up!" came the response.

"Look, mister, we're sorry. We're just awful hungry and we needed to try to get some food. We'll just leave. We didn't hurt any cows or anything, we'll just go away," one of the rustlers said.

Todd turned on a flashlight to see two men standing in front of him. They had ropes and large knives in sheaths hanging from their belts. They were dressed in filthy clothes, although there was no way to tell if the clothes had been filthy when they arrived or just gotten that way in the struggle with the cattle.

"Good. Good, that will work. You go on, get out of here and don't let me catch you here again," Todd said firmly as though he were scolding a child.

"No, that won't work," Alex said firmly from the shadows. He had managed to sneak up on the men while they were distracted by Todd to their front.

"Holy shit!" one of the rustlers screamed as he jumped and fell to the ground in the cow manure and mud at the sight of the huge man emerging behind them.

"Go to the barn," Alex commanded.

"We won't come back, we swear! We'll leave y'all alone," the other rustler cried.

"No you won't. You'll be back, now go to the barn. Now!" Alex repeated as he leveled the shotgun on them.

Todd had no idea if it had been loaded or not and was hoping he wasn't about to find out. He pointed his rifle at the men and proceeded to help Alex march them over to the barn. They arrived at the same time as Gordon, who lit an oil lantern to give them some light inside the large, open building.

"C'mon man, we weren't going to hurt anyone, we just came for a cow," whinier of the two rustlers pleaded.

"Is that a fact?" Alex asked them suspiciously. "Tell me, *Todd*, once they turned to walk away, what were you going to do?"

"Go back on patrol," Todd answered.

"And when they shot you in the back, what then?" Alex asked.

"Sh-Shot him? We don't even have guns, man!" the whiner cut in.

"Ah, is that a fact as well?" Alex asked as he turned the quiet one around and pulled the Glock pistol from its holster on his lower back.

"I didn't see that," Todd whispered to Gordon.

"Alright boys, you're liars and you're rustlers, and I'd imagine you'd be killers if needed. So, who's first?" Alex asked flatly.

The two men looked at one another and then at Todd and Gordon as Alex leaned his shotgun against a wall and set the pistol down on a hay bail. He took off his jacket and hoodie and hung them from a nail in the huge 8X8 post that held up the roof of the barn. He turned around to look the two men in the eye.

"What, um, what are you doing Conary?" Todd asked carefully.

"Well, they need to learn a lesson. They don't get to come here and take what isn't theirs without repercussions. So I'll ask again, who's first?" Alex answered him.

"I'm not going to fight you! You'll kill us!" the whiner screamed.

"Nope, I'm going to beat your ass. Either you choose who gets it, or I will," Alex said as he curled his huge arms and brought his massive hands up into a fighting stance.

The quiet one lunged forward unexpectedly and drew his knife from its sheath, swinging down towards Alex's left forearm. The big man deftly stepped back and pulled his arm out of the way. He threw a right cross and landed it on the chin of the quiet rustler, who went down in a pile. As the smaller man staggered to his feet Alex reached out with his left hand and grabbed the rustler's right arm by the wrist, pulling it taunt from his shoulder.

"So, you're right handed?" Alex asked as he brought his own right elbow crashing down on the limb.

The sound of bone snapping and the shoulder joint popping out of the socket was deafening in the barn. It had happened in one, smooth move and it seemed as though Alex could have actually ripped the arm off if he had so wanted. He dropped the limp, rag doll arm as the formerly quiet rustler became the screaming and wailing rustler.

"Jesus, Mary, and Joseph!" Gordon yelled.

Just as the other man opened his mouth to protest the hulk of a man spun around let out a thunderous clap as he slapped his hands together with the whiner's head immediately between. The look of shock and confusion on the man's face belied the fact that he never heard the thunder as his eardrums burst inside his head, resulting in severe hearing loss.

"I thought you said only one of us would get it!?" the howler screamed.

"I asked who was first, I never said nobody was second," Alex grinned as he put his hoodie back on, "now collect your partner and get the hell out of here."

The man with the broken arm crawled over to his friend on his knees, holding his shattered arm with his good hand and then helped the sobbing mess of a man to his feet. They were making their way to the barn door and were almost to the darkness outside when Alex chimed in again.

"Oh, and boys, if I see you around here again, I *will* kill you," he said menacingly.

The two rustlers took off into the night, stumbling in the darkness with one yelling for the other to stop crying and the other yelling back asking what happened and "what did he say?" Alex couldn't help but chuckle to himself a bit as he pulled his hair back and tucked it up under his beanie, then put his Carhartt jacket back on. He picked up the pistol, dropped the magazine and cleared it, locking the slide to the rear and putting the loose .40 caliber round back in the magazine.

"Todd," he said as he offered the pistol and magazine to Todd.

Todd looked at the pistol in the large man's hand, knowing it was unloaded, he looked past him to the shotgun.

"Did you load that?" he asked.

"Didn't need to," Alex answered with a grin as he reached in his pocket and pulled the two shells out.

"You could've killed that man," Todd said faintly.

"You should've killed him," Gordon chimed in.

"I didn't need to," Alex replied as he put the shells back in his pocket, "they won't come back unless they are really looking for trouble, and then I think they'll find more than they bargained for. Now, do you want this or should I put it in my pocket? My arm is getting tired." He gently shook the Glock back and forth in his hand.

"Keep it. If you wanted to hurt me you just had every chance and didn't take it. I see the monster you told me about, but I hope you see the good man I told you about," Todd replied as he turned back to Gordon.

"Go get some rest. If nothing else those two sure as Hell aren't coming back tonight, but let me know if anything else comes up," he said.

"I'm sure we'll be okay, after all, one of 'em will never hear me coming!" Gordon howled.

He thanked Alex for his help and chuckled to himself at the sounds the two rustlers made when they were each dealt their hands by Alex. He kept giggling and making Rice Krispies jokes at the expense of the one he now called the one-armed bandit.

"You know, for a man who used to run a prison with murderers, rapists and drug dealers you're awfully trusting," Alex said as he and Todd waved goodbye to Gordon.

"When you spend all day with men you know you can't trust, it becomes all the more important that you give everyone else a chance," Todd replied quietly.

"Well, that may have worked in the sanity of the world we used to live in, but it could have gotten you killed tonight. That magazine isn't full. There's only 12 rounds in it and it holds

15. My money is they've used it three times before," Alex told him as he watched his breath curl in the cool evening air.

"Maybe," Todd conceded, "maybe I need to be more like the warden you knew and less like the Todd my family knows, but if I become him all the time, then what's the point of living?"

"How about you just become him when there's someone that's trying to kill us?" Alex chuckled half seriously.

"Deal," Todd laughed back.

Alex and Todd continued their patrol around the farms in the area. Todd showed him where their water came from, a wind powered pump on an underground well. It didn't go anywhere, but it filled a huge plastic tank in a metal cage that was held up on a set of wooden posts at almost chest height. The tank would hold 275 gallons at a time and the wind turbine kept it full, but in order to water the animals, cook or clean, or get water for themselves they would need to carry it in buckets and it had a tendency to go dry by the end of the day and refill at night. Todd said there was a manual pump as well if they ever needed it, but it was a real backbreaker.

Alex recommended building a series of <u>solar stills</u> in the area. He told Todd that he knew how to put them together, and if they could come up with some wood, glass panes and caulk he could set them up closer to the house for small amounts of water. Todd seemed to like the idea and suggested they circle back on it when they had time.

Alex learned where the pigs were kept, the chickens, which areas grew which crops. He felt a little more at ease about being given the grand tour and being entrusted with a weapon now that he had had the opportunity to prove his commitment. It was odd that he was so suspicious of Todd until he had a chance to prove himself to him. It became clear that the real reason he was uneasy was because Todd trusted him without evidence, and the last person who did that ended up a bloody mess who'd never feel the wind in his hair again. They had walked the entire property twice and were into their third time when there was a commotion over at the chicken coop.

"Damn, they aren't letting up tonight!" Todd cursed as they ran towards the coops. Unlike before Todd just lit the area up with a flashlight and they saw the coyotes' eyes glowing low to the ground.

"Damn coyotes!" Todd yelled as he charged them and ran them off.

They hadn't gotten into the coop yet but it was easy to see where they were scratching and pawing at the dirt around the bottom and a few areas they had even tried to gnaw their way through the chicken wire. There were also older grooves in the wood and spots in the dirt that had clearly been filled back in where previous attempts had been foiled.

"I wish I had a .22 for those bastards, but it's not worth a real rifle round. Need to just keep chasing them off," Todd said and the last of them ran off yipping in protest.

"I'll rig up some traps tomorrow, see if we can't convince them it's not worth it," Alex replied as they double checked the fencing and doors to make sure there was nowhere that was loose.

"You know trapping?" Todd asked him.

"Yeah, I, uhm… I used to trap a lot when I was a kid," Alex answered him, "lived off trapping and fishing for a while."

"Well you just tell me what you need and I'll find a way to get it. Those damn dogs get chickens and goats all the time. If it's not two legged rustlers it's four," Todd griped.

That was the last of the excitement for the two men that evening as the sun slowly rose in the East. They headed back to the farm and were greeted with the smells of eggs and bacon and coffee wafting from the main house. All of the neighbors had been invited and Jessica and Donna were working with a couple of other women cooking up a storm for the large group.

There was a gathering of men drinking coffee on the front porch as Alex and Todd walked up. Guille, Walton and Ramirez were enjoying coffee with the other men as Grady sipped a glass of raw milk and Oscar was animatedly telling a story. Everyone quieted their laughter a bit as the two sentries approached from their night of patrols, even Oscar once he realized what was going on.

"I'm going to come right out and ask it," Guille piped up, "did you really break a man's arm with <u>The People's Elbow</u>!?"

"Nah man, it was more of an arm-bar-elbow-strike," Alex grinned back.

The story had apparently already grown a bit and Oscar immediately started doing a reenactment of how he thought it went down, complete with tossing imaginary wisps of hair from his face and slapping his chest multiple times before delivering a massive elbow drop to his invisible opponent's arm. He then proceeded to dance around in the dirt at the bottom of the stairs, whooping and kicking the invisible foe before delivering a massive Hulk Clap (as he called it) to the head of his next opponent.

The men were back to laughing and chuckling as Oscar proceeded to mime out the asswhooping he wasn't even present for, complete with a whimpering rustler running off holding his arm and a, for some reason *blind* and deaf rustler bumping into the railing repeatedly before falling down the stairs and stumbling off.

He had the stage presence of a young Eddie Murphy and any one of them would have been happy to see the skinny, high-energy comedian on a stage at the best of times, so this entertainment seemed a real treat. As he finished his retelling of how Alex had saved the day and ran off the two rustlers, he turned and bowed to the crowd, receiving a well earned round of applause.

Things calmed down as the story came to an end and the men sitting on the porch were introduced by name and what their farm had to offer. Max the goat and sheep farmer, Paul the chicken and pig farmer, and of course Gordon the cattle rancher. Each farmer had a little garden planted and had allocated more space to crops that the group had figured would be most valuable. They'd chosen potatoes, corn, and roughage for the animals. The idea had been passed around to do wheat as well, but even though they had seed there was concern over water usage between corn, wheat and roughage. The decision was made to hold wheat until they had a better idea of water availability or rotate it with one of the other crops.

"Guess we'll be cooking Vodka instead of whiskey, but it'll work," Ramirez mused.

"It's a lot easier to make potato flour than it is to get full bellies off of raw wheat," Gordon replied.

"So what do you need from us other than security?" Alex asked the men.

"The main thing is going to be running water. It's a huge challenge and we are going to need to figure something out," Paul said, "we've been toying with how to come up with some horses, but we haven't found a way to get any yet."

"Hmmmm... I mean, we could probably get some if we really wanted them," Oscar said to no one in particular.

"No. No stealing," Gordon said firmly, "we broke a couple of guys last night because they tried to steal. No hypocrites here."

"Okay, okay," Oscar grumbled, putting his hands up in mock surrender, "looks like you're stuck pulling the wagons, hermano."

"We'll figure it out. I'm hoping that young bull out there takes a fancy to one of the cows and we can trade her off for a horse or two," Gordon offered, "but it might work with goats or sheep or whatever."

"Well, I can get a few chicks real quick," Paul said, "but it'll take a hell of a flock to get a horse out of it."

"Yeah, we may need more than that, but let's keep our ears open and try to organize something. It would make a lot of the work around here easier if we had a horse to pull wagons and carry water," Todd chimed in.

About that time Donna came out and called the men into the dining room for breakfast. The spread wasn't a feast by any means, but everyone had a chance to get some food in their bellies and some coffee. Alex sat and listened to the conversation to find that there was very little coffee left and some of what they were eating was being pulled from the bottom of the stores. There was talk of slaughtering a pig in the next day or two and breaking it down.

The children were eating upstairs and staying out of the way, but would occasionally peek down from the top of the stairs and wave at the new men sitting at the table. As best Alex could count there were at least four of them, two he recognized as Todd's and the other two were around the same age. He waved to them and watched them giggle and run off. When he turned his head back to his food he saw Todd smiling at him then going back to his meal.

After everything was done Todd and Alex went to get some rest from their night of guard duty and the rest of the men divided up to go do chores at various places on the farms. The women cleared the table and planned their days of making meals, teaching the children and helping around the farms as they could.

As Alex walked to the barn he could feel his arms and eyelids weighing down. The food in his belly and the warming sun on his shoulders wasn't even remotely affected by the caffeine in the coffee he had just drank. There was nothing he wanted more than to stretch out on his bunk and get some rest. Todd had told him he needed to go back to the prison that afternoon and wanted Alex and Guille to go with him, so it was important he got that much needed rest.

He could hear the children playing in the yard behind him and Oscar and Gordon walking out to the field where they were going to work the cows, Grady and Paul dragging a wagon with crates to collect eggs. It was peaceful. He breathed in deeply, smelling the scents of the farms and the still lingering bacon and coffee in the air. He relaxed his shoulders as he threw the door to the bunkhouse and saw Walton standing by Oscar's bunk, going through his stuff.

Chapter 4

"What the hell are you doing?" Alex asked him.

"Um, uh," he stammered back, "Oscar asked me to grab his beanie for him."

"Bullshit, he was wearing it," Alex returned, "wanna try again?"

"I, um, I meant his gloves, yeah, his gloves," Walton said as he pulled them out of the bag on Oscar's bunk.

"Don't start screwing with people's bags, man," Alex warned him. "I'm going to check with Oscar later."

"It's all good man, yeah, his gloves, I got it," Walton continued to stutter as he turned and slinked his way out the door.

Alex just mumbled to himself as he went to his rack, kicked off his prison issued work boots and stretched out. He'd decided to keep his riding boots as nice as he could and would wear the size 16 work boots through the mud and muck of the farm. He leaned back onto the bed of 2X4s and a prison mattress and stuck his legs through the two vertical posts at the end. His legs stuck out up to the mid calf area but it allowed him to rotate his ankles freely.

The bunk above him was empty, not just because everyone had gone out to do their work duty, but because nobody lived there yet. He could remember how some guys would talk about how odd it felt to "live" in a bunk when they first got to prison.

It had never seemed odd to Alex, he hadn't had anything more than a bunk, a bag, and a bike since he'd left his grandmother's. He'd become so used to that he felt disconnected from stories that told of the warmth of home and the fellowship of community. In his head there was no fellowship with the Rebels. They were an alliance. A necessary gathering of individuals that would keep their mouths shut and not mess with him. It was a place to eat. A place to sleep. It was income to put gas in the tank of his bike and to keep his ass covered.

He never cared for most of them, but learned quickly to take a "not my problem" approach to the club's inner workings. They'd run dope or guns around the city they were in or maybe boost some cars and bikes, but not a huge deal. Some of the guys were hotheaded and known to throw down over stupid shit, but it wasn't a problem for him unless they did it in the clubhouse or he had to iron out wrinkles with another club.

He had been in surprisingly few fights in his life, since most of the time he could simply bow up and people would back down, but the times he had it had been a mess. The first time he'd ever broken a bone on someone else he had only meant to hit them. He shattered their jaw, nose, cheek and orbital sock in one strike. Another time he'd punched a man in the stomach so hard it ruptured his spleen. He'd learned to pull his punches when fighting unless he really wanted to hurt someone.

Except when he hit Fragnet.

He couldn't help it then. It was like someone else was in control of his body and he was locked in the corner of his own mind. He was looking through his eyes like two large windows, watching his hands land on his friend and mentor, watching as he struck the closest thing to a father he'd ever known. Fragnet wasn't much smaller than him, but Alex could never figure out why he didn't fight back, or at least block. He laid there and took the blows to his head and body without so much as a flicker of anger in his eyes.

As Alex thought about the fight with Fragnet he closed his eyes and relaxed, stretching out his frame to the maximum length he could before folding his hands behind his head and regulating his breathing, in through the nose, out through the mouth, his focus on trying to find calm.

No matter how hard he tried to release the demons in his head and find some form of peace so he could drift off to sleep, the rest of his story was determined to play out on the back of his eyelids like a horrific movie at a drive-in. He remembered his final days in South Carolina and the ride from Columbia. His "brothers" in the Rebels had given him an escort to the city limits, then sent him on his way down I-26 to I-95 South.

The president in Columbia had made him ride down to Savannah, Georgia to drop off a package of God only knows what. Then he turned West on I-16 through Macon and up towards Atlanta. As he tore down I-75 he had been tempted at Macon and again at Forsyth to turn off and head towards the Piedmont National Wildlife Refuge. He could have gone home. They'd have never found him, hell, they probably wouldn't have even looked for him. Just assumed he had been tracked down by a group of Sin Eaters and handled.

As the big bike rumbled down the highway and he debated with himself on what to do he thought of what the years would have done to his grandmother's possessions, what mildew and mold and animals would do to the books and bedding. If not for Mother Nature there was a small chance someone else had moved in, and he would have to fight a squatter's claim on the cabin. The thought of someone else in his grandmother's bed, reading (or more likely destroying) her books was too much.

He continued on to Atlanta, resting up for the night before heading West on I-20 for Memphis delivering more of the packages at each stop and bedding down at the Memphis clubhouse for the final time before heading to his new stomping ground in Texas. He was cautioned by the Rebels in Tennessee that the Texas law didn't play with bikers, they were out to get them.

He finally left out of Tennessee, riding his Fat Boy across the huge Mississippi River on I-40. He had delivered all of the packages and his next stop was to be his new home. If he was honest with himself he'd half expected one of the packages to include payment for a hit against him, but it never came to be. Either the messages weren't calling for his death or the members of each club had decided they didn't want to take on that task with him.

It took a little while for him to adjust to his new digs. The heat was different, not nearly as humid as Charlotte, so that was nice, but the entire area felt dead. There was still more green than out West, but nothing like the hills of Georgia he'd grown up in or the forests of South Carolina he'd learned to ride through. That was another thing, they had a *totally* different definition of what constituted a "hill" in Texas compared to where he was from.

His new clubhouse was nice, oddly enough it was an old firehouse the city had put up for sale and the club had bought it. There wasn't much to it, just off an exit from I-30 to the Northeast of the city, three large garage-style doors that opened into one massive area where the bikes could be parked or people could party. The area that used to house offices, gear, and such had been turned into private rooms for the staff of the club, including Alex. They'd installed a bar and a few pool tables and made the upstairs loft a place for people to do everything from play cards to sleep to have sex and anything in between.

He took his time getting to know the local club members, a pretty clear split between some classic, hard nosed old schoolers that rode mainly Knuckleheads, Panheads and Shovelheads. They were a pretty stark contrast in what they thought the Rebels were about and how they should be run compared to the younger fellas that rode mainly the more modern TwinCams and Milwaukee Eights.

The older riders were content to make some money through drugs, guns and stolen goods, party when they could and do their best to coexist with the other clubs in the area without giving up any of their hard won credibility and territory. The younger guys had it in their minds that they should be out claiming territory, running off other groups and trying to own the DFW area as the only club in town, owning all of the crime and all of the profit.

While the president fell into the older crowd, the vice did not and was often the cause of some pretty serious infighting. He'd authorize guys to do runs into other clubs' territories or to start fights at large events and if it didn't go in their favor it was on the president and the Sergeant at Arms to figure it out.

After getting to know some folks Alex figured out where he fell in the lineup and tried to start smoothing things out in the clubhouse. The vice president wasn't happy to find out that the biggest dude in the clubhouse wasn't looking for excuses to bash heads in and take more territory, but he also wasn't sure about crossing him just yet. Alex had been there for about a year before things dusted up the first time.

It was a pretty major fallout, but not the worst it would get. They were having a party one night when a couple of guys came riding and brought a brand new Ford Raptor with them. The six-figure truck had another thirty-thousand dollars in lights, wheels, tires and body armor added to it and the very clear outline of a rival club's logo in vinyl across the back window. They claimed to have messed up a half-dozen of the other club's members and lifted it from their own clubhouse while they were out.

The party came to a screeching halt and everyone who wasn't a member or a prospect was kicked out. The general consensus was split, with the old-timers saying they had no interest in spilling blood over a truck and the younger group welcoming the challenge. It was up to the Sergeant at Arms to keep the peace while the president came to a conclusion. The president and vice were arguing back and forth when the other club came riding up.

They had already made their decision about the truck, and barely had their kickstands hit the ground when they came piling into the clubhouse doors, swinging all manner of bats, chains and clubs. The resulting brawl cost more than a few broken bones and bruised bodies, but in the end the infringing club took their truck back with them and left. While the battle may have been over, the price was left to be paid.

Somewhere in the dustup the Sergeant at Arms had been stabbed twenty-six times and bled out before anyone even knew what had happened. Even though he was incredibly young for the role at only 22, the president appointed Alex as the new Sergeant at Arms and the rift between the two groups split even wider.

After the brawl the two sides of the group had to do some patching up, so they went on a long ride through the desert of West Texas, into New Mexico, up through Arizona and back to Dallas. The trip worked wonders and brought everyone back together for the most part. There was still a bit of dissension in the ranks, but at least there were some shared stories and nights around campfires that could bond them together. The vice was still working his angles and had his own little circle of loyalists, but most of the club was back to the middle.

This continued on for a few years, the bikers would be good, then grow apart as the younger guys felt like they needed to do more ass kicking and less bubblegum chewing. They would ride up into the Black Hills of South Dakota, through the Badlands, another year they went to Branson, Missouri then up into Canada and back. It became a regular practice that they would plan one long trip each year to pull the crew back together.

It's not like they completely quit growing their territory or any of their illegal practices. It was basically how they kept the lights on. Members would run whatever gig they were into, drugs, stolen vehicles, guns, protection rackets, then take the money they "earned" and do a public "donation" back to the club to keep the money above board and keep the club in the clear. If someone got caught, they were just a one-off and the club stayed clean.

Five years after the first trip through the desert the President was planning a ride out West to take Highway 1 from Capistrano Beach all the way up to Dana Point. The club would ride all 655 miles of the classic highway this year, hopefully continuing the trend of realigning them long enough to make it through another year and on to the next ride.

Alex had told the president that things were worse that year. He'd told him that people didn't want a ride. They'd been talking about splitting the club, even trying to set up a spot over in Fort Worth. It wouldn't be the worst thing ever, other than the fact that it would kill the Dallas club's legitimacy and the nationals would start looking in.

The president told him to take it easy, that nobody was splintering anywhere and that the ride would take care of it all. He believed that he and the vice could iron it out and all would be well. They'd ride Highway 1 and come home to a massive barbecue with kegs and girls and dope and celebrate another year in the books.

It sounded good, but that's not how it worked out. Nobody seemed to see anything, but the vice swore it was a rival club that came in and tuned them both up. The president was dead when everyone else got there. He'd been beaten with a thick chain, and was no more than a bloody mess. The vice was tuned up pretty well, but he managed to recover, bringing one of his faithful in as the new vice when he was back on his feet.

Alex watched as the upper ranks began to close and more and more of the old timers were being cycled out. They found excuses to ride less and less, even avoiding the clubhouse all together. There were still plenty of people kicking around, and recruiting was actually up because of the aggressive nature of the new leadership and the way the club members were spreading into new territory. Alex maintained his role as Sergeant at Arms, if for no other reason than because his sheer size solved most conflicts in favor of the Rebels.

He'd been under the new leadership for about two years when they threw a massive party. 75 years of the Rebels and it was time to get crazy. The Dallas chapter had experienced more growth than any other club in the whole Rebel nation and the national leaders were coming in to celebrate.

There were kegs galore, women, drugs and all manor of debauchery. Nobody was going to hold anything back and the party was even bigger than Sturgis. The club was wild and maintaining control of anything was pretty much out of the question. Alex took it as a sign that if things got crazy maybe he shouldn't bother trying to stop it and wandered out to the edge of the party. He was walking around the outskirts and rolling bikers who were passed out drunk onto their sides and picking up used needles and other paraphernalia to toss so a cop wouldn't find it.

He wandered around the side of a building and could hear angry voices and sobbing. He continued down the alleyway and into the back door of the club's outbuilding. The polebarn was used to store spare bike parts, illegal goods, a couple of grills and some tools. "Out of sight, out of mind" was the motto for storing things there and the idea of organization was laughable.

As Alex wound his way through the boxes of parts and grills, stolen goods and cases of beer, he found a large tool chest that he could duck behind. He looked around the corner and saw his president, vice president and two other ranking members of the Phoenix chapter that were in town for the celebration. On a filthy mattress in front of them lay a young woman, wearing torn clothing and gently sobbing as the four men passed a joint back and forth.

Alex knew what was happening, and turned and walked out the door of the barn. He had no intention of participating, but they were all ranking members. He couldn't do anything. He walked back into the firehouse, fighting a path through to get to his bike. He wouldn't sit around and ignore that that was happening out back. He needed to ride off for a bit. Maybe ride off all together. He could just toss the black denim and leather vest and head North. Maybe find his way to Deadwood. He'd loved looking up at Devil's Tower when the club had visited the Black HIlls. He could live there.

As he tried to push through the massive crowd he heard a crash behind him and turned to see that someone had bumped into a table, shattering glass everywhere. Something in him snapped. These people, these animals, they couldn't have anything nice. Every time someone tried to breathe some semblance of community into them, some type of normalcy and brotherhood, they destroyed it. They got drunk or high or angry and destroyed it.

Now it was his turn.

"Rise and shine, inmate!" The voice boomed.

Alex instantly shot up in his rack, smacking his head into the 2X4 that ran as a brace for the bed above him. He swore loudly and laid back down, grabbing his forehead and trying to clear the stars that dotted his vision behind closed eyes.

"Chingow! Sorry man, I was just messing around," Oscar said apologetically from the other side of the room.

Of course, he hadn't been on the other side of the room when he yelled in Alex's ear, but after he saw the titan crack his head on the board above him he was gone like the shot from a gun. He peaked out from around the corner of a bed and looked Alex over, waiting for any indication that he would need to run in fear for his life.

Guille was howling with laughter as he yelled, "You ran faster than la cucaracha when someone his las luces!"

"Oscar," Alex grumbled as he untangled his massive frame from the bed and stood on bare feet by his rack, "*someday*– not today, but *someday* I am going to get you for that."

"Aww come on, man, it was just a joke," Oscar pleaded as Alex stood and stretched, his arms as wide as the beds were long and his head now looking over the top bunk Oscar hid behind.

"Like I said, *someday*. Is Todd ready to go?" Alex asked.

"Si, hermano. He's waiting for us on the porch," Guille answered as he handed Alex a bottle of water.

"Alright man, let's go see what he needs us for," Alex replied, sliding his boots back on and pulling his jacket over his massive shoulders.

As the two large men walked to the door Alex turned and stomped a massive boot in Oscar's direction, causing the thin Hispanic man to yelp and dive behind a set of sawhorses in the corner. He instantly scrambled to his feet, ready to run at a moment's notice. Guille and Alex just chuckled as they left the barn and bunk house behind them.

Todd was standing on the porch talking to Jessica quietly as the two men approached. He gently pushed her hair back behind her ear and kissed her forehead. Hearing the boots on the gravel she turned and smiled at the giants approaching, nodding her head and returning into the house.

The whole thing still struck Alex as odd. He'd never had any reason to meet with the warden when he was inside, but here he was, walking up to his home where he was kissing his wife goodbye. Just two days ago his life was at the whim of the man standing on the porch, smiling down at him and the other complete stranger he was walking with, but now things were different. Alex could feel the pistol tucked into his beltline and knew that if he wanted to he could pull the Glock and shoot the warden dead where he stood.

"Afternoon Conary, you get some sleep?" Todd asked.

"Yes," Alex answered shortly.

"Well, we are going to go into town. I need to make sure the prison has been cleared out. The guards were supposed to take care of the, um, well, you know. They were supposed to do all of that yesterday. After that we are going to try to trade some eggs for some other supplies on the way back through," he informed them.

"Hey warden, what if there's stuff we want to trade for? Like personal stuff? Can we get some eggs or something?" Guille asked.

"It's only fair. We'll work out some kind of pay system when we get back. As of now, just let me know and I'll take care of it," Todd nodded as he scratched at the stubble on his jaw.

Alex simply turned and walked towards the van, loading up in the back where he could keep an eye on his traveling companions. Guille climbed into the driver's seat with Todd taking shotgun. An appropriate location since he had the double barreled shotgun he'd had Alex carry pointing down between his legs and resting the muzzle on the floorboard. Guille fired the van up and turned it around as Todd gave him directions on how to get back to the prison.

Todd would occasionally flip through channels on the old radio, listening to static as the scan feature ran through the cycle of FM stations between 88 and 108 MHz, then they'd switch it over to the AM band and run from 540 kHz up to 1700 and back around again. There was nothing in the static that would provide either answers or entertainment, so after a few miles Todd just shut it off.

They had the windows down, rolling down the highway in between cars that had been pushed off to the side when they stopped working. As they approached a roadblock Guille became visibly nervous. It seemed he was still trying to wrestle with the idea that this might be some kind of mistake or setup and they were headed right back into the pen. As they slowly approached a man walked around the side of the barricade they'd erected in the highway and approached the driver's window.

"Afternoon fellas, where y'all headed?" he asked politely.

"Need to make sure the prison has been closed out, then maybe down to trade a bit," Todd replied.

"Well, the prison is clear from what I hear. If not, I'd sure as hell like to know where that's all coming from," the guard gestured to a large vertical plume of smoke curling in the sky from the other side of town.

"All the same, it's my job to make sure it went off without a hitch," Todd replied sadly.

"Well, I don't envy you warden, but I won't keep you," the guard stepped back and waved them forward between two large eighteen wheeler trailers that were angled to the sides of the road.

As they wove through Alex thought he recognized one or two of the men standing guard but he certainly couldn't be sure. He knew a handful of guards and Alberto by sight, but otherwise he hadn't memorized a face in the five years he'd been inside. Part of him missed that, just being able to count the days, knowing that you had 3 meals, an hour in the yard, books to read, clothes as needed. It's not that he was one of the institutionalized rats that didn't know how to function on the outside, it was just that now there was no countdown.

He could tell that this world was doomed. He hadn't been out more than 48 hours and he knew nothing would ever be the same for those living in this world. Most of them weren't ready for what was coming when everything started to fall apart. Alex remembered reading a book his grandmother held dear by a Roman named Cicero. It wasn't particularly pleasant reading, but he'd never enjoyed the Greeks or Romans. They were too long winded for him.

Despite the fact he didn't care for him, he remembered Cicero describing how Rome had fallen apart and what the Roman Empire was struggling with. He'd been able to draw a number of parallels, but the Rebels weren't exactly known for their philosophical debates. He knew that as the former US started to circle the same drain that had swallowed the Romans, things were going to continue to get worse until the herd was culled and the strong could start to right the ship.

"You are by far the quietest man I've ever met in my life," Todd said, breaking from whatever conversation he and Guille had been carrying on.

"I just like to think," Alex replied absently as he stared out the window.

"Yeah? About what?" Guille asked.

"I was thinking about the Roman author and politician Cicero and his accounts of the downfall of Rome," Alex answered. The truck went quiet and Guille and Todd shared surprised glances.

"Man, are you some kinda genius or something?" Guille asked him.

"It is better to sit silently and be thought a fool than to open your mouth and remove all doubt," Todd interjected.

Alex just smiled and nodded. There was more to this humble prison warden than he had thought. He had expected him to be a jock, a condescending, arrogant quarterback from an 80's movie that had risen to the top of the ranks by being more of a prick than everyone below him. He was finding that to be an errant assumption on his part.

"Alright, you two stay out here in the van. I'll go check on things inside," Todd said as they pulled to a stop just inside of the now open gate at the prison.

A thick black plume of smoke was curling up into the air from the C-Yard area on the backside of the prison. It didn't appear to be thinning out at all, but the flames didn't reach high enough to be seen over the buildings. There were small ashes that would occasionally fall on the hood and windshield of the vehicle, almost like a fine snow.

"Bodies?" Guille questioned.

"Likely," Alex replied.

At one point a guard came out with a large laundry cart and knocked on the back of the van. Alex and Guille got out and were told to load the supplies into the back. They tossed blankets and jackets, socks and coveralls, some hand tools and finally a wide variety of books that Todd had tossed in. The selection was vast and covered everything from planting and woodworking to some of the classics, even a few that Alex happened to know had *not* been made available for the prisoners.

They had turned the vehicle off and as best they could figure had been sitting there for about an hour when Todd came back out the door he had entered. He sat two large, military style duffle bags on the ground and shook hands with another man and then clasped his hand on the man's upper arm, giving one final hard shake to the hand before turning to the van and closing the distance. He opened the back, tossing the duffles in and shrugging a large backpack off his back into the pile before finally climbing into the vehicle and settling back into his seat. It was obvious he was trying to look out the window to hide the tear streaked stains down his face.

"You good, Todd?" Alex asked.

"Yeah, um, yeah. Just had a lot of blood spilled in there," he replied sadly.

"You didn't do it, why do you care?" Guille mused as he turned the van back towards the gate.

"I didn't pull the trigger, but I ordered it. Every one of them is on me," Todd answered with exasperation

"Let me ask you, Warden, what do you think they would have done if you'd cut them loose like us?" Alex pushed.

"I don't know," Todd replied as he waved dismissively, obviously not wanting to continue the discussion.

"Sure you do," Alex said as he leaned back and stretched his legs out to the side of the van, "rape, murder, pillage… they would have created a fifedom that would have rivaled the most horrible reigns of the most vile leaders in human history. You may have ordered the executions, but your only other choice was to condemn the innocent at the hands of the evil."

"Thanks Conary, that actually helps," Todd acknowledged softly, "alright, enough of that. Guille, turn left up here and we are going to go do some trading."

Chapter 5

"I've got meat! Fresh meat! Cat! Dog! Armadillo!"

"Gold and Silver! Copper too!"

"Car parts! If you've got a junker, we can get it running!"

The calls across the market created a cacophony of noise and competing cries for various goods that made it impossible to really tell what any stall held. There were smells of meats and vegetables cooking, the exhaust of generators that could be rented to charge radios, portable batteries, or anything else someone wanted to put juice to.

A man in one corner of the huge church parking lot had a massive antenna sticking out from behind his tent. He was taking requests from people, but not for top 40 hits.

"Hey, Todd," Guille said as they approached the radioman, "can I try to reach out to my sister in Escondido?"

"Let's see what he's asking," Todd answered as the group of men walked to the tent.

"Hello gents, what can I do you for?" the radioman asked politely.

"Got a man here who wants to try to reach his sister," Todd replied.

"That's the business, need her name, address, who's calling, some personal info only she'd know to confirm it's really her and whatever message you want to send," the man smiled as he slid a small pad of paper and a pencil over to Guille.

"What's the cost?" Todd asked, covering the pad with his hand before Guille even reached for it.

"Well, if I don't get in touch with her, no cost at all. If I do, then I ask for something before I give you her info or response," he answered, "can't really set prices, but most folks will give me a water bottle full of gas for my generators, a handful of 9mm bullets or a plate of food."

"Sounds fair," Todd smiled back as he moved his hand and Guille started to write.

"Just make sure it's clean and easy to read, son, my eyes aren't great and I need to be able to read it real clear," the radio operator replied as he watched Guille start to write.

Alex was standing to the back of the group, keeping watch on the crowd and scanning the booths down as far as he could see as he waited for Guille to finish up and Todd to negotiate a bulk deal on calls so that the other guys at the farm could send in requests as well. He was eyeing a stall in the corner of the lot that he could barely make out, but it seemed to be the only one that was held out away from the others and didn't seem to have anyone yelling about the wares inside the enclosed tent.

"Excuse me, sir, do you know what they charge?" came the gravelly voice of a white haired man to his right.

"I'm sorry?" Alex replied as he realized the question was being directed to him.

"I asked if you knew what they charged for news," the old man asked again.

"I'm sorry, I don't," Alex answered as he stepped to the side and gestured the older man forward.

The man nodded his appreciation and turned to two very elderly people who were next to him. A man was hunched and bent over the back of a wheelchair that held a woman who would have surely been mistaken for dead if she didn't occasionally nod her head up and down for no apparent reason. He seemed to check on them, tucking a blanket into the thighs of the old woman and making eye-contact with the man. It was at this moment that Alex noticed the handcuff that held the ancient man's left hand to the wheelchair.

"What the hell is that about?" he growled at the white haired man as he glared at the bright chain.

"He has Alzheimer's. It's just to help me keep track of him when we are in big crowds like this," the man replied gently.

Alex stepped over closer to the old couple and looked at the wrist, noticing that there was no redness or visible injuries where the metal touched the skin. The ancient man looked up at him, then down at the cuff and then back at the giant and smiled.

"I appreciate your concern son, but I'm lucid right now. Just keeps me from getting confused and wandering off," he said, gently patting Alex's forearm which was as large as the man's thighs.

Alex smiled gently and nodded to him, then turned back to the caretaker who was watching him. He softened as he took the single large step towards him.

"I'm sorry, sir, I just wanted to make sure your father was okay," he said softly.

"It's okay. It's a horrible situation, but we do what we can with what we have. He's not my father by the way, he was a customer at my pharmacy. I knew the medications he and his wife were on and knew they'd never make it out here on their own, so when they said they were heading West I decided to pack up shop and help them," the other man replied as he turned to the radio table and started filling out a card.

"Do you charge for news?" he asked the radioman.

"News is free if I've got it, but tips are always welcome, where were you wondering about?" came the reply.

"San Antonio, I'm from the Northwest side, so that specifically if you've got it."

The radio operator flipped through his notebooks looking for logs and write-ups. "Military City is a wreck. The Nation of Destiny and the remnants of the US Military are duking it out in the streets. The bangers have the numbers but the military has the gear. Austin is burning and everything between the two is a nightmare no-man's-land between refugees from each city."

"Haven't heard much about the South part of the city other than that there's a bunch of humans moving through like locusts. Used to talk to a fella in Boerne that was part of the Boerne Defense League out there. He said they were putting stuff back together but had some rabble rousers that were making it tough. They have plans to put them down and get the Northwest corner back under control. Should be safe soon. That's all I've got," he finished and closed the book.

"Bullshit. I'm from there and the BDL are just rolling everything up and taking it over. That's propaganda," the old man grumbled.

"Can't tell you more than what I know, man," the operator shrugged.

"Thanks anyway," the customer replied and passed him three travel packets of tylenol, which the operator took and smiled happily about, nodding his thanks for the tip.

"I was a pharmacist in the Boerne area at an HEB before everything happened. The BDL are horrible and they are going to hurt a lot of good people if they get to keep charge," the white haired man bemoaned to no one in particular, but in Alex's general direction, as he walked back to the elderly couple and their chair.

Alex had been watching over them and giving the stink-eye to anyone who appeared too interested in them as he listened to the conversation. Guille and Todd had picked up on it as well and were standing by closely, pretending to look at trinkets on a table.

"Is anyone standing against them?" Todd asked, finally joining the conversation.

"Yeah, but it's an uphill battle. There's one group that was when we left. Good folks. If they hadn't helped us with a really lopsided trade of guns for meds we never would've made it this far. I hope they're doing okay," the pharmacist lamented as he checked on his patients.

"We'd best get going," Alex said softly.

"Us too, though the woods are lovely, dark and deep, I've got promises to keep," he sighed as he rubbed the shoulder of the elderly man who was starting to look around, slightly panicked, seeming to lose his understanding of what was happening.

"And miles to go before I sleep," replied Alex with a gentle smile.

The white haired pharmacist smiled in appreciation of Alex finishing the poem and turned away. The three large men watched as the older trio wandered off to the edge of the market and then down a side street.

"What the hell was that?" Guille asked.

"What was what?" Alex played dumb..

"All that miles to go stuff," Guille continued.

"A poem by Robert Frost about a traveler taking a brief pause to appreciate life and beauty before continuing on," Alex replied.

"You're a really deep dude, hermano. You know that? Weird as hell, scary as hell, but deep," Guille laughed as he slapped a paw on Alex's shoulder.

"The monster who quotes poetry," grinned Todd under his breath when he locked eyes with Alex.

The trio continued through the crowded marketplace, looking at goods, listening to vendors shout their wares across spaces. They couldn't help but chuckle when they came to two vendors on opposite sides of the aisle that were both selling food. Apparently they were cousins and had a booming business going where they would insult the other and his food, claiming theirs to be better. They would trade these retorts until one of them slipped and insulted the wrong person and was reminded that they shared a grandmother and aunts and various other people in their lineage.

The food was probably fine, but the customers would buy burritos and sandwiches and then stand around eating them to enjoy the entertainment that came with it. After five minutes of listening all three of the men were holding back tears and gripping their sides as the two cousins let the insults and food fly.

The trio traded for a few small items they needed according to Todd - some candles, a box of rubber gaskets for canning jars, and a handful of candy bars for the kids. They were stuffing them into prison issued laundry bags they had brought from the van when Todd let out a loud sigh.

"Que paso, Jefe?" Guille asked him.

"I'm really not looking forward to this next stop," he said softly.

"Why's that?" Alex asked him.

"Because I've never been a fan of getting raked over the coals by someone who has something I need and knows it," Todd replied.

"We got your back," Guille answered seriously as Alex just grunted his agreement.

They walked over to the large white event-style tent in a corner by itself. Not only was it the only tent that was completely enclosed, but it was absolutely massive compared to the ten-by-ten festival-style tents in the main market. It was also the only one with a group of armed men walking around it and limiting access through a set of strapped stanchions that had likely been reallocated from the DMV or some other government building.

"I'm here to see him," Todd told the guard at the entrance.

The man nodded and spoke into the microphone on his collar that ran to a radio on his belt. After a few minutes a reply squelched through and the guard opened the black retractable strapping that ran between the stanchions.

"You know where to put the weapons," he said, eyeing the two large men that were stepping forward.

"I know," Todd replied.

Next to the doorway into the tent Todd laid the shotgun and pistol from his belt on the table. Next he pulled out a pocket knife and laid it on the table as well. As Alex watched, Todd gently nodded 'yes' and Alex took that as a message to lay out his pistol as well. He set it and his pocket knife next to Todd's weapons on the table. Guille emptied a homemade shiv and a blackjack onto the table. Todd seemed to relax slightly as the men emptied their meager armaments.

"We are going in to see Reverend Shoener. He's not a good man, but he has what we need. Just stay quiet and let me do the talking," Todd whispered firmly.

The two ex-cons simply nodded their agreement and the group walked through the doorway flap of the tent. They were instantly struck by the brightness inside. There were lights, soft music playing from one corner and stacks upon stacks of canned goods, medicine and first aid supplies, weapons and ammunition, tools, and all means of highly useful survival equipment.

Guille and Alex looked around, shocked by the sheer volume of supplies inside the tent. They had only been out for a day and they already knew this had to be mountains above what anyone else had. They spotted a short, fat man waddling his way around the piles with a pad of paper and a pen, counting and recounting everything he saw.

He wheezed as though every step were the equivalent cardiovascular exercise of running a marathon. Even though it was a comfortable 70-ish degrees in the tent he was sweating profusely, and the beads of sweat ran through his short-cut, thinning hair and looked like glossy beads of glass against his black skin. He would pause, push his glasses up onto his nose as he counted, scribbled, then ran off to count again.

"Beanie! Where are you?" came a yell from another corner.

"Right here Reverend!" the short man yelled in a nasally tone.

"Beanie, how is our count going today?" a man asked as he rounded a corner.

"All present and on track to hit our 10% growth for the week, Reverend," the man answered.

"Outstanding! God is great!" the new arrival replied as he turned and saw the new arrivals darkening his door.

"Ah! Warden Todd!" he glowed as he stepped forward and embraced Todd.

"Reverend Shoener," Todd said as he returned the awkward hug, "these are two of my new hands, Alex and Guille." Todd gestured to the two men who simply nodded.

"Lost sheep who have rejoined the fold! How wonderful!" the Reverend crowed as he took each of their hands from their sides and shook them vigorously.

"This sure is a nice collection you've got here, Reverend," Alex said softly as he looked at the stacks of canned goods next to him, neatly organized by not only which type of canned tomato product they were, but also by brand.

"Ah, God's bounty my son! Donations from those who have to help those who are in need when waters begin to rise," came the toothy reply.

Alex turned and looked at the man in front of him. He had an odd way about him, friendly and incredibly handsome. He almost seemed like he could be an actor, like he could be in a movie with Jake Gyllenhall or Ryan Gosling. But under the immediate draw of his charisma was something sinister. A slight snakelike quality to the way he moved or the way his eyes settled on you.

"I don't know if you've been out there or not yet Reverend, but there's some mighty needy folks," Alex said carefully.

"Well, there certainly are, but where would we have been if Noah tried to fill the ark too early and there had not been enough food for the animals to last. We must wait until the need is greatest, then God will send us a sign to distribute these donations and gathered supplies to those most in need," Reverend Shoener replied, this time with less of a smile.

"I suppose we should be grateful for Genesis 9:15 then," Alex muttered, not trying to hide his distrust of the Reverend.

"I'm sorry? Which verse?" Reverend Shoener asked, shocked at the direct quote.

"The one where God promised to remember his covenant with all living creatures and never flood the world again..." Alex answered him with a cruel smile.

"Ah, yes, the covenant to never flood the world again. I'm sorry, I have had so much going on I haven't been as diligent with my studies of the scripture as I should be," the Reverend replied cautiously, quickly turning his attention to Todd again. "What can I do for you today, warden?"

"I need ammunition, Reverend, 9mm, .40 caliber and .30-06. We are getting more and more rustlers, but we also need a small caliber rifle like a .22 to take care of some coyotes. I can bring you some beef when we slaughter, but I don't have much to trade right now," Todd tried to request rather than plead.

"Ammunition is tricky, warden," began the Reverend, "it is a finite resource. I may be able to help with the 9mm since it's a common round, but the rest are more rare. I would need a fair amount to balance the scales on our stocks. I truly, from the bottom of my heart, want to help. I wish I could give you all that you need and more, but I'm afraid that's not possible."

As the faked desperation spilled from his mouth the Reverend would occasionally stop and lick his lips, savoring the power he had over this man because the members of his church, the largest in the county, had been convinced to provide him with supplies in case they were needed. Todd's shoulders simply sagged under the realization that he was not going to get most of what he needed and was likely going to pay dearly for what little he did get.

"You truly wish you could help?" Alex asked.

"I-I do," the Revered stammered his cautious answer, "but I need to think of all of God's children who are relying on me."

"From the bottom of your heart?" Alex continued, steeling his eyes in a stare that seemed to capture the eyes of the holy man.

"From the bottom of my heart," he replied in an almost trancelike state.

"Then how fortunate for us… I'll help you with this one preacher, Second Corinthians 9:6 and 7, 'each of you should give what you have decided in your heart to give, not reluctantly or under compulsion, for God loves a cheerful giver.'" Alex smiled, "sounds like helping the warden out with his needs shouldn't be a problem at all."

"I, um, six and seven? Yes, why, yes! Thank you Brother Alex, that is most helpful in my decision making," Reverend

Shoener stammered. Once again the forgetful father had been ensnared by his own traps and was now between a rock and a hard place. "Beanie! Come collect a list of the needs of the warden here and get him what he requires, I'm needed elsewhere."

"Yes, Reverend," the short, round little man replied as he materialized from between two piles of crackers, salted and cheese flavored.

"Thank you for the spiritual realignment, Brother Alex," the Reverend hissed as he extended his arms for an embrace.

"Don't mention it Padre, happy to help," Alex answered as he squared his hips and shoulders, rolling his body up and making sure the Reverend knew he was not welcome for a hug.

The Reverend diverted to Todd, who had also read the situation accurately and had moved his body into the pathway to intercept. Guille was simply trying to keep himself from laughing hysterically at the exchange. They had only arrived at the market twenty minutes ago, but the mysterious giant with the demeanor of a monster, who quoted poetry and The Bible by verse, had turned the entire afternoon upside down.

After the awkward embrace the Reverend left and Beanie took down a list of what was needed. He said he'd have it all ready at the back of the tent when they came back through with their vehicle to load it in, rather than trying to walk through the marketplace with such precious commodities. They were as likely to get mugged as they were to get overwhelmed with offers for the newly acquired goods. They walked back out the front doorway and put their weapons back in their respective places so they could go get the prison van.

"When do I get a Glock?" Guille asked as Alex loaded the weapon and slid it into the small of his back.

"When you break someone's arm and take it," Alex grinned back at him through the dark strands of black hair that framed his face, holding a massive arm out to one side.

"Easy, El Cucuy, I was just curious if there was a plan, nobody wants to take tu premio," Guille said with his hands up in mock surrender.

"I'm messing with you man, we bueno," Alex replied with a chuckle, slapping a massive paw down on Guille's shoulder.

"We'll see what we can do Guille, I might have something for you," Todd chimed in.

"Okay, okay, if not I'll just keep an eye out for rustlers then," Guille replied, still off his game from the look in Alex's eye.

They left the market and loaded into the van, settling in before Todd breathed heavily and then turned in his seat to confront Alex.

"I know you were trying to help, and I know you think you did, but pissing off the Reverend will only make my life harder in the long run," he said, exasperated.

"How's that, Todd?" Alex asked.

"He's not only very popular with the folks around here because he lets the market set up in the parking lot of his church, but he's also got a lot of pull with town leadership because of that hoard. If he gets pissed at me it will be tough," Todd replied, frustration clear in his voice.

"It'll be fine. I didn't do anything he couldn't save face from and it wasn't in front of a crowd. It's my experience that a lot of holy men can't really quote their own scripture anyway. It just reminded him that other people can read the Bible too," Alex mused.

"Speaking of that, did you memorize the entire book, chapter and verse?" Todd asked him.

"No, just those two," Alex lied with a sinister smile.

"Screw you, Alex," Todd couldn't help but smile.

They drove down the closed road to the back of the tent where one of the guards handed a bolt-action Savage MKII .22lr with a small scope on it out to the waiting van. It was followed by a double layered grocery bag with ammunition in it. The 9mm, .40 caliber, .30-06 and .22lr rounds were all simply dumped in and mixed together. As they said thank you and drove away, Guille passed the bag over to Todd in the passenger seat.

They made their way through town, and Todd opened the bag to try and get an idea of what their ammunition situation looked like, then started laughing hysterically.

"What's up, Jefe, you good?" Guille asked, more curious than concerned.

Todd just kept laughing and held up a small, yellow sheet of lined paper with a simple message on it:

"Please do not bring the Biblical scholar back without notifying me." - Reverend Shoener.

Chapter 6

The three men arrived back at the farm with their haul of weapons and ammo and other supplies. They were unloading things from the back of the van when Oscar came walking up to offer a hand. His face sank when he saw stacks of books and a handful of clothing. He begrudgingly helped to unload the goods from the back of the large van, quickly thumbing through the titles of the books. The rest of the little farm co-op walked up as well to see what had been acquired.

"Ooooo… Candy," Grady said as he held up a bag with a few chocolate bars and Reese's cups in it.

"For los niños," Guille grinned as he snatched the bag away.

"I can be a niño…" Grady pouted.

"Una bebé grande!" Oscar chided, then looked over the gathered supplies. "Man, this stuff looks helpful and all, but couldn't you have grabbed something by Tiffany Sunvale?" he asked.

"Tiffany Sunvale? You mean those lady-porn books?" Ramirez asked with a chuckle.

"I believe the accepted term is 'Erotic Romance Novel'," Donna replied with a cheeky smile.

"Call it what you want, Ms. Donna, I won't argue," Ramirez replied between laughs.

"Tiffany Sunvale is the smut queen of the Southeast. All her stories take place in Georgia, Alabama, and Florida. I like JoAnna Gonzalez, she writes about Texas and Mexico," Guille added in.

"She's good too. You know, I have a fair collection of both of them and some others if you gentlemen would like to borrow some," Donna offered kindly, making Todd obviously uncomfortable at the idea of his mother collecting that type of book.

"That would be great, ma'am," Oscar replied sheepishly. It hadn't occurred to him that the conversation would spiral quite like this.

"I might like to borrow a couple as well," Jessica chimed in as she flipped through cookbooks in the boxes at the back of the van. She gave a devilish smile as her husband squirmed.

"Alright, enough talk about... that. Stuff. I need some help getting something from the side doors," Todd said as he desperately tried to escape the conversation.

"I'll help, Boss," Alex volunteered. He wasn't entirely comfortable with the conversation either, but he hid it much better than Todd.

The two men walked around the side door and pulled out the two large duffels and backpack that Todd had loaded at the prison. They brought them around to the back of the vehicle and Todd opened them for all to see. One duffel was full of tools from the prison, shovels, rakes, pitchforks, hoes and other, smaller hand tools. It took Oscar all of five seconds to start with hoe jokes until Alex reminded him that there were ladies present. He bashfully apologized and was quickly forgiven as Donna and Jessica pointed out that they had been either married to or the mother of prison guards most of both of their lives.

The second bag and duffle weren't opened, but Todd took them inside the house, returning with a black shotgun furnished in orange Magpul furniture. It had a small red-dot sight on top and a bandelier of shotgun rounds. As he approached, he laid the shotgun on the ground and held the bandelier out in front of him.

"I'm sure you gentlemen don't need a reminder, but this is a less lethal shotgun. It's set up to fire three different types of ammo. The rounds are all clear, so you'll need to pay attention. The ones that are packed with what looks like orange sand are OC Pepper blasts, the ones with the black spots everywhere inside fire a rubber pellet version of buckshot. Finally, we have the 'Super Socks' which are exactly that, a little sock filled with sand that acts like a slug. This is the most likely to go lethal under a certain range, so we are only going to use these if we have to. I'm going to put together three shotguns that will be stored at the bunkhouse," Todd said as he walked them through the different configurations.

"These will each hold seven rounds, plus one in the chamber, so they'll be loaded with three rounds of pepper, then three rounds of pellet, then two socks. You're going to get more lethal as we go through, but if you get that deep, maybe you need to." He continued, " this is a circle of trust thing guys. There are those out here that don't want you armed, so this was the compromise. After what happened the other night with Alex and I, I'd rather you have options. Ramirez and Walton will have one each, the other will be available to whoever is on guard duty that night."

"Sounds like a plan. I like having *something* to use when I'm out there," Guille answered. "I've never used a shotgun though. Can I look it over?"

Alex stepped away as Todd gave a quick class. He'd used guns of every type and didn't need the rundown. It was clear what was in the other bag now, and Alex had no doubt it wasn't only less-lethal options. If he ended up leaving he may need to see what all Todd had squirreled away from the prison.

He walked over to the huge live oak in front of the house and leaned back against it, sliding down the rough bark into a squat. It's not that it was hot or even that he was physically tired, but there was so much going on. He had been a prisoner two days ago, now he was sitting under a tree at the warden's house with a Glock in his waistband and a pair of matching scabs healing over brands on the inside of his wrists. He was musing about the situation with his eyes closed when he heard a small voice.

"Are you a bad man?" the tiny voice asked.

He opened his eyes to see the little girl from inside the house standing about six feet in front of him. Her olive skin was an interesting contrast to her sandy blonde hair and pale blue eyes. She was a curious mix of her parents, but had obviously gotten her mother's beauty. He looked over her shoulder to see the two boys hiding behind the wooden railing that rounded the house on the porch. He brought his eyes back to the little girl in front of him. She had her head up, eyes locked on his, feet planted squarely on the ground. It was clear that she either wasn't afraid or was a master at hiding it.

"Yes. Yes, I am a bad man," Alex said softly. He held out his wrapped wrists, "these marks mean I'm a bad man. All men who have these are bad men," he peeled back the bandages so she could see the outline of the healing scars of 'BSPR' on his skin.

"Daddy said that the men he was bringing out here weren't all bad. They were redemdable," she replied as she stepped closer to look down at his wrists.

"Redeemable?" Alex asked gently.

"Yeah, that. That you still had good in you and you'd help keep us safe. Is that true? Are you going to keep me and my mommy and daddy and brothers safe?" She asked with bright blue eyes behind curly brown locks of hair. She was now only a foot or so from Alex.

"What's your name?" he asked her.

"Patti," she answered him.

"Patti, I think you're probably smart enough to know that the world changed not long ago, aren't you?" Alex asked her.

She simply nodded sadly.

"Well, Ms. Patti, then you're smart enough to know that in this new world there are monsters, and sometimes, you need monsters to fight monsters," Alex said as he slowly stood up. He allowed himself to unfold to his entire six-foot-ten-inch frame, rolling his shoulders back and squaring himself off, opening the massive paws that he called hands.

"I understand, but isn't a monster that protects people just a different kind of hero? Like the big green monster in the superhero movies daddy used to watch?" she asked as she looked up at the behemoth before her. She hadn't moved back one inch as he rose.

"I guess that's one way to look at it, Ms. Patti," Alex smiled. "I am here to protect you, and your family, and I will do my best."

"I know," she said as though he told her water was wet or the sun was bright.

She turned and ran, not so much away from Alex, but just ran the way playful children do. She collected her brothers and took them inside to color. Alex realized he had been holding his breath the entire time and slowly released it. Outsmarted by a kid. Go figure. He turned and walked back towards the van to see Todd, Ramirez and one of the farmers standing there smiling at him.

"That one is a pistol," Max the goat and sheep farmer chuckled.

"When God made her he forgot to put in the fear," Alex grinned back.

"Tell me about it, you weren't there when she did her flying 360 kicks off the back of the couch at four," Todd lamented.

"She's got your number though, hermano," Ramirez added.

"Maybe," Alex conceded, "but she's also been told that all of us out here are 'redemdable.'"

"Hey, she's only seven," Todd laughed, "and you are 'redemdable' whether you want to believe it or not. Just one more example. You could have grabbed that little girl and made a huge stink about loading supplies into the van and taken off with guns and food and who knows what else, but instead, you're over here talking to us."

"Hey warden--" Alex started.

"--Todd," he interrupted.

"Todd," Alex corrected himself, "screw you."

At that Ramirez lost it and began laughing hysterically, the infectious chortle spreading until all four men were almost doubled over. Todd reached up and slapped a hand down on Alex's shoulder, shaking his head. As the group gained control of themselves, Todd wiped tears from his face and cleared his throat.

"I haven't laughed that hard in a long time," he said with a still gravelly voice, "you and I are on guard duty tonight Alex, so you might want to get some sleep. I know I am."

"Oscar pulled some stuff together to make his famous <u>prison paella</u> tonight for dinner, so we'll wake you up when it's ready," Ramirez said as Alex turned to the bunk house. He could hear Max questioning what "prison paella" was as he walked away. He'd find out soon enough and Oscar's was notoriously good.

Alex stepped into the empty bunkhouse and grabbed a glass of water from the pitcher by the sink. It was room temperature, but clear, and he'd felt like his throat was covered in dust ever since little Miss. Patti had delivered a reality blow to him from the perspective of a seven year old. He walked over to his bunk and tucked the Glock away under the pillow, kicking off his boots and stripping down to his skivvies before finally laying down.

He generally kept some kind of shorts or something on, but the cool air inside the bunkhouse felt good on his legs stretched out on top of the covers. He could feel the uneven lump of polymer and metal under the pillow and rather than drive him crazy from poking and jabbing where it really shouldn't, it gave a sense of peace. He'd never really needed a gun before, choosing to settle most of his issues with intimidation or shear force. There had always been long-term repercussions that needed to be considered when using a gun before, but in this new world, he felt at ease knowing that anything that happened would be handled the old way.

He'd snapped a man's arm like a twig and stolen a gun in front of a prison warden and a retired senior guard, not one word was said. No sirens. No lawyers. They hadn't even taken the gun away from him. It was almost like that old Sci-Fi movie he'd seen with the bald dude that also raced cars. He couldn't remember the title, but he remembered the tagline: "you keep what you kill." Man, what a world that would be.

Alex stretched in the bed and tried to set a mental reminder that he needed to start meditating again, and also needed to find some two by fours and build a platform to hold the almost foot and a half of his calves and feet that stuck out the bottom of the bed. He could remember his grandmother telling him stories about the monster from the Okefenokee Swamp near the Florida border and that if he didn't stay in bed at night it would come to eat his toes. As an adult he knew of course that she just wanted him to stay in bed and not be out running wild in the woods, but he still couldn't get comfortable with his feet hanging off the bed.

He drifted off into a dreamless sleep, and even though he felt rested and disconnected from the world, every groan from the wood of the old barn against the new siding of the bunkhouse kept him on edge. He never opened his eyes, but he could still tell the sun was setting and even though he barely moved on the bed he could feel the breeze shifting and cooling into the night.

After a while he decided it was time to get up and swung his legs over the side of the bed, pulling on his pants and boots, returning the pistol to the small of his back and following the smell of cooked food to the main house. He paused halfway between the bunkhouse and the main house to watch the sun finish going down. He could hear the laughter and conversation from the backyard, but watching the yellows, ambers, oranges and golds of the west Texas sunset streak from one side of the sky to the other in a 180-degree show was too much for him to pass by.

Sure, Georgia had its beautiful sunsets, but they were usually framed by mountain ranges and valleys or stolen in glances through the forest canopy. This was different. West Texas didn't have anything taller than a telephone pole to stop the spread of the colors and the sky was awfully proud of its wonder when it showed off. Nothing felt as big or as beautiful in all his life as watching the sun sink in this area.

As the colors faded he turned to the house and opted to walk around the side of the house in the yard. He could smell the food and the campfire before he ever got to them and heard the laughter and chuckles of the family as he closed around the side of the house. In another world it would have been just another backyard barbecue with close family. Oscar could have played the crazy cousin that talked too loud and joked too much and Ramirez would have been the weird uncle that liked to throw out stories of his glory days.

Alex was about to take a step forward into the light when he noticed shadows shifting out in the field. He pulled back against the house, trying to shrink his massive frame into the corner of the covered wrap-around porch. He reached back and pulled the pistol out of his belt, thankful he'd checked the chamber and magazine before leaving the bunkhouse.

He hadn't loaded any extra rounds from Todd's haul at the marketplace earlier that day, so he only had the 12 the pistol had in it when he acquired it. Hopefully there weren't too many of them to deal with. Alex looked around and figured that if he took a few steps back he'd be in enough darkness that he could make it to the little shack off in the corner of the yard. It wasn't much, but he could at least hide behind it and go from there.

He started his movement, erring on the side of caution and staying further back. He truly hoped that the interlopers weren't going to ambush the family, but it was a risk he had to take. He settled in on the back side of the shack and listened as they approached. It was tough to tune out the festivities around the campfire, but he was pretty sure he could hear two different people walking.

He watched as Patti played with Jessica, doing a Jacob's ladder with yarn. Ramirez was telling Oscar how to cook his paella while Guille and Grady gave them both a hard time, laughing it up as the two would rile one another into speaking Spanglish. The farmers were comparing planting plans and talking about what kind of trades would be worth pursuing and which ones were going to be less valuable than others. They had no idea they were being stalked.

If these were the two from the other night, or two from the same camp, Alex knew what he would have to do. He didn't relish the idea of taking another life again, but one of them would surely have to die to deliver the message. One dies to seal the message and one lives, at least for a little while, to carry it back.

It was Todd that noticed the man first, he had no firearm on him, but jumped up and shielded his wife and daughter just the same. Alex didn't see the two younger boys and assumed they were inside sleeping, but he watched as Gordon gently pulled Donna behind him. The five inmates caught on quickly, but inmate instinct took over and their initial reaction to run had to be consciously pushed down. Instead they opted to try and fan out until a gruff voice rumbled out of the distance.

"Everyone stop right where you are!" it shrieked.

The assembled group froze. Alex couldn't believe that with the haul he assumed Todd had brought back from the prison there was not a firearm in sight. He adjusted his grip on the pistol and stared into the darkness, trying to locate anyone else in the ambush. One figure emerged, thin and short, only about five foot three and with a waist no bigger around than Alex's thigh. He strode towards the group arrogantly, his long, thin black hair twisting around the hooked end of the crowbar he was holding over his shoulder, and pulled up a chair that Ramirez had left empty when he went to give Oscar a hard time.

Since he didn't have a gun or knife visible Alex decided to wait and let things play out a bit. There was no way this guy was going to try and take on the entire group with just a crowbar. Guille and Grady alone could handle him if he tried, but the rest of the group would surely help as well. Alex noticed that the entire group seemed to be having the same thought and visibly relaxed. Everyone except for Todd.

"Evening folks, nice little dinner you've got here," the stranger said with a wicked smile, "any chance you've got enough to share?"

"Sure thing, friend," Todd said through semi-gritted teeth, "how many bowls do you need?"

"Oh, I'll only need one. Just one man after all," he smiled back.

"Nobody wanders around alone in the darkness with only a crowbar," Gordon observed.

"No, I suppose they don't. So you're actually curious how many folks I've got with me?" The stranger asked, "why didn't you just ask?"

"Because I don't know you, and I don't know what your intentions are," Todd replied as Jessica grabbed a bowl and spooned out some of the paella into it.

She started to approach the man when Todd stood up and blocked her path, taking the bowl from her and gently ushering Patti to her mother's side. He turned and approached the man. He was in dirty clothes, unshaven and reeked of body sweat, unbrushed teeth, and other rotten scents. Todd offered him the bowl with a spoon, just slightly out of reach and the man had to stretch his hand out to accept. The sleeve of his coat came up a bit and Todd could see the bandage wrapped around his wrist.

"Well now, isn't that just about the way of it? You don't know me, so you can't trust me. I don't know you, so I can't trust you. Yeah, I've got a couple of folks out there in the darkness. They're making sure I'm okay here, then they'll come in and get their food. It's security, you see?" The stranger rested his crowbar against the chair with the hook on the ground by his feet. He took a sip of the paella broth and an odd look came over his face.

"I've had this before…" he reminisced, clearly searching his memory for where the familiar flavor could have come from.

"Yeah? What did you trade for it, inmate?" Todd asked in a steel voice.

The man shifted nervously in his seat, and the arrogance faded from his eyes. He looked up at Todd and his eyes cut to his crowbar and back, the paella cooling in its bowl resting on his knee.

"You won't make it inmate, best idea is to call your buddies in and let us all talk," Todd said.

"How'd you know I was an inmate?" the man asked.

"Your brands. They work," Todd replied.

"Holy shit! I recognize you! You're the warden!" the man yelled as it suddenly dawned on him.

"That's right. I'm the one that set you free, now how about you call your fellows in and let's talk about your situation," Todd said as Guille and Grady pulled up to either side of him.

The seated man licked his lips nervously, then sounded off with a sharp whistle, like he was calling a dog. The sun was now completely down, with only the faintest glow over the horizon, but Alex could see movement in the darkness and realized there were actually still two figures out there. They seemed to be arguing over who would go in and one slowly started to walk forward. This was his chance and Alex moved quickly on soft footsteps.

He had hunted deer and turkey in his youth that required stalking and had learned how to hide his footsteps in the sounds of other noises in the forest. In this case it was easy to hide his sound under the stumbling and grumbling of the man who had won the debate walking towards the fire, he just had to hope that the darkness and surprise were enough to hide his size. He took an angle that would bring him around behind the remaining figure. His plan worked perfectly and he was able to close the gap and get a large hand around the man's neck as he pushed the barrel of the Glock into the area where the skull and spine met.

"One noise and it'll be the last sound you ever make," Alex growled into his ear, "nod if you get me." The man nodded, trembling at the monstrous claw wrapped tightly around his throat.

"Do you have any weapons?" Alex asked quietly.

Nod.

"Gun?"

Shake.

"Knife?"

Nod.

"Where? Speak quietly,"

"Machete, on the ground by my right foot," came the hushed reply.

"Anything else?" Alex asked as he tapped around on the ground to feel for the handle of the blade.

Shake. Alex finally found the handle with his boot and used it to pull it back behind him. Now that it was out of reach he needed to test the honesty of this man.

"On the ground, belly, flat, *slowly,*" Alex grumbled in his ear menacingly.

The man slowly dropped to his knees, the speed of descent controlled more by the hand around his neck than his own muscles. The hand loosened as he lay forward and starfished out. He'd been through this routine before. When he was arrested, when fights broke out in the yard, when he was being searched. He knew what was coming as Alex used a massive hand to get *very* familiar with his body, checking every angle and space. It occurred to the man on the ground that this was either a prison guard or a former prisoner himself with the thoroughness of the search. He suddenly regretted his choices in life.

Alex found the mid-sized folding knife tucked behind the belt buckle in the front of the man's jeans. He wasn't angry, he'd have tried the same thing if someone got the drop on him, but a lesson needed to be taught. He took the knife and put it in his own pocket. Then put the sharp point of his knee between the shoulderblades of his prisoner and shifted all of his weight onto him as he leaned forward as far as he could. Even though the man on the ground wasn't small by any means, he wasn't anywhere near big enough to fight what was about to happen.

"You lied," he growled quietly.

The air was pressed out of the smaller man's body as it felt like he was under a parked car. He remembered something from a TV show about the middle ages where they had pressed people with rocks and suddenly he had a better appreciation for it. He flailed slightly, but it was pointless. Even if he could get his arms into a solid pushup position there was no way he was coming up from the sheer tonnage on his back.

"You lie to me again, and I will stay here for an hour and watch you suffocate. Slowly," Alex threatened as he shifted his weight and took some of the strain off the man.

There was still no way he was going to get up quickly, but Alex wanted to listen in on the conversation at the fire. He could barely make out anything but it seemed that the two inmates were enjoying their paella and behaving. Alex would have given anything to be able to send Todd a telepathic message that he was out there with another one.

"Name?" Alex asked.

"Marco Fernandez," Marco wheezed.

"What were you in for?" Alex asked him, not taking his eyes off the group at the fire.

"Dope. I used to cook meth for my cousin to sell," he replied.

"Tell me about them," Alex said to the man under his knee.

"Grover and Devon. Grover has the bat, he's a real sicko, man," the man gasped. Alex let off a little more pressure so he could speak, "I don't know his real name, he was in PC. He talks in this voice like a cartoon character and calls himself Grover. Got a real thing for kids. Devon is pure evil, man. We were cellies and he told me stories about what he did, but he was never caught. I'm only with them because I had nowhere else to go."

"Convenient that you're the victim. Alright, here's what's gonna happen, when I stand up you stay down. I'm going to pick up that machete back there and then kick your feet. You stand up, slowly, and we are going to join your traveling companions by the fire. Got it?" Alex finally looked down at the man beneath him.

"Got it," he replied.

Alex slowly took the weight off the man, but never his eyes. He backed away and picked up the machete when he found it. To his prisoner's credit he never so much as flinched while waiting for his signal to rise. After the kick came, he slowly got up and felt the tip of his own weapon pressed into his right kidney, the Glock hanging loosely in his other hand.

"Walk," Alex commanded quietly.

The pair walked forward, attracting attention as the light revealed them to those gathered in the backyard. One of the newcomers noticed everyone's eyes looking into the night and turned in his seat to follow them. He saw his partner first, not noticing the huge shadow that prodded him along.

"Marco, what are you–" he cut off as Alex's huge form emerged, dark hair hanging over his face.

"Evening, Alex," Gordon grinned as he recognized the dark silhouette.

Chapter 7

Alex crept forward, using the machete to push his prisoner and his size to keep the other two quiet for a moment. He moved around Marco to stand in front of the two seated men, then handed the machete to Walton. The former trustee took it and let it hang by his side loosely.

"Nobody else in the field that I saw, warden," Alex said softly.

"Thanks, Alex. Why don't you get yourself some food while we continue our talk with these three," Todd replied, stepping to his side so he was in front of all three men.

"I'll grab you a bowl," Jessica added cheerfully, as though the county sheriff had just rolled up in the middle of a family dispute and put it to bed.

"Thank you Ma'am," Alex replied, not taking his eyes off of the man who had carried the bat and called himself Grover, "I'd like to recommend that the young lady go inside."

"A wonderful idea, I'll take her in," Donna said as she gently grabbed Patti by her shoulders and turned her toward the house.

Alex watched as Grover's eyes followed her, his lip quivering slightly over his twisted yellowing teeth and his brown eyes showing sadness as she got further away. Marco may have lied about a few things, but it seems he had told the truth about this Grover sicko. He reached back and ran his hand through the twisted brown mop on top of his head. Jessica handed him the bowl of paella and he returned the pistol to its place in his waistband.

He took a bite and listened to the tales of woe from the prisoners. Apparently they hadn't had anywhere to go when they were released, so they tried to stick around Big Spring and find "honest work." In their version of the story they were run out because people didn't want any "branded" around their families, so they grabbed whatever they could find and started walking. They weren't really headed anywhere and claimed to be looking for a place to settle down and work the land.

The whole thing stank of bullshit to Alex, and he couldn't help but hope that Todd was picking up on it too, although it didn't really seem like he was. He was asking questions and offering food and water, sitting relaxed in a chair across from them. After a lengthy conversation about the state of things, he stretched and looked up at Walton and Gordon.

"Well gents, I'd like to have a moment to talk with some folks about your situation. If you'll give Walton here your weapons some of us will go talk and y'all can just rest up here for a minute," Todd smiled at them.

The three men just nodded as they leaned back and rubbed bellies that likely hadn't been full in days. Walton collected the bat and the crowbar, moving them to another chair slightly out of reach but right next to Oscar if it came down to it. Todd nodded his head around the corner of the house and Alex, Guille, Ramirez and Gordon followed. As soon as they got around the corner and out of earshot for whispers, Todd was the first to speak.

"There is no way in Hell those three are staying here," he whispered harshly.

Alex was surprised by the finality of his statement right off the bat. He had already been preparing arguments for why they shouldn't stay, what the one had told him out in the field and the suspicion of why they were actually run out. He breathed a sigh of relief when he realized he wouldn't have an uphill battle anymore. He was glad to see Guille and Gordon nodding in agreement.

"Glad to hear you say that, because those dudes never should've been let out of their cages to begin with," Ramirez said, "I remember two of them. That dude with the bat had to be moved to PC because he kept talking in a voice like he was on a kid show and talking about how beautiful the little girls on the TV were." Ramirez shuddered with disgust.

"The other that came in first, he's bad medicine too. That dude bragged about rapes, murders, cutting off people's heads... said he did it and was never caught," Guille added, "he was crazy, talking about eating people and how barbecued human is basically just carnitas. Dude was creepy."

"Well, the only real question is what do we do with them? If we turn them loose we're only passing the sins on to the next family that doesn't know it, or even worse, they come back and get the drop on us," Gordon pointed out.

"Anybody know anything about the other guy? Alex's friend from the field?" Ramirez asked.

"He says his name is Marco, claimed he was in for cooking meth, only teamed up because he was bunkies with Doctor Lecter," Alex answered.

"Bullshit, that creep didn't have a bunkie. They tried to keep him solo because he kept attacking them," Guille countered.

"Interesting..." Alex thought aloud. He definitely hadn't expected the truth from Marco, but wasn't sure what the lie was going to be. Guess now he knew.

"Well, we can talk to him if you like, but I don't see much option on the other two. We either arrest them and take them back to town, or…" Todd let the sentence trail off.

"Or we feed them to the pigs," Gordon offered in a half jest.

"I can't do that," Todd said to him more than anyone else, "I can't kill a man that's not a direct threat."

"They *are* direct threats Todd, even if you don't want to see it. They will be back, one way or another," Alex said. "Now, if you really think there's something that can be done back in town, we can bind them for the night and then take them in tomorrow. Otherwise, best to do it at night while the kids are asleep."

"I think we should bind them. If they fight us, we'll do what we need to do," Todd replied.

The men nodded in acceptance, if not entirely agreeing with the choice. They would back Todd's play. The mixed group walked around the corner of the house and up to the three men sitting in front of them.

"C'mon gents, follow me, I'll show you where you'll be staying tonight," Gordon offered with a smile.

The three men stood up and reached for their weapons, but were swiftly told that they wouldn't be allowed to have them until everyone got to know them better. The answer didn't sit well, but it was laid out as a non-negotiable, so they accepted their circumstances.

They followed Gordon through the dark as Todd went inside to talk to Jessica and his mother. Alex and Guille followed as the rest of the former inmates peeled off towards the bunkhouse. Gordon led the men to the barn where Alex had worked over the rustlers a couple of nights before. He opened the heavy door and ushered them inside where he lit an oil lamp.

"You'll be in here for tonight gentlemen, safe, sound and *secure*," Gordon said as he pulled out a length of rope.

"Wait, what?" Marco asked.

"You'll spend the night tied up," Gordon explained as Grady, Ramirez and Walton came walking up to the open doors with the three less than lethal shotguns they had grabbed from the bunkhouse, "we don't know you, so we don't trust you."

"I saw the scars on the wrists of these guys, they're just like us! You give them guns and welcome them in, but you tie us up? What the Hell man?" Devon screamed.

"We know what they did and what they were in for. We don't know you," Todd answered as he walked through the group with his pistol on his belt and a shotgun furnished in wood where the others were bright orange.

"It's this or a hole," Alex said definitively. He was growing tired of the talk and wanted to go on a quiet walk around the farm, pulling security and listening to the livestock in the barns make their calls.

"This is bullshit," Devon complained as he was led to a post in the barn.

Devon and Grover sat down, facing one another with the post between them. They were laid on their side and had their wrists bound together, then to one another on one side of the post, the process repeated on their ankles on the other side. Marco was given his own post and a slightly longer rope to run from his wrists to his ankles.

"Y'all just try to get some sleep, we'll take care of what we need to in the morning," Gordon said as he blew out the light and the free men walked out of the barn, closing the door over the whining and complaining of the three men inside.

They walked towards Gordon's house and onto the back deck where Alex and Todd had surprised him a few nights prior. There were a few chairs, a deck table and a propane grill on the fourteen-by-eight foot deck. The men circled up to discuss the rest of the night.

"I think we need one person to stay here on the deck at all times, rotate them out every so often, but have them watch that barn," Grady offered, "but we can also have a group walking around like we would any other night."

"Don't see any way around it," Gordon agreed.

"Well, I'll take the first shift watching the barn," Guille offered as he sat down in one of the chairs and kicked his feet up on the small table.

"You know that means *watching*, right? Not a siesta?" Grady asked him with a grin in the darkness.

"Si, si, no dormir en el trabajo," Guille replied.

"If anything happens, everyone turn on a flashlight when they move. We know they don't have guns and it may make it harder to find them, but we don't want to shoot each other running around in the dark," Todd added.

Grady took the shotgun he had brought and leaned it against the chair next to Guille. The non-lethal rounds would at least make a loud enough racket that everyone would come running. After the shifts were worked out Gordon went inside his house while Todd and Alex got ready for the night shift and everyone else headed back to the bunkhouse.

"I need to go get my coat and hat," Alex said, realizing for the first time all night that it had gotten a little cold in the last three hours or so since the sun went down.

"Yeah, sounds good, I'll meet you at the oak," Todd replied, rubbing a hand over his own bicep for warmth.

Alex turned and walked to the bunkhouse, almost catching up to the others on his way. As he closed on the door he realized that everyone had stopped and was waiting outside.

"What's up?" he asked.

"We need to talk, just us," Grady answered him.

"Okay, should we get Oscar?" Guille asked.

"Nah, let the little man sleep, but let's step inside," Grady continued.

As the group stepped inside and gathered around the table, Oscar tossed and rolled over in his bunk. Alex told them he didn't have long as Todd was expecting him, but he was interested in what was going on.

"Look, we gotta figure this out. It's not going to work," Grady started, "I'm all for not hurting people, but we've been here, what, three nights? We've had people walk up on us on two of them. You don't need to be a genius to run those numbers."

He was right, of course, but Alex didn't want to think about it. He knew what Grady was getting at. They didn't have very many people and it was a large piece of land they were trying to care for. Sure, food and water weren't going to be a problem, but other than Todd and his family, none of the farmers were under sixty, maybe even sixty five. How much medicine did they have saved up? What happened then?

"So what are you suggesting?" Ramirez asked.

"I'm suggesting we figure out how to start being more of a help than labor. I'm not a sadist or anything, but we may need to start delivering some more permanent messages to get things to calm down here. It's only going to get harder as people get more desperate," Grady replied.

"So, again, what are you suggesting?" Ramirez pressed as Oscar tossed and turned from his dream.

"I don't know, but we need to figure something out to help these folks and keep us all safe," Grady answered desperately.

"Grady, you were a highschool teacher before you made a stupid mistake. Leave the hardened stuff to us hardened criminals," Alex said, listening as Oscar's movements intensified and he began to really throw himself around.

Alex got up and crept silently to the side of Oscar's bed. The way it was positioned both sides were open and the head of the bed was against a massive wooden upright that ran through to support the ceiling. Alex pulled his hair loose and let it hang down in his face so his eyes cut through it and took a flashlight that Todd had given him and held it so it would light his face from the bottom like he was telling a scary story at Boy Scout camp. The men behind him just sat at the table, confused by what he was doing, but not willing to get involved just yet. He put his face inches from Oscar's before clicking the light on.

"Good Morning, Sweet-lips," he growled loudly but in the lowest, most sinister voice he could muster.

"AY DIOS MIO!" Oscar screamed in a shrill voice and attempted to shove himself back from the terrifying visage in front of him.

He doubled over, falling out of the top bunk and landing squarely on his back with a loud thud. He continued his panicked retreat in a scrambling crab-walk away from the bed towards the showers, escaping from his sheets on the way. The men at the table cut loose with an uproarious laughter that reverberated through the wooden panels inside the bunkhouse and into the clapboard siding. Oscar was almost into the shower room before he realized what was going on.

"PINCHE PENDEJO!" He screamed, this time far more aggravated than scared. He came up from the floor, debating his next move carefully as he squared his shoulders and balled his fists.

"Easy amigo, just a little payback for making me knock my noggin'," Alex grinned as he pulled his hair back and grabbed his knit watch cap off his bunk.

At that same moment, with the men gathered at the table slowly regaining control of themselves, Todd came bursting into the room with a shotgun leveled and at the ready. He swung it back and forth, trying to identify where the danger might be and gain an understanding of what was going on.

"Eaaasssyyy warden, just a little fun," Ramirez chuckled as gently as he could as he wiped away the tears from his eyes.

"I thought there was a problem in here, someone was under attack or something," Todd said as he slowly lowered the large barrel of his weapon.

"Nah, just settling a little prank score, that's all," Alex grinned as he held a massive paw out towards Oscar.

"This is why I hate the top bunk. A lot farther to fall when a puta madre wants to be funny…" he grumbled in response as he took the large hand and shook it.

"Well, if everything is good, you guys get some sleep. Alex and I are going to go on patrol for a bit," Todd replied, "grab your stuff Alex."

"Got it right here, let's roll," Alex said as he pulled on his gloves and adjusted his hat.

The two men walked out into the night and patrolled quietly for almost an hour. They hadn't talked much, almost nothing other than a brief explanation of what was going on in the bunkhouse and some talk about expansion ideas for the farms. Alex wanted to broach the subject of security, but he wasn't sure how to do it without upsetting Todd.

"We need to find a way to lock this place down a bit," Todd mused randomly, unknowingly opening the subject for him.

"Well, we actually had some thoughts on that, boss," Alex ventured, "but I don't know if you're going to like them."

"Hit me with it," Todd replied, stopping to take a drink of water from a metal bottle that hung in a pouch on his hip.

"Well, for one we should start doing more random patrols, and have us split them up. You can't be on all of them," Alex started, "the guards in the prison used to walk through at random times rather than on a schedule and it kept guys from getting *too* stupid at night."

Todd dropped his head and shook it from side to side, capping his bottle and putting it back in the pouch on his belt. He took in a deep sigh and looked up at the stars then let it loose.

"That is the problem Alex, that right there," he started sadly, "you know, I started that policy? The random patrols were one of the first things we did when I came on as warden. We saw a huge decrease in issues at night, but with all the stress of running this place, trying to keep everyone safe and track everything going on… I didn't even think of it."

"At some point you're going to need to sleep," Alex reminded him. He could hear the exhaustion and frustration in Todd's voice.

"We'll start that tomorrow night. I could use the sleep," Todd said, "as for the next twenty-four, we're going to have to figure out what to do with those three."

"You know what we need to do, warden, you just don't want to do it," Alex answered.

Todd stopped dead in his tracks and turned toward the big man standing next to him. The look on his face was vacant of any emotion other than rage. Even in the darkness it was like his eyes were two burning coals staring directly at Alex with no fear, no holding back. The wind softly blew past the two figures, the creaking and groaning of the windmill that powered the water pump and soft rustling of grass were the only sounds.

"Alex, I ordered the murder of hundreds of men at that prison. Not three, not thirty, *hundreds*," he said coldly. "I reconciled in my own head that people were generally good, but the ones at the prison were the gathering of cast-offs that were not. They weren't representative of people at large in my mind, but now I'm seeing that even the ones I tried to save, the ones I gave a second chance to, may have been a mistake. People may just be evil, and I brought six of those people to my home around my family."

"Yeah, you did," Alex replied as he turned and squared up with the smaller man, "and you can't just try to run us off

120

because we know what you have and how light your security already is. So, what's it going to be? You going to kill us too? Or are you going to trust that maybe you misjudged those three, but not us? You want nine more souls on your head, or just three?"

Todd deflated, his head hanging low, shoulders falling forward and breathing slowing to an inconsistent hyperventilation that bordered on a sob. His rifle barrel that had been at chest level for Alex fell to the ground and hung loosely towards his feet.

"Alex, I can't get myself to kill those three, even though they probably deserve it. How am I going to kill you when you've been nothing but helpful and respectful and kept my family safe?" he asked.

"You're not, warden. You're not going to kill anyone, but in the morning, you're going to let me and the boys take care of what needs to be done. I'm not sure all three of them need to die, but two of them definitely do," Alex answered him softly. "You need to learn to let people live in their own space. You know most of what I've done, and you've put together some of why I did it, but that's not you. Before I was a Rebel, I rode with Sin Eaters. Have you ever heard of them?" Alex asked.

"Vaguely. They're a military and first responder group aren't they?" Todd looked up, gathering his emotions as the two started walking again.

"Yeah. They do a lot of good in a lot of communities, but they walk the line between legal and illegal in some areas. They don't run drugs or guns or anything, but they deliver beatdowns and may have been known to make people disappear. They run a protection racket, but the 'fees' are always donations to charity, and the protection is from actual criminals," Alex replied.

"They sound like they can't decide if they are good or bad," Todd observed.

"In some ways they can't. I guess it's in line with their people being soldiers and cops and such. They don't have to follow an ROE anymore, so they do what they think will work, and it usually does even if it's not 100% legal," Alex continued. "I wasn't military, so I couldn't get past being a tagalong, but I did learn a lot with them. One thing that I came to understand is that our leaders sometimes need to look clean and pure, which means those under them need to get dirty. You don't do it for glory, you get the job done that needs doing for the greater mission."

"You're asking me to give you permission to kill those men, Alex," Todd lamented into the night air. It wasn't a question.

"No, I'm recommending you just sleep in a bit. You won't ever have to ask anything. If the boys don't want to help me, that's okay too, but it'll still get done," Alex encouraged him.

It wasn't a bloodlust that fueled him, rather a practical understanding of the situation. He knew what letting them live meant. The crazy one would go on to harass and maybe even kill someone else. He would find someone else to prey upon, and when he had guns and resources he would come back. Ones like that always came back.

The meth-head, eh, he might be okay to let go, especially if they made him watch what happened to the others. He might even spread the word to leave that particular farm alone. Worst case he'd come back eventually as well, but he seemed to be more of a "path of least resistance" type that would rather move on and find an easier scam.

The pedophile, well, he had to die. If he was allowed to live, he'd do the same perverse evil to more children, and in this new world he'd probably be able to find kids who had no parents to defend them. That one had to die, and he was the one that

Alex planned to use to make an example to the meth-head of what he was capable of.

"Alright, here's the plan," Todd broke into Alex's thoughts, "in the morning, we take them to the roadblock with the Sheriff's department and try to turn them over. Maybe they have something setup to handle them and we don't have to get our hands dirty. If that doesn't work, we'll bring them back here and you and the boys can do what you think needs to be done."

"I think that's a mistake, Todd, but it's your show here," Alex replied quietly.

"I know, and it might be, but I've ordered enough death for a thousand lifetimes, I need to at least *try*," Todd replied, "the Sheriff was a worthless bastard before everything happened, but maybe his deputies are stepping up for once."

"They seemed real responsible when we met them on the road the other day," Alex chuckled.

"Yeah, Deputy Carver in particular has always been corrupt and pompous as hell. He's had a dozen internal investigations, accepting bribes, using his authority for discounts at businesses around town, even one about him demanding a woman 'satisfy him' on the side of the road to get out of a bogus traffic ticket that probably wouldn't have held up anyway," Todd replied.

"People like that only get worse in worlds like we have now. They become warlords and tyrants, especially when they have family and close friends they can prop-up in their new empires," Alex said as he scanned an area of pasture to their west.

"Ha! If you only knew, Alex! You want to know how deep it goes? Carver is the acting Sheriff because nobody can find Sheriff Beauson anywhere. There's whispers that he either took off or was taken out of the picture, and most of those whispers point back at Carver as the prime candidate because he was so ready to step-in and run things," Todd whispered as though there were spies lurking in the tall grass of the field or behind the tomato plants in the garden they walked past.

"And to top that tidbit, you remember the good Reverend Shoener? His wife's maiden name was Carver..." Todd grinned into the darkness.

Alex had never been one for gossip, but this was more local politics and information than true gossip. If the Reverend had all the food and medical supplies and God (and Beanie) only knew how many weapons and how much ammo, then it would make sense for his brother-in-law to position himself over security of the town. The only other domino they needed in line would be a threat to the town and they could redesign the government as they wanted.

"Curiosity's sake, Todd, but who recommended the release program at the prison?" Alex asked.

"Huh? I mean, I was the one who kept bringing up the population and supply issues at the town meetings, but Reverend Shoener devised the plan. Carver wanted to just unlock the cells and lock the gates and let y'all starve, but the Reverend said that was inhumane and unchristian," Todd replied, a curious tone to his voice.

Now it made sense. It was really no different than the Romans letting the Germanic hordes inside the gates, then being destroyed from within. The prisoners had nowhere to go and no resources to survive. Few of them would have skills to be able to contribute to society, so they would turn to what they knew, crime. The safety would drop, crime would skyrocket, and people would panic. There would be a call for someone to do something and the dastardly duo that were the Reverend and the makeshift Sheriff would step to the lead.

"Todd, who sits in on the town meetings?" Alex asked as they continued their patrol.

"Well, there's me, Carver, and The Reverend. Beanie is usually there as well but just to give reports on what is going on," Todd started, "the Mayor is in the meetings with the City Manager, but they are more figureheads. We used to have the City Council in there as well, but the meetings would spiral, so the City Manager suggested they set up another meeting with each of them for discussion on specific needs. That hasn't happened yet though."

"So it's just the five of you. Mayor and City Manager pretty close to the others?" Alex continued.

"What are you getting at, Alex?" Todd pushed back, growing confused by the former inmate's line of questioning.

"Just humor me a minute longer," Alex replied.

"Well, the Mayor can't stand Carver. He's dialed him back multiple times with curfews and punishments for petty crimes," Todd replied cautiously, "but the City Manager, Maddie, is fine with them. She was in the choir at Shoener's church for years. She was the one that recommended we bring him in as the spiritual leader of the largest congregation in the county."

Todd's voice slowed as though he was putting something together. Alex stopped walking and shook his head, letting out a loud sigh.

"Do you see it?" Alex asked him.

"They're going to take over," Todd said, shocked by the clarity of it.

"And you're their patsy," Alex added.

"Wait, how's that?" Todd asked, he wasn't that deep in the rabbit hole yet.

"They'll tell everyone that it was actually *your* idea to let everyone loose from the prison, and that it's *your* fault that the town is falling apart from scumbags like we have in the barn. They'll say the Mayor isn't handling it, and call for his removal. The City Manager will be in charge of the politics, Carver will run the security, and the Reverend will be the spiritual leader who pulls the strings from the shadows," Alex detailed the plan clearly.

"Son of a bitch…" Todd was stunned.

"We can go through with your plan, Todd, but tomorrow needs to be the last time we go to town for a while. They are going to count on you being at one of these meetings so they can take you out and parade you around as the cause of the problem," Alex continued, "don't give them an Augustulus to martyr."

"Who?" Todd asked, clearly confused.

"Augustulus was the last emperor of the Western Roman Empire. He was defeated and killed by a barbarian chief. They let the barbarians out, and now they are going to pin it on you so they can take power," Alex responded.

"What the hell, man. You do realize that most people don't know this stuff about history, right?" Todd asked in a bewildered voice. "Like, it's not normal to know that stuff. You're incredibly smart."

"I just read a lot," Alex replied sheepishly. He had never been comfortable with compliments, especially around his intelligence. He was a dumb biker from the backwoods of Georgia, and that's all he wanted anyone to know he was.

"Uh-huh…" Todd chuckled, "I bet. Well, we are going to start off with my plan tomorrow and see where it goes. I'd like you, Guille and Grady to go with me, just in case. Having three very large ex-cons at my side should deter any violence."

"Or kick it off," Alex answered with a shrug, the movement of his massive shoulders up and down and thick arms out to the side visible even in the darkness of night.

The two men were sharing a chuckle at their new found indifference to the end result as they continued their patrol past chicken coops near Paul's house. They only had a circle left past Max's place and then back to Todd's and the first round of the evening would be complete. It took about an hour to do, but wasn't horrible in the cool night air.

They were on the stretch of shared tractor trail that ran between the pastures and allowed both farmers to access the fields with their tractors. You could hear coyotes yelping in the distance, so the pair agreed that later they may want to bring the little .22 they'd gotten from the Reverend and a bright spotlight.

They were discussing the best way to set up their little ambush when they heard an explosion back towards Gordon's house. Then three more in rapid fire.

Both men seemed to realize exactly what the shotgun blasts were and where they had come from at the same time. No words were said, they simply turned and took off running as fast as they could, turning on the flashlights they carried as they ran so nobody would mistake them as rustlers. They rounded the corner of Gordon's house to see Gordon and Grady standing on the back porch and a handful of flashlights being carried at a dead run from the bunkhouse.

"WHAT THE HELL IS GOING ON!?" Todd yelled as he caught his breath at the bottom of the stairs.

"They're loose!" Grady yelled.

"Dammit!" Alex bellowed and turned towards the barn.

"The only one left out there is that Marco fellow," Grady said softly, "the other two took off."

Gordon was holding a hand towel on Grady's forehead trying to sop up the blood that was running down his face. As the other men came running up with weapons of various types Todd was giving them sections of the farm to go search and instructing them to *carefully* knock on the doors of Max and Paul's homes and tell them what was going on.

"What happened to you?" Walton asked, stepping up to help Gordon tend Grady's busted noggin.

"I heard a sound out in the barn and thought they were trying to get loose, so I went out to check. As soon as I opened the door they hit me in the head with a shovel and I went down," Grady told the men still gathered there. "Luckily, I never let go of the shotgun and they didn't realize I had it since I'm left handed. I got one round off but forgot it was just pepper. It burned like hell in the cut but just scared them off. I dumped three more shots to try to get to the stuff that actually threw something at them. One of them yelped but it didn't slow him down."

"You did good, Grady, you alerted us that there was something going on," Gordon reassured him.

"I wish I'd have changed the order or something," Grady lamented, "I should have dumped everything I had."

"It's alright, Grady," Todd added, " Okay, you two tend to Grady and check the bonds on the one still in the barn. We need to find the other two before they get too far."

"We need to check your house first," Alex said seriously.

"You really think they'd go after my family instead of running away?" Todd asked Alex as they took off at a run towards the house.

"I think that pedophile hasn't touched a kid in a long time and he's jonesing," Alex huffed.

Todd just looked at the large man and added speed to his run.

Chapter 8

They hit the back porch at the same time, Alex's long strides having helped him keep pace with Todd who was running faster than he had ever run before. Todd grabbed the doorknob to the back door and threw it open, slamming it against the wall and causing various pictures and tchotchkes on shelves to rattle.

"Bedrooms are upstairs, top of the stairs is our room, down the hall is a bathroom, then the boy's room, then then Patti's," Todd told Alex as they quickly checked the downstairs.

Alex turned behind Todd and followed him up the stairs. There was a new problem now that he wished he knew the answer to but didn't dare to ask and distract Todd with it. Alex hoped the bags of guns that Todd had brought in the house were locked away somewhere that they weren't going to be a problem.

They climbed the stairs, with Todd hitting the doorway to his bedroom and throwing it open as Alex turned and walked down the hallway. He knew the two boys would be scared of him, but if they were hiding from him, it would simply have to do as proof that they had managed to hide from the pervert too. He opened the door and saw the two beds, lumps under blankets on top. He slowly walked in, holding his hand over the end of his flashlight and turning it on, fingers separated just enough to let a small slit of light out into the darkness.

He saw the blond and brown hair of the two boys on the pillows, blankets slowly rising and falling. He turned the light off and backed out of the room, taking their peaceful sleep at face value. Maybe they had managed to make it here before the escapees? Or maybe Todd was right and they'd just decided to get the hell out of Dodge? Alex gently closed the door and heard talking coming from Todd's room. He assumed Todd was talking to Jessica and telling her what was going on, so he decided to simply go downstairs and let them have a moment.

Something started itching in the back of Alex's brain. Something he couldn't put his finger on. It was in the back of his head, and he felt his gut start to tighten into knots. Something wasn't right though. Had he really *seen* the boys' blankets rising and falling? Had he just heard something? Yes, there it was again, a muffled whimper. Something quiet.

Something coming from Patti's room.

Alex turned and walked slowly down the remaining few feet of hallway, careful to place his heavy boots as close to the edge of the worn carpet as he could. He didn't know exactly where the old farmhouse would creak and groan under his weight, but his experience said that floorboards were noisier in the center of a pathway than on the edges. He took a finger and traced it across the center of the doorknob, holding his breath and hoping against hope that there was no keyhole there, which would mean the door had a lock and he would have to knock it down.

"I'm so sorry little one," he whispered silently, "you should never have to feel this. You should never have to see what's about to happen."

He slowly opened the door and found Patti sitting in Grover's lap in a rocking chair. He exhaled in relief as he saw that both of them were fully clothed. Grover was rubbing her back through her nightgown, smiling as he whispered in her ear. Patti sat perfectly vertical, sobbing gently, wincing ever so slightly each time the man whispered in her ear.

"I think we should let the little one get some sleep, Grover. Let's go for a walk," Alex said gently.

"But why would I do that? We're having so much fun!" the twisted man replied in a voice that would have belonged in a kid's show, had it not been for the sinister undertone.

"Are you having fun, little one?" Alex asked her.

She didn't reply, but shook her head, turning large, sad eyes up at Alex in the light of a little battery powered LED light by the bed. Grover just started to grin an evil, twisted smirk, reaching his arms around her and rubbing his hands together.

"She's got a point," he started in his horrible voice, "this is getting tiresome. Maybe we should find another way to have... fun."

"Not today," Alex replied flatly, producing the Glock from his waistband.

"Are you really going to show her what you are? If I say no? If I refuse to leave? If I threaten to break her sensual little neck?" the pervert grinned back at Alex.

"Little one, I need you to get up and come over here," Alex said softly. "He's going to hold onto your hand, or try to stop you, but he can't. He can't stop you because all you need to do is walk out the door. Go ahead, walk out the door."

The noise from Todd and Jessica's room had grown to a yelling match. There were three clear voices now, two male and one female. The conflict between the three was impossible to ignore, with clear threats and pleas being exchanged.

Patti slowly turned and put her feet on the floor. Grover leaned forward and whispered something in her ear before kissing her on the cheek. She winced and swallowed hard, freezing in her steps. When she opened her eyes again she was staring at Alex.

"He can't hurt your brothers, little one. The only one he could hurt is you, and you're going to walk away from him," Alex smiled as he squatted down in front of her, holding one arm out to her and the other as a gesture towards the door.

Patti continued her movement now, revitalized that the huge man in front of her knew what this creep was saying and that he was already a step ahead of him. Patti took a few steps forward as Grover held onto her arm. When she had reached the end of the lead he was giving her, she turned and ripped her arm away from him as powerfully as her small frame could muster.

Alex smiled and waved both hands in a "go ahead" manner, showing her the door. She took a step through and held a small hand back towards him, offering to lead him into the hall as well.

"Sorry little one, but I need to take this one back to the barn first. Go to your brothers' room," Alex instructed her gently, "oh, and when you get out there, just yell to daddy that Alex said everything out here is okay. Can you do that for me, please?"

"Yes Mr. Alex," she whispered as she walked into the hallway and pulled the door to her room closed behind her.

Alex rose and stared at the man in the chair who had remained still the entire time. It was almost as though he had accepted his fate, grinning like a Cheshire cat as his prey slowly walked away.

"Daddy? Mr. Alex says everything out here is okay," you could hear her yell from the hallway as the distinct *thunk* of a door closed.

"It's not nice to lie to children," Grover said to Alex, "everything is certainly *not* okay here."

"Not for you," Alex said as he took a step forward.

Suddenly, two shots rang out from the other end of the hallway, causing Alex to turn and look at the door. In that split second Grover launched himself on the gigantic man, plunging a homemade shank into his shoulder. The pain shot through Alex's body like lightning. Fortunately for Alex this was a sensation he'd felt before, and he knew how to ride it out. He grabbed Grover's forearm and twisted it as hard as he could, causing him to let go of the shank and drop to his knees.

Alex grabbed the man by the neck and threw his knee into his head as hard as he could, watching the body go limp and crumple to the floor. He pulled the shank out of his shoulder, putting it in his pocket and grabbing the man on the ground by the collar. He opened the door to see the three children standing in their doorway, staring at their parents' room.

"Back in bed, close the door," Alex said firmly as he dragged the unconscious body by them.

Patti ushered her brothers back inside and locked eyes with Alex as she closed the door to their room. He continued down the hall, standing outside of Todd's room.

"Warden?" he yelled.

Todd swung around the edge of the doorway and almost lost control of his pistol as he slapped it against Alex's chest. He pulled back and leveled the barrel again before realizing what was going on. He looked past Alex, down the hall, then at the unconscious man being dragged along, then back at Alex's face.

"It's just me, Todd," Alex said softly.

"Yeah, I, uhm, yeah. Where are the kids?" he asked.

"Down the hall, in the boys' room. They're pretty freaked out and need their mom and dad," Alex replied, staring at the gun that was still pointed at him.

"Yeah, um, yeah…" Todd slowly muttered as he came back around to reality but stood there, still clearly in shock.

Alex looked around the corner of the doorway and saw Jessica standing over a body on the floor. She had a small pistol in her hand, and was holding it firmly on the lump at her feet. She briefly looked up at Alex, then returned her focus to the shape on the floor.

"Can I help with something Ms. Jessica?" Alex asked into the room, returning his stare to the still in-shock Todd in front of him.

"I think he's dead, but I'm not sure. I need someone to carry him out," she replied softly.

It was at that moment that Ramirez and Oscar came running into the house on the first floor. They'd heard the shots and came running, not sure what they were running into. They came in much slower and louder than Todd and Alex had, yelling as they entered.

"WHO'S UP THERE!? WHAT'S GOING ON!?" the two men were yelling.

"We're up here, it's okay!" Alex replied.

The two men came up the stairs, looking at the pile of unconscious pervert at Alex's feet and Todd staring at the door to his kids' room. Ramirez froze in front of Oscar and looked at Alex with terror in his eyes.

"Tell me you weren't too late," he whispered.

"No, just in time in fact," Alex assured him, "Ms. Jessica is in there and needs a hand with a mess." He nodded his head into the bedroom as he bent down and grabbed the collar of the other man.

The two climbed the stairs and gently walked past Todd, although Ramirez's foot did "accidentally" hit Grover in the head as he passed by. Hard. They checked the body at Jessica's feet, finding a circular hole in the lower right corner of the left eye, and a significant portion of the skull missing. There was no doubt this man was dead, but the trauma of having killed him seemed to be too much for Todd and Jessica and they couldn't seem to process it.

"You don't need to cover him anymore Ms. Jessica, we've got it," Ramirez said softly.

"You should go to your kids," Oscar told her, tossing a towel over the missing part of the man's head.

"You're sure you've got him?" she asked, panic creeping back into her voice, "if he wakes up, are you sure you can handle him?"

"That's not going to be a problem," Oscar sarcastically quipped under his breath.

"*Cállate!*" Ramirez hissed at him before turning back to Jessica, "we've got it, go to your kids."

Jessica laid the pistol on the bed and ran to the boys' room, her maternal instincts kicking back in through the shock and pressing her on to check on her children. Alex snapped his fingers inches from Todd's face and put a slight crack in his stupor.

"Go check on your kids, Todd," he said firmly.

Todd blinked a few times and looked down at the limp body in Alex's hand, he slowly curled his right fingers into a fist

136

and started to pull his own pistol from his belt with his left. The stupor of trauma that had painted his face a few moments ago was gone now, replaced by pure hatred and rage.

"Not now," Alex told him, holding his hand out to block Todd's pistol from taking aim, small drops of blood dripping from the knuckles where it had run down from the wound on his shoulder, "I swear he'll get his, but not here. Your family is traumatized and needs you right now."

Todd slid the pistol back into the holster and locked eyes with Alex, his chest rising and falling in a rage filled breath.

"Wait for me," he replied, "don't do anything to him without me there."

Alex nodded and let Todd cross by him in the hallway, headed towards the bedroom that was now filled with sobs and calming hushes. Alex dragged the unconscious man down the stairs as Oscar and Ramirez used a sheet to wrap up the body so they could carry it. Grover's feet dragged limply down the stairs, thudding with each tread they passed over.

As Alex made his way out the back door of the farmhouse Grover began to come around. He wasn't fully conscious yet, but was beginning to moan and groan as the fog cleared his head and the cold night air swirled around him. It took him a few minutes to realize that he was being drug along the ground in an almost seated position, his feet stretched out in front of him as he levitated backwards, held up by the armpits of his shirt and the scruff of his neck.

By the time Grover was able to process his surroundings and what was going on they had made it to the barn. Alex stood Grover up at the same post he had been tied to before, except this time he was tied with his arms behind him at the wrists. Grady, Walton and Gordon were there, and were joined by Oscar and Ramirez shortly. The only missing members of the group in Alex's mind were Guille and Todd.

"Mr. Gordon, do you have any tools around? Particularly a spike or large hook?" Alex asked.

"I've got some 12-inch logging spikes, what do you need them for?" Gordon returned, not entirely sure he wanted the answer.

"Security," Alex answered him dryly.

After a moment or two of silence Gordon realized that Alex wasn't going to give any further explanation and he went to get the spikes and some tools. When he returned, Alex took one spike from him as well as a large hammer. He held the spike up to the man's stomach, pressing in as he did. Grover winced from the metal jabbing into his body, but Alex stopped before he even drew blood.

Instead of trying to drive it through the pedophile, Alex reached as high as he could and used the large hammer to sink the massive spike deep into the vertical wooden beam. Every blow from the hammer sent a shockwave of pain through his arm, but he refused to let the pervert see him wince. He grabbed ahold of it and tried to lift himself, seeing that it wasn't going anywhere he let go and took a deep breath. He untied the bonds that held Grover in place and brought his hands up in front of him.

He started by tying a <u>poacher's knot</u> in the rope, taking a <u>bight</u> from the middle and looping the knot over itself, then back around through the hole to create a center loop that wouldn't shrink or tighten. After that he tied a handcuff knot by centering the poacher's knot and crossing the loose ends of the rope over one another, then passing the resulting loops back through one another. These loops would tighten and only loosen if all pressure was taken off of them, and Alex had no intention of this man taking pressure off of them.

He grabbed Grover's hands and put the loops over them, lifting the center loop to tighten the sides. Ramirez and Oscar gave him a hand lifting the man up as he started to kick and fight. Since Alex was the only one able to reach the spike above he had to use his one strong arm to hang the loop of the poacher's knot.

After they had tressed the man up by the spike and rope his feet hung about four inches from the ground. He spent about five minutes trying to shake his rope bonds or slip the loop off of the spike before the strain on his arms was too much. Although his arms were beginning to turn into limp noodles from exertion and blood loss, his mouth seemed to be working fine as he continued to cuss Alex and the other men, making endless threats. His creepy character voice made them even more menacing, allowing them to worm their way into even Alex's mind. Marco laid in the corner the entire time watching the events unfold but said nothing.

"Now that he's handled, let's talk about you," Alex started as he turned to Marco. "Why didn't they free you?"

"They said I shouldn't have told you anything. They called me a snitch and left me here to take their punishment," Marco replied from the ground.

"How did they escape?" Alex continued.

"There's a metal piece at the bottom of that post. Looks like some kind of old nail or something and they wore through their ropes. Once they had one hand done they just untied everything else," Marco informed them.

Ramirez went to the bottom of the post, approaching from the back so he didn't get kicked. Sure enough, there was an old wooden framing nail sticking out at the base of the post, bent at an angle where it would have a decent snagging angle on a rope. Ramirez picked up the hammer that Alex had set down and drove the nail deep into the wood.

"Did they tell you what they were going to do?" Alex asked the prisoner on the floor.

"They didn't say anything to me, just called me a rat and left," Marco answered again.

"See!? You are a rat!" Grover screamed at him, "shut your damn mouth, rat!"

In one smooth, swift motion Alex spun around and delivered a half-power blow to Grover's <u>solar plexus</u>, relieving him of his ability to speak for a few minutes. The punch hit hard enough to suck all the air from Grover's lungs and knock the wind out of him, leaving him gasping and panicking.

"Quiet," Alex commanded calmly.

"Where is Devon?" Marco asked carefully.

"Devon is in a wheelbarrow outside, getting ready to go into the pig pen," Ramirez informed him, "guess you could say he lost his head when things got tough."

Grover continued to wheeze as his diaphragm started to work again. His head hung down, staring at the 4 inches that would have provided him relief from the growing pain in his arms. It may as well have been four miles, because there was no way he could even stretch his feet and tiptoes to reach the dust that still hung over the floor where the men had lifted him up. Todd came walking into the barn with Guille behind him. The two walked over to the gathering and Guille looked up at the spike in the pillar.

"That had to be your handiwork," he whispered to Alex, "nobody else can reach that high."

"Yeah, he's not escaping again," Alex replied back. Walton began to tear pieces of a sheet and tend to the wound Alex had been ignoring.

Todd walked in a slow circle around the post that held Grover suspended in the air. He looked over the now silent man in his dirty denim jeans and sweat soaked button down shirt. He was a pathetic sight. Next, he approached Marco, who lay on his side facing the center of the barn, wrists and ankles still bound together. Even in his submissive, undefendable state he still managed to cower away from Todd as he approached. Todd regarded him curiously, as though he hadn't quite decided what to do with him yet.

"Sit him up, tie his hands behind the post," Todd said coldly, then turned away from Marco and back to Grover.

Oscar and Walton were closest, so they proceeded to prop Marco up in a seated position and tie his hands together behind the post. Everyone appeared uneasy as the cold, collected former warden simply stood and stared at the process. Once Marco was in position and bound, Todd turned his focus back to Grover. He dragged a wooden block they had used for putting under the tongue of trailers over to Grover's feet and put it under them. It wouldn't allow him to get all of the weight off of his arms, but he could at least relieve the tension enough to breathe.

"So, what was the plan, exactly? You go in, and you rape my little girl while that other shit-bird raped my wife, then what?" Todd started, "you had to know we'd find you eventually. You might have been able to get started, but we'd have found you before you finished."

"Just wanted… a taste… before… dying…" Grover panted, "just… one more… time." He had to flex his ankles to lift himself up for each word.

"A taste, huh? Well, you didn't. The punk you traveled with might have copped a feel on my wife, but I broke that up. She shot him in the head and blew his skull apart before he could do much else. You heard that, right? The shots?" Todd asked with a twisted smile.

Grover simply nodded.

"Yeah, Jess has been a decent shot her whole life. I always wondered what would happen if she had to use it in an emergency situation. Turns out that once she knew ol' Alex there had you under control, she let two rounds fly like it was any other day at the range," Todd told the hanging man.

"That a girl, Jess," Gordon grinned, congratulating her in her absence.

"Now what was your plan? What were you going to do if Alex hadn't stopped you?" Todd continued the macabre line of questioning.

"That's… for me… to live out… in my head… for the… rest of… my… life," Grover huffed at him with a demonic grin.

"Well, it won't be long," Todd said firmly as he turned back to Marco.

"Why didn't they take you?" Todd asked him.

"We covered that. Marco didn't know what they were going to do, and they didn't free him because they thought he was a rat for spilling to me like he did in the field," Alex chimed in.

Todd simply nodded his head, pondering the story.

"Well, good. That's good, Marco, because we need a messenger, and you just won the award," Todd informed him.

Marco looked up from the spot his eyes had been locked for the proceeding portion of the conversation. He had tears in his eyes and his face belied the terror in his mind. Todd moved over next to him and crouched down, his face only a foot or so away from Marco's, and pointed at the desperate figure hanging on the beam.

"You see, Marco, that thing up there has committed some of the most despicable crimes against man and God that anyone ever could. He hurt children, and he was going to do it again. And likely again and again until somebody stopped him," Todd said softly but loud enough for everyone assembled to hear him. "So we are going to be those somebodies. We are going to stop him."

He stood from his crouched position and walked over to Grady, looking over his head and whispering something in the injured man's ear, making him nod and driving a lone tear from his eye. He then proceeded over to Guille, Oscar, Ramirez and Walton, shaking hands and nodding to each of them. Finally, he arrived at Alex, looking up into the hardened eyes of the large man.

"If it hadn't been for Alex here, there's no telling how this night would have gone. It may have been different from the very moment you saw our campfire. No matter, now it's my job to see it through, but I want to say, Alex, that my family and I are forever indebted to you. I can never repay what you did for us tonight," Todd smiled as he shook the massive paw in front of him.

"It's in that spirit that I am taking Alex's advice," he said loudly as he turned to Grover. "Grover, you're going to die tonight, but I'm not going to kill you. I am going leave you there, to suffocate. To die hanging from your arms, gasping for breath, thinking of every miserable thing you have ever done."

"You see, crucifixion, not unlike how you are hanging now, kills by suffocating people," Todd continued, "and you said a minute ago that what you were going to do to my daughter was for you to know in your head. Well, I hope you think of it. I hope you think of it until that spark that makes you the twisted monster you are burns out. I hope it takes you hours to die, and all you can think about is my precious, sweet daughter who you couldn't hurt."

On that note Todd kicked the block out from under Grover's feet and his arms went taught again. His bodyweight was pulling down hard enough that he was unable to take a full breath unless he pulled up slightly, which was already a struggle for him. Todd heard him groan and smiled, turning back to Marco.

"Marco, tomorrow we will take you back to town, and you'll be handed over. I don't know if you deserve to live or not, but I won't kill you," Todd told the now sobbing man. "I'm going to turn you over to the Sheriffs, and let them decide. But I will tell you this: you're going to spend this entire night listening to him die. You're going to be the first one to know when he stops breathing. When the occasional shallow wheeze becomes a deafening silence and you can't remember how long it's been since he breathed last. You're going to carry that story however long you live, and you will tell it. Tell them that when you come to *this* ranch to hurt *these* people, *that* is how you die."

The men in the barn shifted uneasily. It wasn't that they disagreed with anything that Todd was saying, only the way he was saying it. He sounded so passionate, so eloquent in the delivery, as if he took joy in knowing it. It made sense to Alex if he did. He was just glad that he was able to spare Todd the sight of sweet Patti sitting on the monster's lap, shivering every time he whispered in her ear. Alex would carry that burden, and he was okay with that.

"So you're not going to kill me?" Marco asked hopefully.

"No, we aren't going to kill you," Todd replied, but after a brief pause he added, "but we aren't going to save you either." Then he turned to the gathered men and nodded.

"If you guys can iron out the security for the rest of the night, my wife and kids need me," he said as he walked out of the barn.

Chapter 9

The men put together rotations for the rest of the night and the next morning, after Todd and the family were up and had made breakfast, they met the men in the bunkhouse. The family was cheerful, bringing in the mounds of eggs and piles of bacon that had been prepared. If it wasn't for the lack of electricity and collection of ex-cons it would have been like any other Sunday morning celebration.

Patti sat next to Alex, drawing a picture for him with crayons and talking his ear off about her former favorite show on TV and how she wondered what would happen with all of the puppet characters. She believed that maybe the people that worked with them would take them in and take care of them. Alex didn't have the heart to tell her that they weren't real and the people likely didn't care at all about what happened to them.

The family poured out genuine praise and thanks, making the former thugs, drug dealers and general criminals around the table uncomfortable, but they understood the intention behind it. Donna was running non-stop, making sure milk glasses were full and plates didn't go empty. She had even tapped into the emergency supplies they had set aside and brewed fresh, strong coffee for them.

After the meal was finally over, the men gathered to figure out their daily chores and who was going to handle which task. Grady was told to rest and heal up a bit, while Ramirez and Alex were tapped to go with Todd to the checkpoint and drop off Marco and the bodies. Everyone else divied up the farm chores and lined out their day.

Ramirez and Alex joined Todd on his way to the barn where Marco and Grover were being held. There was no conversation on their way there, the men preparing themselves for the deathly scene they were sure to see. The doors creaked open and the sunshine cut through the dust that twisted up. Marco looked up at them and coughed slightly.

Ramirez walked over to Marco and cut him loose, lifting him up and letting him stretch his limbs. He kept an eye on him as Todd and Alex moved to take Grover down from his perch. They were shocked to see him shudder when they touched his clammy skin.

"Are you kidding me?" Todd yelled, shocked.

"Nope," Alex answered, pulling his right shoulder back and releasing a massive right fist at full velocity to the abdomen and solar plexus of the man.

Grover let go of a whoosh of air with a low, guttural sound. Whatever oxygen was stored in his lungs up to that point was expelled, and he hung loosely, beginning to heave and gag on his own empty lungs.

"Solved," Alex said frankly.

"You didn't have to do that," Todd grumbled as he turned to Alex. He made no effort to save the man, but felt it needed to be said.

"You pronounced 'get to' wrong, Boss," Alex replied with a smile.

Todd simply grinned back and shook his head, he wasn't upset, but it felt like something he should have said. He started watching the struggling muscles in the man's chest and abdomen try to draw breath, but to no avail. Todd turned around and grabbed Marco by his shoulders, pressing his head against Grover's chest.

"Listen," he growled menacingly, "listen to his last breath. Tell this story when people think we are easy pickings."

Marco stood silently with his head against Grover's chest. He heard the gurgling of his stomach as his body struggled to divert resources to only the most essential organs. He heard his heart slow as the life giving organ struggled to function on its reduced ration of oxygen. The lungs wheezed as they fought to fill.

Then silence.

After a few minutes of nothingness had passed in the void of his chest, Marco pulled his head back and closed his eyes. It wasn't like he'd lost a friend, after all, he saw Grover as nothing more than a sick monster that deserved to die slowly and painfully, but it was still unsettling to actually listen to his last breath. To hear his organs cease to work.

"He's dead," Marco said solemnly.

"Good, then he won't mind hanging around for a bit to make sure," Ramirez quipped.

"Dark man, that's dark," Alex said, shaking his head.

"Fuck that petter," Ramirez shrugged.

Todd offered Marco a couple of pieces of bacon and some water to eat while they waited. Alex checked Grover for a pulse, holding his fingers over the carotid artery in his neck. He held his fingers there for what felt like five minutes with no response. He wasn't medically trained, but he knew what no pulse for that length of time meant. He wrapped his arms around the body's waist, doing his best to stay out of the urine and fecal matter on the pants, then lifted him pulling the rope over the spike and then laying the shell on the ground. It wasn't remorseful or gentle.

"Good, it's done," Todd nodded. "We'll load him and what's left of the other into the back of the van. Wrap them in tarps first to keep it clean. You, messenger boy, will ride next to Alex in the middle seat so you don't get froggy."

"Yes warden," Marco gently sobbed.

"Hey warden, if there's a chance today, should we stop by the market and see about getting some news from the area? Maybe check-in with the weatherman and get some supplies for solar stills?" Alex asked.

"We can try, Alex," Todd lamented, "but I honestly don't think we'll be welcome long. I don't think this visit is going to be a pleasant one."

"Understood, but figured I'd throw the idea out there," Alex replied as he rolled the body in a bedsheet they'd brought out before lifting it over his shoulder and heading for the van.

Ramirez made sure that Marco was loaded in the middle seat as Alex and Guille put the bodies in the back. The pillowcase that had been put over Devon's head was sticky and black with old blood and clumps of brain matter. The most disturbing part to Alex was the waste of what looked like a nice, high thread count pillowcase.

Guille wished them good luck and reminded them about the radio guy who may have heard back from his sister. Alex told him they'd try but that Todd didn't think they'd receive an overly warm welcome. Guille simply shrugged and said thanks as he headed for the bunk house. Alex climbed in the middle seat, pinning Marco against the far side of the vehicle as Todd climbed in behind the steering wheel and Ramirez rode shotgun.

The old trustee was chatting Todd's ear off about some concoction he hoped to be able to make with vegetables and chicken from the farm. Something about rice being stuffed in the chicken with peppers and spices, but to Alex it sounded like he was talking under water. After a night of adrenaline dumps and heavy activity, the road seemed to drag on forever, and no matter how hard he fought it, the world seemed to close in around him. He saw the tunnel vision forming as his eyelids grew heavy and his head began to loll back and forth.

Alex looked down and all he saw was blood. Blood on his boots, on his hands, running down his forearms. He could feel it on his face, small circles that coagulated at the edge and felt tight like drying mud. He looked at the filthy mattress where the naked woman had curled into a ball. She was bleeding profusely from open wounds on her face and arms where she had been struck, as well as from other places Alex didn't want to look at.

At his feet was a body. One of the members of the Phoenix crew, his head cleaved nearly in half, was laying on his back with his right shoulder on top of the toe of Alex's left boot. The blank, dead stare looking up at him, his face twisted in a look of confusion and rage, a slowly burning joint hanging out of the corner of his mouth with the lit cherry against his cheek, making his skin burn.

As Alex moved his eyes around the room he saw more. He saw a body crumpled at the foot of the bed, his pants wadded around his ankles, exposing his thighs and genitals which were covered in blood as well. He had no shirt on, and there was a large gash between his shoulder blade and spine, clean cut white rib ends protruding out slightly.

Against a wall, the body of his Vice President was slumped over, the head twisted at an unnatural angle and his jaw hanging open in an eternal, silent scream. He had an odd diamond imprint centered almost perfectly between his eyes that looked as though it were set into the bone of his skull.

A final, familiar body lay in the corner behind Alex, a large square hole in its head oozing brains down the front of his leather vest. The open front of the vest exposing his bare chest and stomach, the latter of the two torn open with a wide gash that ran from hip to hip and made his internals become his externals.

He had to force himself to remember what had happened. It all seemed blank, but it started to come back to him when he saw the rusted Estwing shingling hammer in his hand, still dripping blood from the bladed end and with a thick gray goo with small white speckles on the blunt, square head. He remembered earlier in the day, which seemed like ten lifetimes ago, that he had stood next to the toolbox and watched these men take turns at the poor woman in front of him. He saw the hammer sitting on top and thought that it would make a good weapon in a pinch, but he'd just walked away.

Hadn't he?

Didn't matter now, it was done. The four men were motionless in bloody piles on the floor. Alex turned and grabbed a painter's tarp from a nearby shelving unit and tossed it to the woman on the bed. She numbly pulled it over herself and looked up at him, clearly unsure of whether or not she had been saved, or simply gone out of the proverbial pan and into the fire.

"Go," Alex said as he pointed at the door in the back of the shop, "find the police."

He turned and slid his boot out from under the dead man's shoulder. He had no intention of cleaning this up. To Hell with them. He buried the bladed side of the hammer deep into a two-by-four that ran overhead as a support beam, the murderous edge sticking out the other side by at least two inches. He walked out the door, casually wiping the blood from his face and hands with a shop rag as though he'd just changed the oil on a bike. Even though he was careful to close the door behind him, his ghoulish appearance was too much to hide from those still partying outside.

It only took a couple of minutes before someone had gotten suspicious and slipped in the garage door to find the bodies in their macabre state. The man ran out and raised the alarm, notifying everyone about the murder that had just occurred. Alex instantly regretted leaving the hammer behind, but he pulled out his father's Buck 110 pocket knife and flipped it open, revealing an almost four inch blade.

It felt like he was fighting for years at that point. As though he had wandered into the mythical battles of Valhalla or the depths of Dante's Hell and was submitted to a torture of endless combat. There was no telling how long the fight actually was, because they just kept coming, bearing whips made from chains, wrenches and pipes as clubs, slashing with knives and broken bottles.

The police finally broke up the brawl. Apparently they had been staged at either end of the road leading to the clubhouse to grab anyone drinking and riding, so the woman was able to get to them quickly. They arrested everyone, no exceptions, and carted them off to county lockup. Alex was given his own ride and own cell when the other bikers identified him as the murderer from the shop and the woman unintentionally corroborated it when she claimed he saved her.

It wasn't until much later that Alex would learn what actually happened. His court appointed lawyer had gotten his degree online and passed the bar exam by about two points, but it was what he had. There was a decent chance that Alex could have argued his own case better, but he remembered Abraham Lincoln's opinion of the pro se defendants stance.

The pathetic excuse for a lawyer argued that Alex was fighting in defense of an innocent party and essentially just tried to save a damsel in distress. There were only two problems with that line of defense though: the prosecution argued that with his massive size he shouldn't have needed a weapon to do so. Surely he could have used his large stature and fists to achieve the same result, according to them. The second issue was the testimony of Miss Cynthia Lee Moss. When "Cindy Lee" took the stand she recounted what she felt was a heroic tale of a man saving her from four monsters at once. The court and jury seemed to hear it a little differently.

The 23 year old Cindy Lee had met a charming, dark haired man with a deep tan complexion and well worn leather jacket at a bar the night before the event. They had spent the night flirting, having drinks and smoking cigarettes at a local road house as he tried to invite her back to his club house to hang out and get "friendly."

Cindy Lee had refused multiple times, but just as she was about to call it a night and call her ride, she lost her memory. She described blackness, fuzzy lights and slow tempo music. She vaguely remembered being on a growling horse (later realized to be the man's motorcycle) as lights flashed by and wind blew through her hair. The next thing she knew, she was laying naked on a dirty mattress in the shop.

Alex tried to tune her out as she recounted for the court what the men had done to her. The hours on end she had had to endure, the countless people that came and went delivering food, drugs, and beer so the men could stay and have their fun. She had remembered seeing Alex in the corner at one point, but then he left. She said that that was when she prayed she would just die so it would be over. Instead, she lived, and remembered when the huge man had come back.

She began to refer to Alex as "her Angel" in the story. Saying that her Angel came back and grabbed a hammer off the toolbox, instantly swinging it into the forehead of one of the men, causing him to fly across the room and land with a sickening thud against the far wall. She recounted how the remaining three were so shocked that they didn't even move, she took the opportunity to try to get away, but all she could manage was crawling to the head of the mattress and curling into a ball.

Next, her Angel swung the bladed side of the weird hammer into the back of the man who had been between her legs only moments before. He let out a soft gasp and collapsed to his knees, slumping forward on the mattress, his body going limp almost instantly. He turned and slashed the bladed side across the stomach of the next man, spinning the weapon in his hand and then striking him in the head before lifting his now limp body by the throat and throwing it against a wall.

The final man had made an attempt to fight back, but to no avail. Her Angel simply swung his weapon with a mighty bladed blow at the top of the head, splitting it like a cantaloupe and causing the body to drop in a heap at his feet. She said it was the most horrifically glorious sight she'd ever seen. Her Angel, her avenging Angel, had killed four large, evil men in the blink of an eye.

By her account she knew she was safe, although Alex remembered the fear in her eyes as she looked at him. Next, he took a huge cloth from the shelf and threw it to her, telling to run and get help. To stay safe and find the police, and that he wouldn't let anyone follow her before he bravely turned and walked out to fight the rest of the motorcycle gang.

Of course, Alex knew that wasn't what he'd said, but the semantics didn't matter. Maybe her flowery version would help his case anyway. When it was his turn to take the stand he simply replied that he had mentally blacked out and didn't remember anything. As far as he knew Ms. Cynthia Lee Moss's account of the event was completely accurate. The jury seemed to take no issue with this and was satisfied with the tale of one man standing against an entire gang of evil menaces.

The trial was relatively short, a handful of the semi-trustworthy bikers were paraded through to discuss the event and speak to Alex's demeanor and character before his rampage. It wasn't until the prosecution stood and called their final witness that Alex actually felt fear and regret for what he'd done. Not to the bikers in Dallas, but for something else.

"The prosecution calls Christopher "Fragnet" Lamb," the Prosecutor said loudly.

Alex watched Fragnet roll down the aisle in his wheelchair, the Prosecutor holding the swinging doors to the courtroom <u>well</u> open for him.

"Mr. Lamb will need to testify from the well as he cannot get out of his chair to enter the witness stand," the Prosecutor said in an accusatory tone as he looked directly at Alex.

Fragnet went on to tell the story of how the two met and some of their adventures from his riding with the Sin Eaters. He recounted the lessons learned by Alex and ultimately the fallout from his being denied membership. He told the jury about the event at the rally, about gifting Alex his motorcycle, and about how he had moved on. At the end of his testimony he looked sadly at his former protege as the Prosecutor promised just one more question, and then proceeded to ask three.

"So, you would say that you two were close? That he was closer to you than anyone else?" the Prosecutor asked.

"I would say he was like a son to me, in every way but blood," Fragnet announced sadly.

"And do you think he is capable of doing what he is accused of?" the Prosecutor finally asked.

"I think that the Alex I knew, almost seven years ago would have done literally anything to save someone he felt was in danger, but I don't know the man in front of me today," Fragnet said, turning his back on Alex, revealing the Sin Eater's colors sewn to the back of his wheelchair.

The jury found him guilty, but recommended a lighter sentence because of the nature of the crime. He was given 32 years in prison with the possibility of parole in 20 if he maintained good behavior. He stood as the judge and jury exited the room, keeping his eyes locked on the red, white and blue colors of the American flag.

He knew that the colors of the Sin Eater's patches had been officially matched to the exact colors of the flag. He had memorized and then drilled into others what the colors meant and why they were important. Now, he would be locked inside where the colors he'd see most often would be orange, tan and gray, but the image of the Sin Eater's colors burned into his mind.

He was escorted by two bailiffs to the holding cell in the court, then loaded into a Sheriff's van and taken on the long ride to a little dot on the map of Texas called Big Spring. It was the last time he would see his clothes for thirty two years as far as he knew. His father's pocket knife and his zippo lighter were put in an evidence bag that was checked in with his beloved black leather pull on boots and the rest of his clothes. He was stripped and physically searched *in depth* before being given the prison issued jumpsuit and escorted into the hole where he would live for the next three decades.

Todd swerved to miss a pothole in the road and jostled Alex out of his sleep. He looked over to see drool pooling on Marco's shoulder with a string running up to his mouth. Apparently being bound as he was didn't amount to a good night's sleep either. Alex looked out the window and had no idea how far out they were or how long he'd even been asleep.

"How much longer, Todd?" Alex asked groggily.

"About five minutes. I slowed down a little to let you get a few minutes sleep," Todd replied into the rearview.

"I'm good now," Alex replied as he tried to find an angle in the van where he could stretch his massive frame.

"Good to hear," Todd answered.

They pulled up to the checkpoint that now stretched entirely across the road. Alex wasn't sure how many people had been on the barricade when they came through a few days ago, but there were certainly more people now. Men and women both stood guard with weapons, spike strips from the police cruisers ran across the street. A full sized piece of plywood that had been warped and had chunks missing out of it had been propped up on top of an 18-wheeler trailer that created a high point in the barricade. It was painted in thick white spray paint with a clear message:

BRANDS NOT WELCOME

"Well that's encouraging," Alex whispered as he leaned forward between the two front seats.

"That's new," Todd said, "You two stay in here with him. If things go wrong, just take off."

"Not likely," Ramirez replied quietly.

Todd got out and approached the barricade, hands out to his sides. He was stopped a few feet from the spike strips by Deputy Carver, the deputy they had run into the day they'd been released from the prison. Carver looked over Todd's shoulder at the van as he spoke, but the passengers couldn't understand what he was saying. He was getting animated, waving a hand back and forth and shaking his head, laughing as Todd told his story.

"I don't like this," Alex said.

"No bueno, Mijo," Ramirez agreed.

Marco began to come to, slowly rolling his head upright, blinking and smacking his lips as he awoke. He looked around, rubbing his eyes and trying to make sense of where he was and what was going on. He looked between the driver's seat and the B-pillar of the van, watching the exchange. Then his eyes shifted as he dipped his shoulders forward to look at the sign on the barricade.

"They aren't going to take me," he said bluntly, "you're going to have to either let me go, or kill me yourselves."

"Could go either way, so don't push your luck," Alex replied with no emotion.

Ramirez couldn't help but let a chuckle slide from the front seat as Marco stared at the side of Alex's unmoving head. The men inside the vehicle continued to sit silently, watching the discussion at the barricade become more and more intense. Finally, Alex reached for the handle on the door to get out.

"Bad move, Mijo. I've got a feeling you'd only make things worse. Stay here," Ramirez said as he opened the passenger door and stepped out with his hands leading the way in plain sight.

Alex sat back in the seat and continued to watch as Ramirez slowly walked up, keeping his hands above his shoulders at all times. More than one person started to get antsy from their posts around the vehicles and on top of the box trailers that made up the barricade. As Ramirez got closer, Deputy

Carver leveled his rifle at him and started to yell commands as Todd tried to step in between them and deescalate the situation.

Carver said something directly to Todd who turned and started waving at the van. Alex opened the door slightly and could just hear Todd yelling for him to bring the prisoner forward. He pushed the door the rest of the way and unfolded himself out from the cramped seat into the open air, seeing shocked and terrified looks on the people of the road block as his frame filled their view at full size.

"Get out," he demanded of Marco.

"They're going to kill me. They won't take me in," Marco lamented to his captor. It wasn't so much a plea for help as it was a verbal statement of his internal acceptance for his future.

"You made a piss poor decision in teaming with those two, and now you're going to have to deal with the reckoning. Get out, *now*," Alex commanded again.

Marco crawled out of the back seat and stood in front of his massive escort. The two of them walked forward, slowly. Alex kept one hand on Marco's shoulder to prevent him from trying to run or do anything stupid that might get them all killed. His other hung loosely at his side, a dull ache from where he'd been stabbed the night before radiating down it.

"Well, well, well," Carver started with a sick smile, "the meth-head is back for round three, huh?"

"Round three?" Alex asked.

"Shut up, inmate. You speak when spoken to!" Carver screamed. "This piece of shit was already kicked out twice for stealing food. He was traveling with two other scumbags when he left, way worse than him. Those the two you have in the back of the van?" He nodded at the prison van sitting about fifteen feet away.

"Yep, neither of them will be a problem again," Todd said frankly, "but we didn't know he was on his third strike."

Todd turned and glared remorsefully at Marco. If there was anything he could have done to help him, any sweet talking or favors to call in, they vanished when he heard about that. This man was now considered beyond saving and would be subject to whatever penalties the town leadership wanted to put on him.

"Yeah, he's out alright," Carver leveled the rifle at Marco's head, who simply took a deep breath and closed his eyes.

"WAIT!" Ramirez yelled, "You can't really be talking about executing a guy for some petty theft? He stole food!"

"Which is a crime punishable by death now," Carver said over the front sight post of his AR15.

"This is crazy… you're going to kill a man for refusing to starve to death," Ramirez couldn't let it go, "isn't this still America?"

"This isn't anywhere anymore," Carver boomed as he lowered the weapon and took a step forward to get in Ramirez's face, 'this is *us*. This is *Big Spring*. This is *our* community and we are going to protect it! He broke the law multiple times, he's not redeemable!" Carver gave the old trustee a solid shove with the barrel of his rifle, jabbing him in the sternum and causing him to fall backwards.

Once again, things went black for Alex.

Chapter 10

It was difficult to actually make out what anyone was saying with all of the screaming and threats being lobbed through the air. As the light cut back through the darkness of Alex's rage he realized that his hand was firmly wrapped around Carver's neck, holding his feet about a foot off the ground as they kicked the air ferociously.

"Put him down!" screamed a dark haired Latino woman with a bolt-action rifle from behind a car.

"Somebody do something!" yelled a blonde man from his position on top of the 18-wheeler trailer.

"Cálmate, Alex," Ramirez whispered from the ground, his calm voice somehow cutting through all the noise.

"Everyone relax!" Todd was screaming back at the crowd.

There had to be a dozen weapons pointed at them, and even though Alex and Todd had pistols tucked away, they would never get them out before they were cut to shreds by the defenders of I-20. Ramirez slowly stood and gathered himself as he placed a hand on Alex's massive bicep.

"Put him down, Hermano. You're only going to get a lot of people killed with this, including Todd and I," Ramirez said calmly.

"When I put you down," Alex grumbled, "if they take a shot, or you get froggy, you will die before I do. I promise."

Carver just nodded back ever so slightly, his feet no longer swinging, his eyes starting to bulge slightly from the lack of oxygen but burning with a pure, hateful rage all the same. Alex slowly lowered him to the ground, allowing his feet to take up the weight of his body before starting to release the hold on his neck. Once his hand was clear, Carver struggled to catch his breath again as he stumbled a little, stooping to pick up his AR15 that lay on the ground where he'd dropped it.

The strike from the giant had been far faster than Carver thought possible when he had closed the distance and jabbed the mouthy old inmate with his rifle. The large man had managed to shove the meth-head to the ground and jerk Carver into the air in a fraction of a second. One arm, one hand, was all he needed and now Carver knew it.

"Everyone calm down," Carver croaked as loud as he could through his recently crushed vocal chords, "just a little misunderstanding. Everyone stand down!"

"Glad we cleared it up," Alex replied menacingly.

"Well, even with that cleared up, we still aren't taking him in," Carver replied as he tilted his head towards Marco on the ground, "and I'll identify the bodies if you want, but we aren't taking them in either."

"So what are we supposed to do with them?" Todd asked.

"I don't give a damn," Carver answered as he rubbed his sore neck, "toss them on the side of the road on your way home and feed the buzzards. As for that one there, if you leave here without him, I'm just gonna kill him and roll his body off into the dust."

The three men from the van took a step back and turned to one another to talk. They agreed that the bodies didn't matter much, but the idea of leaving Marco to be simply executed when he was nowhere near the monster the others had been just didn't sit right with them. They opted to take him back and cut him loose on the road, letting nature figure it out.

"By the way, warden," Carver said as they picked Marco up and started to walk back to the van, "you can't take that with you."

"Take what?" Todd questioned, genuinely confused by the vague statement.

"The van. We're going to confiscate it for use by the town. New rule, all running vehicles are to be confiscated at the checkpoints," Carver grinned.

"And when was that rule passed? I don't recall hearing about a town meeting," Todd replied, frustration and anger clearly rising in his voice.

"Yeah, after the little debacle your prison release caused with a sharp rise in crime and all, you were elected *off* the town board," Carver was still grinning his arrogant smile as he informed the former warden of his loss of authority.

Todd started to shake with anger, balling his fists and rolling his shoulders forward. The rage was becoming physical, oozing from his pores and dripping from the corners of his mouth. He started to take a step forward, intent on letting Carver know exactly what he thought of this development, when the lightning-like speed of Alex stopped him with a gentle hand to the chest.

"Easy Augustulus, we can't have both of us lose our cool," he whispered.

Todd stopped and took a deep breath. This was it. This was the moment that the town leadership had planned. They would kick him out for some kind of "legitimate" reason, then, when he fought and got angry, they would point to him as being unstable and dangerous. He was playing right into their trap.

"Well, Carver, I'd love to say I was sad to see it come to pass, but I'm not really. It was becoming a bit of a haul to come in and handle things, and frankly, a waste of valuable fuel," Todd announced in his sweetest "church-Sunday" voice. "I'll tell you what, since we have two bodies to get out of your hair and didn't bring any supplies to walk over 10 miles back, why don't we take the van for now and I'll bring it back in a day or two, ready to leave it."

"You'll bring it back *tomorrow*," Carver said angrily.

He was obviously annoyed, but whether it was because Todd hadn't taken the bait or because of the van situation was anyone's guess. Everyone except Todd and Alex. They knew exactly what was under Carver's skin.

The four men slowly walked back to the van, climbing in and backing away before turning around and driving off. For a while, nobody said anything, until Marco actually broke the silence.

"So, what are you going to do with me?" he asked.

"We're going to take you out to Coahoma and drop you off," Todd answered him, "you're going to die eventually, Marco, but I'm not going to kill you just because you stole some food and made piss-poor life decisions on who to hang out with."

"Consider this a blessing, chico, because the only thing standing between you and Jesus is the morals of the people in this van," Ramirez added.

"Thank you," Marco replied genuinely, "I swear you'll never hear from me again."

"See that we don't," Alex said absently, his mind already turning over other problems.

"What about the bodies?" Ramirez asked next.

"I guess we just kick them out the door on the way home," Todd answered absently, as though he wasn't really sure what to do with them.

"Not to be a monster, but I want to point out it's unwise to waste much of anything in our current state," Alex pointed out.

"What do you mean?" Todd asked him.

"Well, just that we have pigs, and pigs will eat human remains…" Alex just kind of let the words hang in the air.

"Absolutely not!" Todd yelled, "you do realize that we would then be eating those pigs and that's just cannibalism with extra steps!"

"Not necessarily," Alex continued, "I mean, we pull three or four pigs into a separate pen, feed them the bodies, then trade them off. It's just a thought."

Todd came to a screeching halt in the middle of the road, throwing the van in park and jumping out. He walked angrily to the back of the vehicle, ripped open the doors and grabbed a tarp in each hand, yanking the bodies roughly out onto the ground. He slammed the doors shut and climbed back into the van, slamming it in drive and taking off so fast the tires squealed slightly.

"There, problem solved. Now no more talk about feeding people to pigs," Todd yelled angrily.

"Okay then," Alex replied in a deadpan tone.

"What about feeding pigs to people? Because… me gusta mucho el carnitas…" Ramirez chided with a smile.

"Ramirez… don't," Todd tried to shoot a glaring look in the old trustee's direction while fighting his own laughter.

It didn't work and within minutes all four men in the vehicle were chuckling softly. They pulled up to the outskirts of Coahoma, Texas on I20. Coahoma wasn't much more than a gas station, a school, and a few small shops, but it was something. The sign on the edge of town proudly displayed that the town was home to not only the Coahoma Bulldogs, but also the famous rodeo clown Quail Dobbs.

There was an older man sitting in a chair in front of the gas station just off the highway. He was flanked by two men with shotguns while two more with rifles patrolled the parking lot. The gas prices had been taken down and somehow a bed sheet that was painted with the word "OPEN" had been hung over the giant brand sign.

"Afternoon fellas," the man drawled as they stopped and climbed out of the vehicle.

"Afternoon, sir," Todd replied back, tipping the brim of his hat as he did, "how's things in Bulldog country?"

"Eh, fair-to-middling all things considered," came the reply, "y'all here to trade?"

"Well, might be. We had a man who was looking for a change of scenery and wanted to drop him off, but trading might also be on the to-do list," Todd answered him.

Todd took off his hat and whipped his brow with the back of his forearm, then turned and motioned for Marco to come forward. As the lanky man walked forward with his head hung he tried to look as casual as possible, which only made him look even more suspicious.

"You kick him out?" the shopkeep asked bluntly.

"No, truth be told he's not one of ours. He wandered in and we simply can't take another stray," Todd's genuine Texas accent became thicker as he conversed with the local.

"Well, we can always use more hands," the shopkeeper mused, "you should know ahead of time that if you're trouble you'll either be run out of town on a rail or shot. We don't have time for anything more."

"I'm not going to be any trouble, sir," Marco gently assured him.

"Good, then go around back and clean yourself up in the bucket of suds back there. I'll get you over to the school and they can set you up on a work detail," the man said as he stood and shook Marco's hand.

The men all shook hands with Marco, Todd holding on a little longer than comfortable and staring into his eyes until the message landed. Marco whispered that he understood, and nobody would ever know. He swore he'd never be back and he genuinely had no plans of returning. After the less than emotional goodbye, Marco walked off with one of the guards and the shopkeeper sat back down in his chair.

"Well, what are you looking to trade for?" he asked as he leaned the wooden seat back against the metal and glass face of the building.

"I need horses. At least two, but three would be better," Todd said frankly.

"Well, why don't we just hand over the deed to our oceanfront property on main street while you're shopping!" he bellowed in response, coughing roughly as the raspy laugh grew..

"I know, tall order, but I've got some decent trade for you. Pork, chicken, beef, bushels of vegetables, maybe even a gun," Todd knew all the right words to drop to refocus the merchant in front of him.

"Well now... that *is* something," he grinned as he looked around the parking lot, "but I don't see any of it here."

"Nope. We'll meet out at the corner of Old C-City highway and FM820," Todd said as he pointed to the North of the town, "y'all don't need to know where we came from with our supplies, and we don't need to know where you're taking them."

"Fair enough," the old timer nodded as he rubbed his chin, "I can get you three horses, they aren't exactly thoroughbred stallions, but they'll ride. You bring everything on that list and we'll be good.

Alex and Ramirez just stood by the van, watching the exchange take place. The days of a simple price being placed on an item, paper and coin or plastic 1's and 0's being exchanged and the item walked out with were gone. That was not how business had been done even a hundred years ago, at least not all the time, and it was back to the way it was before. What you had was only worth as much as someone else was willing to pay.

"I can bring a sow, a heifer, and half a dozen chickens, figure how much on the veggies?" Todd asked.

"Figure around 40 pounds? And don't forget the gun," the merchant grinned and pointed at Todd.

"I'm thinking closer to 10 pounds with the gun," Todd pushed back.

"Rifle or shotgun?" the man asked, calculating the different values in his head.

"I've got a Remington 870 and an AR15. Your choice," Todd answered with a half smile.

"Hmmmmm… two guns, huh?" the old man seemed to be scheming out loud with a tobacco stained grin.

"Yes sir, but only one in the trade," Todd grinned back

"Well, you can't blame a fella for trying," he chuckled, "alright, AR15, a heifer, a sow, half a dozen chickens and 15 pounds of veggies. Sounds like a fair trade for three horses *with tack*," he said as he stood again and extended his hand to seal the deal.

"That'll work," Todd replied, shaking the man's hand and nodding his head, "how long do you need?"

"I'll need about two hours to get them together and get out there. It's only about three and a half miles to that intersection, so the travel shouldn't be bad," the old man smiled and nodded.

"Sounds good. We'll likely need about three since we're a little further out," Todd confirmed, again shaking hands before walking back to the van.

The men climbed inside and turned down FM820 to take the route home. Strangely, the town didn't look much different. The small hamlet was filled with small farms and oil field workers, folks used to working with their hands and making do with what they had. Once they were out of town a bit, Ramirez broke the silence.

"You're going to trade all of that for a couple of horses?" he asked.

"Well, when we lose the van tomorrow we're going to need another way to get around. We can spare a couple animals and some vegetables to secure that," Todd replied.

"Still," Ramirez continued, "seems like a lot."

"It is, but three horses with tack is a lot to get back. Let's just hope they aren't old nags," Todd mused as they turned on a dirty back road and headed towards the house.

As the barren fields and worn homes passed by, the air in the vehicle turned heavy. Nobody wanted to focus on it, but they all seemed to have the same thought on their minds. Alex licked his lips in anticipation of the scolding that was coming. He'd never had a strong male role model growing up, and by the time Fragnet came along he was already too big for most men to feel safe chewing him out.

He'd always imagined what it would be like to get chewed out by a father, sitting on a stool in the corner of the room as an imposing man paced back and forth, yelling or ringing his hands. He respected the two men in the front enough to be concerned, but he wasn't exactly afraid. It was an odd sensation for him.

"You need to control yourself, Güey," Ramirez started.

"I know you were just trying to stand up for Ramirez, but killing the head deputy and brother in law of the preacher isn't going to help anyone," Todd quickly added.

"He was just trying to flex for his homies," Ramirez pointed out, "he knew he couldn't take you, but he needed to show them he was El Jefe no matter what. You caused problems when you made him look weak."

"I know," Alex replied softly, "I blacked out. It doesn't happen often, but it did then. I'm sorry."

"You know, El Diablo comes in many forms, Amigo," Ramirez smiled over his shoulder, "you have to remember who is in charge when he tries to speak over you."

"It won't happen again," Alex promised quietly and truly hoped it wouldn't.

"Well, if it does, just make sure you see enough light in the darkness to know who's on your side," Todd added as they turned into the farm.

Once they returned to the ranch Ramirez told Oscar and Guille about the encounter at the roadblock and apologized to Guille about not being able to gather information on his sister. He was understanding, but clearly disappointed.

The next few hours were spent gathering the supplies for trade. Oscar and Ramirez were tasked with making sure everything on the list was loaded into the van. They'd tie the heifer to the back bumper and have someone ride in the back to make sure they went slow enough she wasn't hurt. They'd taken the rear two sets of seats out of the van and rigged a ramp so the pig could be walked into the van and hobbled. The chickens were put into a dog crate that was in one of the barns and the setup between the pig and the baskets of vegetables.

Everything seemed to be set, so Guille and Paul, Walton and Max split up into teams to head down the road and try to get into position where they'd be hidden but able to cover the men on the road if anything happened. The farmers carried ARs from the prison and the prisoners carried bats and spare magazines.

It was interesting to Alex that Todd had just pulled up to the farm, rounded everyone up and told them what was going on. There was no arguing, no laying claim to a horse "belonging" to one particular family simply because their goods had been promised for it. Everything was communal and Todd's word was the binding agent that gave it weight.

He couldn't help but chuckle at the execution of communism on a local scale. Everything belonged to everyone and it was working. The unique factors weren't lost on him, of course, but he couldn't help his amusement. He chuckled to himself as he walked towards the live oak by the house.

"Something funny, inmate?" Todd asked with a grin as he approached. He held out a tin cup of water that Alex accepted gratefully.

"You're all communists," Alex chuckled.

"Say what now?" Todd asked, stunned.

"You, sir, are a commie," Alex grinned as he drank the water.

"You know, saying shit like that here in Texas would get even your big ass whooped back before everything went to Hell," Todd said, stone faced.

"Hey, you don't have to like it, but it's true. This is a commune. Everyone is giving what they have for the collective good, no concern for central ownership or profit," Alex waved a massive hand around the farm. "You are collectively making decisions to barter, dividing work, and providing for one another regardless of who does what in the grand scheme. This is textbook communism."

"We are neighbors helping neighbors, not commie scumbags or hippies," Todd shot back, his offense showing in his tone.

"Easy, Todd. It's not an insult, or if it is, it wasn't meant to be. Hell, at anything it's a compliment," Alex chuckled as he showed his palms to the land owner in front of him, "you've managed to do something here that people have been trying to figure out since the mid-1800's."

"Alex, I know you're smarter than you let on, and I'd suspect smarter than most people you've ever been around, so you've got to see how calling a bunch of Texans commies is a bad idea," Todd said, concerned.

"Communist isn't an insult, Todd," Alex began, "it's an ideology. It's no different in status than Republican, Baptist or even Texan. It's a way of identifying people based on their principles," Alex started. "Now, I'll grant that most communists at least evolve into scumbags, murderers, and corrupt bigots, but the idea of 'to each according to his needs' is pretty strong here. In many ways you're making sure that everyone contributes and gets what they need for the greater good. It's not a bad thing! On paper Communism is a fair system, but in practice… let's just say that forms of government are like forms of religion, it's the human factor that usually screws it up."

Todd couldn't help but be confused. He'd spent his entire life hearing how horrible Communists were, seeing pictures of them starving in the streets in North Korean markets and Soviet bread lines. It had to be a bad thing, right? He'd never really stopped to put a definition to how things were run on the farms, but now that Alex had put it out there, it felt like an itch inside his skull. Was he really a dirty red?

Todd could see the wheels turning and the smoke of concern curl out of Todd's ears. It was entertaining for sure, but he didn't want his new friend and benefactor to worry or think he was ungrateful. He'd only meant it to be a discussion point... a casual observation, not an insult.

"Look, Todd," he started gently, "I'm not saying you're Mao or Stalin here. One of the key differences is that you aren't *forcing* anyone on any of these farms to give anything up they don't want to. If Paul had said 'I'm not giving up a pig *and* a half-dozen chickens, it's too much from just me' then you wouldn't have made him. You'd have figured it out fairly."

"That's what's missing from most forms of communism. Most of them force people to be members under the banner of the 'greater good' whether they want to contribute or not," Alex put a large hand on Todd's shoulder, "you're not forcing anyone. That's a *really* important distinction."

"Yeah, I guess that is how we are different," Todd smiled, gladly accepting the lifeline of logic Alex was throwing at him.

"It's okay to dabble in it, as long as people's free will is respected. You take that away, and I'll start calling you Kim Jong Todd," Alex chuckled.

"I will bury you under the corn, capitalist American dog," Todd replied with a horribly mixed accent of Korean and Texan.

The two men were laughing hysterically as Oscar came walking up with a confused look on his face. He smiled his classic grin, bright white teeth cutting through the dark brown skin and assorted facial tattoos from his previous gang affiliation.

"We're ready, Jefe," he cut in.

"Oscar, you and Ramirez ride in the back of the van and watch the cow, Alex, up front with me... capitalist American dog," Todd chuckled.

Chapter 11

The van crept slowly down the road, watching men behind them riding the horses. The exchange had gone off without a hitch, even an occasional chuckle breaking the tension.

Apparently the men of Coahoma had arrived at a similar idea and sent men out to cover the exchange as well. The kicker was that the two teams from Todd's group had arrived first. Guille and Paul had set up near a shed that sat behind the barn on a property not far from the intersection. Paul knew the owner and knew they'd cleared out and headed to Oklahoma to meet up with family, so the place was empty.

They were settled in and quietly exchanging tales of their youthful prowess when two men came wandering up from the road and took cover behind the barn not 100 feet from their position. Guille and Paul stopped talking when they saw them and had to stifle their own laughter as they listened to the two former Bulldog linebackers talk about a cheerleader they'd both hooked up with in their prime.

The van came rolling up slowly from the left of their position and the football studs became quiet as well, watching the exchange go down. They didn't know the man by name, but the one that seemed to be in charge of the other group got out of the van and walked around the horses, inspecting them.

Guille was pleased to hear them say, "he won't find anything wrong with them, even if he does know what he's looking at, even if the tack had seen better days."

They were excited for fresh vegetables, but did complain about the "tip" the old man from the store had brought Todd, a bottle of Gentleman Jack from the liquor store. They lamented that they were now down to only a case and there wouldn't likely be more anytime soon.

The exchange on the road was calm, both leaders looking over their goods and, after approving, shaking hands for all to see. Everyone seemed to relax as they realized that nobody had any trickery in mind and men from Coahoma began unloading the goods and livestock into a truck bed of their own, putting the cow and pig in a horse trailer they'd brought. The two men at the barn seemed to relax and Guille could hear them exhale from his position behind the shed.

"Damn, I really thought they were gonna try something. Glad they didn't though," the burly blonde man said.

"Yeah, it's not often you meet honest folks nowadays," the other replied.

Paul stepped out from behind the shed, rifle slung over his shoulders and hands out to his sides and gently replied, "Well, *honest* might be a stretch."

The two men jumped at the sound and spun around to face him, unsure of what was going on.

"What can I say, we thought you might try something too," Paul chuckled as he stepped forward, "I'm with the farmers out there. No harm, gents."

It seemed to hit the two former football players at the same time, that this was just the 'other side' of why they were here. They started laughing hysterically, even going so far as to slump to the ground and set their rifles down, one holding his head in his hands as his laughter escalated into a howl.

"Jimmy!? You okay??" the old man in the intersection yelled as everyone became more tense and rifle barrels started to float upward.

"Yeah, yeah, Pops, we're good," the blonde yelled back, "c'mon mister, we better walk around the corner here before they get jumpy out there and start shooting over a misunderstanding," he said to Paul.

Paul, Guille, Jimmy and his partner walked around the corner of the barn laughing together, their presence and demeanor relaxing everyone in the road. After they told everyone what had happened the laughter spread like wildfire and soon every man there was laughing hysterically at their initial distrust and good fortune to stumble on one another.

"C'mon in Max!" Todd yelled, now satisfied that this exchange would go well regardless of security.

"You too Cory!" the old man yelled as each team appeared out of their respective hides not three hundred feet from one another, "we don't have anyone else out."

"Sounds good," Todd replied.

"Y'all got a radio wherever you are out there?" the old man asked as the two other teams came walking in.

"No Sir, no way to charge it if we did," Todd answered him.

"Jimmy, let me see your radio," the old man said.

Jimmy handed over a bright orange walkie-talkie and the old timer started messing with buttons on the face of it. He was pushing buttons up and down as he told one of his men to grab some batteries from the vehicle. When he was done, he handed the radio to Todd.

"This is a <u>GMRS</u> radio, I figure y'all can't be more than 5 miles from here to get here in the time you did. This ought to get you in range for us, or you'll need to come a little closer, but you can manage," he started, "I've cleared out all the channels except 1 and 9. Now, 1 is our general channel to talk about anything we don't consider special or secure. Y'all want to meet up and trade again or have any weather information or anything you think we should know, you just give us a call on channel 1 at sunrise or sunset and we'll do the same."

Todd nodded as he accepted the radio.

"Now, if things get wild and y'all need some help, you just jump on channel 9 and give a holler. That channel is for emergencies only and we monitor it all the time form a pretty powerful base station that can reach out a ways," the old man grinned, "you'll need to trust us with your location, and I'm not saying we'll come running, but we may be able to help a bit."

"I appreciate it, mister..." Todd let the words float.

"Tim. Just Tim," the old timer smiled back as he shook Todd's hand a final time.

As everyone exchanged final handshakes and chuckles over the fortune of the trade Paul, Max, and Walton mounted up to ride the horses back to their new home. Alex, Todd, Guille, Oscar and Ramirez loaded into the van and slowly crept down the road.

They arrived back at the farm to a highly unexpected welcoming party as Donna and Jessica stood in the driveway with Gordon, and Max and Paul's wives, all of them watching the three steeds ride in as Patti and her brothers begged to ride them, give them carrots, and brush them out.

Walton was terrified as Todd handed a young boy up to him in the saddle, another going to Max and finally Patti landing in Paul's lap as they trotted the horses in circles. The three grade horses trotted around as though they'd just won the Triple Crown, everyone cheering and joyful as they circled.

"What are their names?" Patti asked excitedly after the ride had been finished.

"Whatever you want them to be, you each get to name one," Todd told her as he lifted the little girl up on his hip to pet the horse's nose.

The little boys chose Brownie and Peanut Butter, or PB, for their selections, fitting since one horse was a deep brown and the other more of a deep tan. Patti circled the remaining horse, a paint with giant splotches of brown and white.

"Hello, Geronimo," she said softly.

The horse pulled its ears back and bowed its head so she could scratch under its mane on the forehead. She giggled and nodded her approval as the horse grunted and snorted under her tiny hand.

"Brownie, Peanut Butter, and Geronimo. What a mix," Todd chuckled.

"Geronimo was a great warrior. He fought for his people and escaped danger many times. I read about him in one of my history books," Patti told everyone gathered, "he protected people."

"That's right, little one," Alex said softly.

"I like Brownies!" her youngest brother crowed.

"I like Peanut Butter more!" her middle brother fired back, not to be out done.

The two boys began to playfully squabble and push one another around, taking off towards the house and arguing about Brownies being like poop and Peanut Butter having pee in it. The large group chuckled about their antics as Patti gently pet Geronimo and whispered to him, the horse snorting gently and nudging her with his nose.

"Well, let's get these ponies put away," Gordon said as he took the reins from the riders who had dismounted, "we'll need to see how they handle a yoke for plowing. Pretty sure I still have one in the barn."

"I'll give you a hand, Jefe, I grew up around horses and always loved them," Guille offered as he gently stroked the fur on Brownie's hind quarter.

"Grassy-Ass, Amigo," Gordon replied in a clearly "gringo" attempt at Spanish, causing half the group to chuckle quietly.

"I'm going to go get some sleep before tonight," Todd yawned, "I suggest everyone else do the same if they can. It's been a long day and we didn't sleep much last night. Tomorrow we go in and turn in the van at the 120 road block."

"That's going to be trouble," Alex started.

"I think we should come up with another plan for that," Ramirez added gently, "they didn't seem overly interested in the van, as much as they were in you, warden."

"We'll handle it tomorrow when we plan it out. It's going to be fine, they just want the van back. There's nothing for them to gain by messing with us," Todd said confidently, although clearly exhausted.

The group parted ways and most went to bed down. Grady and Oscar opted to walk the property for a bit and just keep an eye out on things. They took the shotguns with less lethal rounds in them and decided they would check the far corners of the goat and sheep pasture first. They wandered off as Todd and his family headed to the main house and the rest of the farm families found their ways home. Soon, it was just Alex and Ramirez standing together on the bone-white caliche of the driveway.

"You know what's coming, don't you?" Alex asked the old man.

"Si, and they don't understand," Ramirez sighed.

"They think the turn-in is going to go down as smoothly as today, and it's not," Alex continued.

Ramirez simply nodded, staring off at some unseen point of interest, just over the horizon as the sun started to sink in the evening sky. The first hues of orange and pink stretched from one side of the infinite horizon to the other. He took a deep breath, slowly inhaling and exhaling again before turning to Alex.

"You know they are going to try to either capture him or kill him, right?" Ramirez asked.

"They will try to capture him. They need him alive to parade through the streets as a pariah," Alex observed, "they can't just kill him without a mock trial. They'll need to legitimize their new authority by getting rid of the one that caused the problems."

"If they take him, this place will fall apart," Ramirez replied, "he leads, and the niños y viejos will never make it if he's not here. Not to mention Ms. Jessica and what could happen to her."

"We can't let Todd go, but we need everyone to know we aren't trying to backstab them if things go wrong," Alex continued, "let's go talk to Gordon."

The two men began to wander towards Gordon's barn where they could hear the horses whinnying as they were unsaddled and brushed out. Gordon and Guille were talking about the horses they had grown up around as Alex and Ramirez arrived.

"Afternoon, boys," Gordon smiled as he saw them enter through the large barn door, "you know Alex, if you weren't on our side you'd have given me a heart attack watching you walk up."

"I don't do well being sneaky," Alex grinned, "kinda hard to hide anywhere except in the dark of night."

"I can see that," Guille chimed in.

"Gordon, we need to talk to you about what happened at the roadblock today and the turn-in for tomorrow," Ramirez said seriously.

They recounted the events of the roadblock and what had led to the urgent need to find horses. Alex told Gordon, Ramirez and Guille about the conversation he'd had with Todd before the inmates had snuck up on them. Gordon listened quietly, occasionally nodding or shaking his head in agreement with what was said or what someone else did. After the stories had finished Gordon sat silently for a few minutes, then cleared his throat.

"Seems you boys have something else in mind," he stated frankly.

"I've got a plan, but Todd isn't going to like it, and it won't make friends," Alex said, "but it'll give them their damn van without Todd being endangered."

"What do you need?" Gordon asked.

"Real guns. Rifles if you can get them. We'll need the horses and the van and nobody questioning whether or not we had their best intentions at heart," Alex replied.

"Wait here," Gordon answered.

He walked back to the house and after about twenty minutes came back carrying a long gun in each hand, with another slung over each shoulder and a duffle bag. He set the rifles against a bale of straw, setting the duffle on top and then unslinging the others and lining them up.

"I've got two ARs, both of them have optics on them, this one has magnification up to 8, the other is just a red dot. These two are bolt action rifles, a .308 and a .243. Either one will drop a man, but if they're behind anything I'd use the .308. This is a lever action .30-30, not ideal, but it's what I've got," Gordon went down the line.

He opened the bag and pulled out a Glock19, locking the slide back to show an empty chamber and set it on the bale, then pulled out four magazines of ammo for the ARs and two boxes of rounds for the bolt-action guns. Ramirez stepped forward and picked up the Glock, deftly loading it and sliding it into his waistband. He then picked up the AR with the red dot and began to look it over. Alex stepped forward to grab the other as Guille picked up the shotgun.

"What are you doing?" Alex asked him.

"I'm checking out my gun," he replied absently.

"We only need 2 for this," Alex informed him.

"No, you don't," Guille replied as he looked over the .308 bolt gun, "let me guess, the Trustee here drives the van up, you wait a ways back with the horses and cover him. Far enough away that they can't yell for you to bring in the horses and lose them too."

He continued on, "then, Abuelo hands off the keys and walks out to you, that way, even if they try to get the horses you have distance working for you. You guys mount up and ride like Hell back here. They don't get Todd, they don't get the horses, and they don't get you. Bueno."

"Well… no actually, but that's a better plan," Alex conceded.

He'd just planned on basically driving up, jumping out of the van and running back to Ramirez holding the horses. It was going to be fast and efficient, but didn't really allow for any kind of discussion with them.

"Yeah, well, it's still weak," Guille said, "you need a third. Just like the exchange with the Coahoma folks, you need someone already in place to help cover you. Someone they don't know is there."

"And you're a good enough shot for that?" Ramirez asked.

"No, but I'm a good enough shot to keep their heads down and not hit you if you have to run," Guille grinned back.

"Should you take another?" Gordon asked.

"Yes, you should," came a response from the door.

The men turned to see Grady and Oscar standing there. Apparently during their rounds they had opted to swing by the barn and check on things, stumbling into the conversation just in time to hear the plan. Guille gave them the short, animated version of what was going on, and Grady nodded in agreement. Oscar wanted to go as well, but Grady pointed out that he had actually shot before with bolt guns. They'd sorted things out in short order and had a plan that involved each of the men playing their part.

"If you'd ever told me that four inmates would risk their lives to save my step-son I'd have called you a damn liar," Gordon mused as they each laid out their plans, "thank you for this."

"Alright, let's try to get some rest, go in early in the morning and try to drop it off then," Ramirez said.

The men stretched out in the barn, relaxing as best they could. Gordon paired up with Oscar to take over the patrols so Grady could rest. They'd come back around <u>midnight</u> and start saddling the horses. The men shook hands and relaxed into their spots, with Alex quickly drifting off into a dreamless sleep.

A few hours later, in the dark of night, he awoke to flashlights propped up, aiming at the ceiling as Gordon, Oscar and Guille saddled Brownie and Peanut Butter. They'd decided that they would leave Geronimo here so that there was at least one horses that couldn't be taken. Gordon had grabbed the keys to the van from inside the main house while Todd slept.

They planned to have Guille ride the horses to about half a mile away from the roadblock, with everyone else in the van to keep them fresh. Then Grady would go to the South side of 20 and Guille to the North and work their way in to where they could see the barricade. After about an hour, which they would time with a sandglass that Gordon had brought them, Ramirez and Alex would bring the van in, following the rest of Guille's plan.

It sounded good in the barn, but it seemed too easy.

As the men walked out and loaded into the van, they heard a shotgun rack a round into the chamber by the house.

Todd had come out and seen the men with horses around the van.

"Stop where you are," he yelled.

"Eaaasssyyy, Todd. It's Gordon," Gordon yelled back from the vehicle where he was watching the men load the back seats back into the van.

"What the Hell is going on, Gordon?" Todd asked as he lowered his weapon and walked towards the van.

"We're solving a problem before it happens," he replied.

Todd was visibly confused as he came out to the vehicle looking around at the horses and guns. Alex spelled it out for him, in detail what they were going to do and why. He didn't ask for permission or give Todd a chance to say no. It was stated as fact. To his credit, Todd took it all in and didn't say much.

"You guys don't need to do this. They aren't going to do anything, there's no reason to," Todd started to protest after Alex had laid out the plans.

"Todd, you're a good guy, and you saved all of us from a terrible fate of either being shot in the head or starving to death. You can't go there, and I think that you know that," Alex said solemnly, "let us do this. If it all goes well, great, they get their van back and we come back here to keep working. If not, *we* are the problem, not you or your family, and anyone that gets hurt has nothing to do with you."

Todd just nodded in silence, accepting defeat that he was outnumbered and out reasoned on this plan. His own pride was the only thing driving him to be involved, and there really was no good reason for him to go to the roadblock. The town leadership wanted the van back and this would get it to them, and since he'd already been "voted out" there was no reason to even go. He was really just another guy now, except for the target on his back from them setting him up as a scapegoat.

Todd shook hands with the former inmates and put the shotgun on his shoulder. He took a deep breath, trying to find the words to thank them for the responsibility they were taking on, but fell short. He simply nodded, turning away and walking back to the house. He paused again at the steps of the wrap-around porch, waving to them before walking back inside.

"Well, that's done. At least he knows the why," Alex said softly.

"Nothing left to do but do it," Guille muttered as he threw a leg over Brownie and wrapped the reins from Peanut Butter's halter around the saddle horn. Gordon had found a rifle scabbard in his barn that would do the job of carrying his rifle.

"Let's go boys," Ramirez announced as he climbed into the driver's seat with Alex taking shotgun.

The men loaded up, waving goodbye to Gordon as they slowly turned the vehicle around and Guille led the way with the horses. The plan was to have him lead out to allow them to set the slow and steady pace and not burn out. Alex looked at the house in the rearview as they went to the end of the driveway, and was surprised to see a small face, framed by curly brown hair shining a flashlight out the window.

It was dark, and he was over 100 yards away, but he could have sworn he saw her crying.

Chapter 12

They rolled slowly down the highway, the horses' tails swaying gently in the dark. Ramirez had the running lights on but no headlights, trying to maintain as low of a profile as possible.

"Damn man, this reminds me of when I'd just graduated from college in Lubbock. Some buddies came into town and took me out for the night," Grady reminisced, "we found these three honeys that we followed all over town. We'd roll up behind them in my boy's whip and just hollered at them all night. They played like they didn't want us, but by the end of the night they were following us around… damn that was a good time."

"Hermano, I hate to tell you this, but if they had asses like that," Ramirez yelled as he pointed at the horses in front of them, "you weren't chasing 'honeys,' you were chasing gorditaaaas!" He let out a raucous laugh as he drew out the word.

Alex started chuckling at Grady's expense, who muttered obscenities in horrible Spanish aimed at Ramirez. The only thing Alex could really make out was "old asshole," but Ramirez simply laughed the younger man off. They began to calm down as Ramirez rolled to a stop where Guille had halted the horses. They climbed out to see what he needed.

"There it is," Guille said, "that's the truckstop billboard that Gordon told us to stop at. This is where Grady and I push out."

"Seems about right," Grady said, looking out over the road.

"I'll take the horses," Alex offered as he extended his hand.

"Don't take off the saddles, but make sure you run that towel in the van over them," Guille ordered, "they only sweat a little on the way here, but we don't want them getting too cold to run if we need it."

"Got it," Alex nodded, "Guille, you know the most about them, if we have to cut out of here in a hurry, who should ride which?"

"We should put you and Ramirez on Brownie since he's the stouter of the two," Guille said as he ran his hands up and down the horse's legs, "Grady and I will jump on Peanut Butter, but she's not going to be able to run long with us. The biggest thing is going to be getting gone and then we can get off the road and walk them."

"Sounds good. If it comes down to running, we'll figure it out, but we're hoping it doesn't go that far," Ramirez added.

Guille took the .243 Roberts and nodded to the others. He wasn't that familiar with the gun, but he'd figure it out easily enough. He had a pocket full of ammo he'd brought with him and five rounds already in the rifle. As he started walking out into the night on the North side of the highway, Grady checked the rifle he was holding.

The Remington 783 was chambered in .308, and unlike the 700 model that Guille carried, Grady's had a removable magazine, which meant he would be able to swap rounds out faster since Gordon had given him 2 extra. He shook hands with Ramirez and Alex and headed off to the South of the highway.

Alex tied the horses to the front bumper of the van, pulling out the towel Guille had mentioned and wiping them down. There wasn't much sweat to come off of them, but Alex didn't know horses the way Guille did and he did what he was told when he was in unfamiliar territory. "Shut up and learn before you ask questions," as Fragnet had said. Alex couldn't help but wonder what his former mentor was up to in this world.

"I flipped the sand thingy," Ramirez said as he walked around the front of the vehicle, "but I'd rather be timing it out with a pack of smokes."

"It's an hourglass," Alex offered as he stood and threw the towel into one of the saddlebags on the horse, "how do you think this is going to go down?"

"Not well," Ramirez answered with a sigh, "I'm pretty sure at least one of us is going to die tonight."

He'd had the same feeling. There was no way this went down smoothly. They'd be lucky if the guards let the van near the roadblock, double lucky if they let Ramirez get out before shooting him. There was almost no chance they let him walk away.

"We could always back out. Just sit here for a few hours. When we don't show up Grady and Guille will figure it out and come back," Alex offered, even though he hated the idea of running.

"Not an option, Hermano," Ramirez smiled in the dark, "if they don't get the van, they'll come after la familia at the ranch."

"I could take it up," Alex continued, trying to provide the old man a way out.

"I'm sure that will go well after the show you put on yesterday," Ramirez chuckled, "I appreciate what you're trying to do, Mijo, but there's no other way. I have to be the one to take it up, and it has to be tonight."

"You're a good man Alberto," Alex said softly.

"Yeah," Ramirez smiled back, "I think we all are *now*. We were different before. We lived on the edges of society and did what we felt we had to do to get by, but I'm not a young man anymore. I learned my lesson when I went in the last time and now, I'm just trying to do right."

The two of them stood in silence for a long while, the only noise from the occasional short screech of a night hawk, the horses shaking out their manes, or some critter scurrying by on the side of the road. They had nothing left to say, just time to kill. Ramirez went back into the vehicle and reached through the open door to check the hourglass.

"It's time," he said frankly.

"You have the pistol?" Alex asked him.

"Yeah, tucked in my belt," Ramirez answered as he gently tapped the pistol grip under his shirt, "clip is in my pocket."

"Good," Alex nodded, "I'll follow you with the horses, but I'm not going to ride yet. I'm going to be enough weight for them when I ride. I'll find a spot to hide out when we get a bit closer."

"Sounds good," Ramirez said absently.

Alex untied the horses from the bumper and led them around the back of the van. Ramirez met him at the back and extended his hand. Alex took it and pulled his friend in tightly for a hug. There was nothing left to be said other than a generic exchange of "Good Luck." Ramirez climbed into the driver's seat and fired up the vehicle, slowly driving forward the mile or so that they had left.

Ramirez noticed in the rearview when Alex stopped walking and waved to him. He waved back in the rearview and turned on the headlights. He'd already decided that he was going to slowly roll up to the blockade to make sure they didn't think he was a threat. He kept one hand out the open window, feeling the slow breeze of the wind and tapping his fingers on the mirror.

As he approached the road block he saw people scurrying around to get in position behind cars and other obstacles as someone blasted a siren over a bullhorn before commanding him to stop. He did as ordered, and when they told him to use both hands out the window and open the door he followed the old song and dance that he'd done before. It was pretty clear this was a cop giving out the orders.

Ramirez stepped out, leaving the keys in the vehicle and the engine running. He left the door open and stepped away from the vehicle, waving to the people at the roadblock before trying to turn around and walk away. He heard the boots behind him rustling around, and couldn't cover his heavy sigh as they began yelling for him to freeze. He kept his hands up and slowly turned around.

"I'm dropping off the van for the warden," he yelled.

"Stay where you are!" the voice commanded from behind a truck.

"I was told to drop it off and come back," Ramirez clarified, "the keys are in it, it's running, I need to get walking because I have a long way to go."

"You'll stay where you are until Deputy Carver gets here, inmate!" the man yelled.

Whoever was giving the commands had obviously been told what to do if someone tried to drop off a van in the middle of the night. He had a deep voice, booming like thunder even without a megaphone at this point. Ramirez had a hard time figuring out exactly where he was because they had turned on the construction lights they had in place and were flooding his vision with light. He couldn't help but chuckle, because it didn't take a tactical genius to know that it would actually help Guille and Grady to cover him if need be.

"Deputy Carver is on his way, you just wait there," the man boomed again.

"Man, I need to get going," Ramirez feigned, "it's a long walk back."

"You'll survive, inmate," came the familiar venom of Carver's voice from behind a vehicle.

He stepped out into the light, rifle slung across his chest, gloved hands resting on top. He walked slowly out towards the van, circling around the vehicle and looking inside before waving someone forward to drive it in.

"We good? Can I get going, deputy?" Ramirez asked in as polite and respectful of a tone as he could muster.

"Where's your master, inmate?" Carver jabbed as he scanned the darkness.

"If you mean Todd, he's at home, likely in bed. He told me to bring it in and drop it off, then walk home," Ramirez lied.

"That's a long walk for an old man," Carver replied as he looked Ramirez over.

"Gets me out of chores for tomorrow, so I don't mind the fresh air," Ramirez continued his tale.

"You seem to think he's still got some kind of authority around here. Like he's still in charge," Carver pushed, "he was voted out, and now, he's just another farmer. I'm the law here, me and this badge, we take what we want, when we want, for whatever reason we want." He flicked the badge on his shirt.

"I can take this van. I can go out to his farm and take his cattle, his guns... I could take his wife and kids if I wanted to," Carver smirked as he said it, "he's a nobody, and he'll get what's coming to him, whether he sends an old man as his errand boy or not. Hell, we've already drawn up the plans."

Ramirez felt something inside of him snap. He may have been older, and life had tamped down his fiery Latino blood, but he was still Hispanic, and his temper was still the legacy of Poncho Villa, Emiliano Zapata, and Miguel Castillo. He cursed himself in his mind, but he knew he'd just lost control.

"You see, here's the funny thing about that badge," he said as he turned to face Carver directly, "you think it matters. Hell, you thought it mattered before, and maybe it did a little, but it's nothing more than a shiny trinket on your chest now. There is no law, except that the weak are meat and the strong will eat. You, you're used to hiding behind that piece of tin."

"For example," he continued, as he raised an open hand faster than lightning and struck Carver in the face hard enough to turn his head, "if I'd have hit you like that before it would have been striking a law enforcement officer. Now it's just shutting up an asshole who has no real authority anymore."

Everyone at the barricade froze in stunned silence as they watched Carver regain his composure. The deputy turned to face the old man who had slapped him like a child who had said a curse word in front of his elder for the first time. Nobody was sure what was going to happen, but Ramirez was fairly sure he could feel Grady and Guille tightening their grip on their respective rifles and he was almost certain he could hear Alex mutter "Shit..."

Alex was waiting tensely as he saw the exchange at the roadblock. He saw Carver's unmistakable, arrogant stride as he walked around the van, making comments to Ramirez as he walked by.

It had almost worked. Ramirez had dropped it off and had started to walk back, but Carver wasn't going to miss his chance to inflate his own ego. Alex couldn't hear what was being said but he could read the changes in body language. As soon as he saw Ramirez slap Caver across the face with an open hand, all he could mutter was, "Shit."

This hadn't really been discussed in their planning. Ramirez was supposed to be the calm, cool, collected one. That was why they'd sent him in. Alex couldn't imagine what Carver had said to get under his skin like that, but it didn't really matter now, it was done.

Alex watched helplessly as Carver butt stroked Ramirez to his stomach. The old man crumpled, but as Carver pointed the barrel at him a round skipped off the pavement from the North side of I20, leaving a loud "ZING" sound followed by a crack from the darkness.

Carver instantly dove behind a car and started screaming orders. He had temporarily forgotten about Ramirez and was focused on navigating his own way back to the safety of the barricade.

Ramirez crawled for a bit until he was near a vehicle and then stood, crouching behind the car that had been placed in the road. He began shooting his pistol blindly over the top of the vehicle. His rounds flew at random and struck all around the barricade, some landing uncomfortably close to Carver as he ran further for cover.

Suddenly, there was another bullet whizzing through the air, but this one struck the generator portion of the construction lights on the same side of the road as Ramirez. The newly created shroud of darkness covered his retreat as he ran back towards Alex.

As Ramirez ran through the dark the barricade began shooting in any direction they thought would find their enemy. Some aimed at the vehicle that he had been hiding behind, others to the North and South at random. They had no idea where the rounds had come from, but they were trying to find a target wherever they could.

Alex was just far enough away that he remained covered in darkness and out of sight from those at the barricade. He had turned the horses and was positioning them where he could help Ramirez up and then mount up himself and ride away. He watched as his friend tried to stand up straight and run, but the impact of the weapon into his abdomen kept him stuped and in an uneven gait.

He was only around a hundred yards from Alex when one of the random rounds fired from the barricade found its mark. Ramirez went down in a pile. For a moment he stopped moving all together, but just as Alex was getting ready to run towards him, he started to climb back to his feet and make an attempt at running.

He was only ten feet or so from Alex when his strength gave out again and he went down in a pile. This time, Alex closed the distance rapidly and scooped the man up, trying to put him on the horses with one hand as he held the reins in the other.

"It's no use, Alex, they got me good," Ramirez moaned as he slid off the saddle, "don't make this some Hollywood bullshit where you waste time arguing."

Alex wanted to do just that, he wanted to ignore Ramirez and throw him over the saddle, slap the horse on the ass like in the old Westerns and turn and fight. He had his pistol, he could take whatever Ramirez had left in his, but he knew it was suicide. He also knew Ramirez was right.

"You have to know, they are coming for the farm," Ramirez coughed, "the deputy said they had a plan. They are coming for the cows *and* the family!" Ramirez was now coughing up blood, the stain in his shirt growing out from his right side where the lung had collapsed.

"We'll take care of them, my friend," Alex assured his friend as he laid him back down.

"Vaya con dios," Ramirez grinned with blood stained teeth, "there's your corny movie line."

Alex made sure Ramirez had his pistol and then jumped onto the darker brown of the two horses. He heard bullets flying left and right behind him, and while he knew many of them were coming out from the barricade, he couldn't tell if any were being fired in. He drove his heels into the animal's side as he rode to where he was supposed to meet up with Grady and Guille.

As he rode, Ramirez's final warning rang in his head. "The deputy said they had a plan... They are coming for the family." Were they really coming for the family? Sure, they would have liked to parade Todd through the streets, but why the family? What did they do?

He stopped at the billboard they had stopped at before and moved off directly under it, tying the horses to the bottom of the ladder that ran up the massive post holding the sign up. He stalked his way back towards the road and hid behind a vehicle that appeared to have stalled out there when everything happened.

He was waiting for the sounds of his partners to come skulking back in, when he heard something else. The sound was unmistakable, but it shocked him as the bright gleam of the headlight came racing towards him. The <u>Shovelhead</u> rumbled and growled as it got closer and he had to think fast if he was going to stop them. He didn't have time to come up with a good idea, so a bad one would have to do. He took the flashlight from his pocket, turned it on, and put it on top of the roof of the car next to him pointed at them.

The Harley rapidly slowed to a stop near another vehicle, with two men jumping off almost before the bike had turned off. They tried to fan out a bit, but there was nothing else to hide behind. Alex could tell by their conversation that they were looking for whoever had helped "the inmate at the barricade."

As far as he was concerned, these were the enemy. These were the people that were going to help hurt Todd and Jessica and Patti. Not if Alex could help it. He had to stop them here. It may only be two of them, but it would be two less to deal with later.

Alex quickly looked around and saw a decent rock on the side of the road, about the size of a grapefruit. He picked it up in his right hand and held his pistol in his left as he maneuvered around the back of the car. He wished they had left the motorcycle running because the rumble of the exhaust would have covered his movements better. He squatted down at the back of the vehicle and waited for the man who was closest to come in range.

Alex heaved the rock at the closest man's head as hard as he could, connecting with his jaw and throat area at only a ten feet or so away. The impact caused a sickening thud, like someone slapping a side of beef as it hangs in a freezer. The target went down in a wheezing, gasping heep as Alex turned his pistol on the man by the front of the vehicle.

Ammo was precious, but Alex still had a wound in his shoulder from dealing with Grover the night before. He would need to trade accuracy for speed and hope he hit him. He began pulling the trigger in measured squeezes, trying to keep tempo as he closed the distance with his new target.

The first few rounds flew off into nowhere, but the fourth shot struck the man in his abdomen, with the fifth and sixth rising to strike him in his shoulder and head. The .40 caliber rounds made short work of him and he was down for good. Alex turned his attention back to the other man who was still wheezing on the ground.

He took the weapons away from him, checking his throat to see that it was severely bruised and that his vocal chords likely wouldn't work quite right again, but he would live. Alex was putting the spare magazines, knives, a multitool and both pistols from the two men into his pockets and waistline, then approached the man that was trying to get back to his feet.

"You carry a message," Alex growled at him as he wrapped a hand over the man's already bruised and damaged throat, "you go back and you tell Carver that the warden's family and property are off limits. If he comes out there – if *anyone* from town comes out there — they die there. Got it?"

The man did his best to nod his head, the fear in his eyes burning bright as the giant in front of him spelled out the warning. It might have been the bruising, it might have been the massive hand wrapped around his neck, but he was already having a hard time breathing and the threat only served to tighten his throat muscles further.

Alex released the light grip he'd had on his throat and lifted the man to his feet. He watched as he walked over and looked at the bike, then turned and did his best to say "I... can't... ride..." in a broken and gravelly voice as he pointed at the bike. He turned and started walking back down the highway towards Big Spring.

After a few minutes Guille and Grady arrived, panting heavily and out of breath from their run back. They told Alex that the only people they'd seen leave to chase him had been the one bike and Carver had been screaming for them not to, so it seemed likely that nobody else was coming. Alex told them about Ramirez since neither of them had actually seen him fall. They packed up, each man taking a horse for himself. Guille and Grady saddled up the two horses for the ride home.

Alex settled into a more familiar saddle on a 1978 Super Glide. He took off, roaring down the road as the world around him began to lighten with the sunrise. The wind whipped through his hair, stinging his eyes and pushing the resulting tears back on his cheeks. He'd been in a cage for five years, and had no reason to believe he'd ever feel the rumble of a bike under him again, let alone this classic.

The horses had no prayer of keeping up, but Alex couldn't help himself. The throttle seemed to turn on its own, roaring down the road. He saw the exit for the ranch and thought about Todd and Jessica, Gordon, Max, and the other ranchers and their families.

Patti. Strong willed, blue eyed Patti.

He looked down and saw the fuel gauge on the bike was pegged at "full." He had no real obligation. He could ride right by and into tomorrow. He'd helped them more than once and Guille and Grady would deliver the message that they were in danger. He didn't need to be there.

As the exit came up, he felt his wrist trying to turn the throttle, but something else caused him to slow down. He turned off the exit, under the highway overpass and towards the place he had called home since his impromptu release.

He had to help them, he felt like he was the only one that could.

Chapter 13

As Alex came rumbling into the driveway he was met by Oscar and Gordon, weapons up at him until they recognized who was riding the black Harley. Todd was almost immediately on the porch of his home and Walton came running from the bunkhouse. Alex sent Oscar and Walton to gather the other farmers. He told them it was an emergency and they needed every person together. Everyone finished gathering in about 20 minutes, just as Guille and Grady made their way down the drive.

"Kinda thought we'd lost you for a minute there," Guille said with visible relief as he and Grady trotted the horses down the driveway.

"Sorry, man... it's just been a while," Alex lied to hide his shame.

He was angry at himself, not for coming back, but for even entertaining the idea of leaving. He'd left when things didn't go his way in the woods, again when the Sin Eaters wouldn't make an exception for him, and he'd walked right past poor Miss Cindy Lee in the garage. He'd done his walking away, it was time to stand.

Guille, Grady and Alex recounted the events of the night. It had been Guille who fired the shot that temporarily saved Ramirez while Grady had taken out the lights to give him passage. They had only fired a handful of shots each and were upset to find that their efforts had been in vain.

Alex was the one who had to tell everyone the details behind Ramirez's message. He didn't have the full story, but he made sure that they understood that the normally jovial and calm Ramirez had been so unsettled by what Carver had said about his plan for the family, he had struck him first. Guille and Grady confirmed that they had seen the same, and they all agreed it must have been truly horrible to break Ramirez's easy-going demeanor.

Alex recounted the message Ramirez had died delivering, that "they are coming for the family," and told how he had been shot in the chest and didn't have long. Walton started to seeth, he'd known Ramirez for many years as trustees and had spent many nights hanging out in the chow hall with no one else around sipping prison wine.

"We have to get out of here," Max broke the silence.

"Yeah, we need to be gone, like, yesterday," Oscar agreed.

"I'm not running," Gordon countered, and the entire group devolved into various ideas and opinions, points and counterpoints.

Alex stood silently, an entire head of height above the rest. He watched Todd, who stood still, looking around the group, then reached out and put his arm around Jessica's waist.

"I'm not leaving," he said firmly, but the crowd roared over his words.

Alex lifted his arms to chest height and swung them forward, resulting in a massive clap that silenced everyone there. "You were saying, Todd?"

"I said, I'm not leaving," Todd repeated, "we'll radio the folks in Coahoma, see if they'll let everyone in. If we move fast we can rig up something to carry a bunch of chickens and vegetables and put together a half-assed cattle, sheep and goat drive. If we can get enough going, maybe Coahomma will split with us and after this is all over, you can all come back out here to whatever is left."

"And you'll do what, exactly? Stand and fight against the entire city of Big Spring?" Donna asked her son, "You're not some John Wayne Lone Ranger character, Todd!"

"He won't be alone," Gordon said in a hushed tone as he hugged his wife from behind, "I'm staying too."

"Me too," Alex announced.

"And me," Grady stepped forward.

Walton rarely spoke in groups, but he stepped forward and grunted a noise of support as he stood next to Grady.

"Well, I'll make an even half-dozen then," Paul the chicken farmer announced as his wife tried to hold him back by the wrist.

"Seven it is," Max whispered as he stretched out a worn and calloused hand to Paul, who shook it with a smile.
Then Max's wife stepped forward as well.

"This isn't some old western movie where the men stand and die and the women run and hide from 'injuns,'" Paul's wife said, "I can shoot, I can mend injuries. I'm staying to fight for my home."

Oscar and Guille looked at one another, then around the group. They were uneasy, and it was clear that they didn't think this was a good idea and they didn't have the same loyalty to the dirt and buildings that the rest did.

"Warden," Guille started, "I'm really thankful you got me out, and I was all for being a farm worker, but this is war. People are gonna die and… and I…"

"And *we* aren't ready to die," Oscar said as Guille faltered.

"I understand, and I'm not asking you to," Todd reassured them with a smile, "I'm not asking *any* of you to. As Alex has pointed out, they really want me. They want to make an example out of me and blame things on me so they look more legitimate. I'm not asking you to stay, but will you at least help us get the families and supplies together before you cut out?"

Both men nodded, somewhat ashamed of their choice now that it had materialized into words. It might have been easier if Todd or Alex or someone else had cursed them for cowards and demanded they leave immediately, but everyone simply smiled and nodded. These people were staring down their death and smiling at the men that were too cowardly to do the same.

The group broke up without another word. Donna and Jessica would take the kids and head into town with the livestock. The plan was to get as much of a herd together as possible and send them into town. Guille and Oscar would help take them in, but they were leaving afterwards. They'd never be able to hold their heads up on the ranch after abandoning the others to fight.

Max and Paul and their wives started gathering bushels of vegetables in any kind of container they could find. They'd run ropes between two and set them on the backs of cows that were headed into town. They repeated the same plan with cages of chickens.

Grady and Gordon began going over weapons as Todd turned on the radio and tuned it to Channel 9. He called the Coahoma folks and after a few minutes was connected to the old timer that appeared to be in charge of things. He told him the situation and the old man assured him that if they sent people and livestock in they'd take them in until they needed to leave, and only asked for a quarter of whatever was sent to stay.

Alex began walking the property, rummaging through old storage areas in barns to find anything he could build traps out of. He set Walton, Oscar and Guille to pulling out supplies and putting together traps as he saw them. They would need to move quickly, but with the pressing nature of the threat they decided that using the last of their remaining fuel to power the old tractor and dig holes and fighting positions was a good investment.

Alex wished that Fragnet and the other Sin Eaters were there. They would have had a field day setting up defendable positions and fighting a good fight like this. But they weren't there and he needed to focus on what he could do. He'd picked up a lot of information and creative fighting tactics from listening to the old vets compare war stories and scars from their battles.

Their collected knowledge spanned Korea, Vietnam, the hundreds of micro-wars in Central and South America through the '80s and '90s, Eastern Europe, The Horn of Africa, Iraq, Afghanistan, and beyond. He was going to leverage every boobytrap and fighting position he'd ever heard of, from punji pits to ranger graves, Vietnamese toe poppers to fox holes. The defenders might die, but by-God the attackers would pay.

The sun was low in the sky as Donna came around with handkerchiefs that each held biscuit sandwiches, loaded with bacon, eggs, a slice of tomato and farmer's cheese. Each man was given three sandwiches, a large cup of coffee, and a bottle of water.

"No matter what happens, they aren't getting this stuff," Donna repeated over and over with a fake cheerfulness to hide the tears forming in the corners of her eyes.

Oscar and Guille tried to deny the food, saying they wouldn't need it or didn't deserve it because they were leaving. Donna refused to hear it and threatened to beat them both with a broom if they didn't stop wasting time and eat. They eventually caved, thanking her profusely with guilty smiles. They split Guille's sandwiches and wrapped the remainder to pocket for later on their journey.

Alex sawed down pieces of ¾-inch PVC pipe to about 1 ½-inch sections as Walton prepared 2X4's for the backing to their little traps. Oscar and Guille were screwing 4-inch screws into pieces of plywood and affixing hinges to one side each so they could attach and swing from the 2X4 frames they were building.

"Alright, how are we going to lock this place down?" Todd asked as he came walking up with Gordon.

"I've got some thoughts, but it's your home," Alex relied.

Todd and Gordon looked around at the assorted trap material on the ground. In their current form nothing looked particularly dangerous, but once fully assembled, camouflaged and armed, they could only imagine the absolute hell the items would wreck on anyone unfortunate enough to trip them.

"Well, the good news is that we are really flat here," Gordon mused as he looked around, "if they bring more than about a dozen folks they'll never get near us without being spotted."

"If they're good shots they could sit in that stand of trees over there and pop-off rounds at us," Grady said as he walked up.

"I figure they'll come for my house first," Todd added, "if I'm the one they want, they'll come looking for me here. I'm pretty sure they want me alive if they can swing it."

"Agreed, and you're right, if they come in the daylight with any number, we'll see them. Anyone know if they have any kind of night vision?" Alex asked.

Todd scratched the back of his head as he thought, "They might. Not much if they do, but some of the guys might have their own and they might have some for their SWAT team."

"Then coming at night might be a thing," Alex pointed out the obvious.

"I doubt they have more than a couple pairs, so unless they plan to send in some kind of 'wanna-be' SEAL team, I'm not too worried about that," Todd assured him.

The men began pointing out the areas they expected them to come from. I20 was a little over 3 and a half miles to their south, and Old Colorado Highway ran in front of them with the driveway leading right up to the front door of Todd's place. It was pretty unlikely they'd try to come from the north because they'd have to add miles of walking or driving to get in position, and if they went out to Coahoma to the east, the folks out that way that they'd come to call the "Bulldog Boys" would radio in and let them know.

"Best guess? They're going to come straight at us from the south. They can get off the highway and walk across farmland and plowed fields, come up on us the same way the last group did," Gordon proposed.

"Probably not wrong," Alex thought aloud, "we should focus our traps around buildings and some of the other options to the South and West, but let's keep an eye out on the north side and see what happens there."

Alex's gaze had drifted over Todd's shoulder, watching the brown haired, blue eyed girl come walking up with a rifle on her shoulder. As her feet crunched over the caliche, the assembled defenders turned and watched her.

"Where do you need me, Daddy?" she asked, as serious as a Ranger showing up to the front lines of a battlefield.

"You're going with Mommy," Todd told her.

"I can help!" she protested immediately, "you taught me to shoot and you need help!"

"Sweetheart, you are only eight years old. I am not going to set you up to be shot at, you are going with Mommy and your brothers and you can take your gun to help protect them. That answer is final," Todd gently scolded her.

Alex couldn't help but feel something for the little girl. It was almost like pride, maybe it was what Fragnet had felt for him when he got the call that the stray kid at the cookout had made it all the way to the club house. It wasn't his kid, but she showed no fear for what was to come, and he found that honorable.

"I want to fight," Patti said bluntly.

"And someday you will," Alex told her gently, "someday it will be your turn to plant traps and load guns. It will be your turn to stare down men that want to harm you, but today isn't that day Miss Patti. Today, you have a more important task, like your Daddy said, you need to keep your family safe on the trail to Coahoma."

"They'll be fine," she grumbled as her shoulders fell and her head sagged.

"You see to it they are, Sweetheart," Todd told her as he kissed her head, "now run along and help your Momma pack."

She turned and walked slowly towards the house, kicking a large rock into the yard as she walked. This was not the answer she had expected in her brave, innocent young mind, but she was ignorant of what was to come. She walked into the house and allowed the door to close slightly harder than usual behind her.

"We may have just saved those boys from Big Spring a whole heap of trouble," Gordon joked.

"She'd likely take them all on, and never stop smiling about it," Todd said, slightly louder than a whisper. "You know, other kids complain about the country life... the smell, the work, being out here away from town, but not Patti. She loves this place more than I do. I feel bad for Jess and Mom if they can't come back out here, because she's never going to forgive us or them."

"Then let's get set up where they can come back, and the people coming this way never forget what they started," Alex said flatly. "We'll need Ranger graves out there in that field. I'd go 5 wide and 8 deep, every 10 yards fanning out from the shack there so we can cover a wide area with them."

"What the hell is a Ranger Grave?" Todd asked.

"It's basically a small trough in the ground, only a few inches deep. You mound up some dirt in front of it and around the front sides in a 'U' shape and it's a hasty fighting position," Alex used his hands to explain the value the positions would offer, "this way, you're down low enough with enough cover to your front that you're hard to hit, but if they make it that far it doesn't give them much cover like a foxhole would, because the back portion is wide open."

"We can dig those out real quick with the backhoe on the tractor," Gordon chimed in.

"It won't take much, just remember that you only want them to be a few inches deep," Alex warned, "if you go too deep they'll have cover when they get to them."

"Got it, anything else?" Gordon asked, he'd pulled out a small pen and paper and started making notes as Alex had described the positions and pointed out how the fan would be laid out to give them fallbacks.

"Yeah, every so often, we need one that has a deep, *deep* pit. We'll make it a punji pit for them to fall into. We can mark it with stakes so we know, but they won't know what they mean until it's too late," Alex grinned as he said it.

"You're a scary man," Grady said as he walked up.

"I try," Alex shrugged.

"I think we should set up at Gordon's. They won't really expect that barn and house to be full of people. Let Max and Paul and their wives stay at their houses to the west. They'll see them coming, and if they aren't targeted, they can help flank them. We need to figure out communications though," Grady laid out his plan as he looked around.

The other men kind of froze, watching his mind work. He went on to talk about points of overwatch and running a flanking maneuver, ambushes and so on. Nobody had expected the mild-mannered former teacher to lay out battle plans quite that way. When he'd finished, he looked around at the bewildered faces and paused for a moment before smiling.

"Oh… I was a highschool *history* teacher. I did my graduate thesis on the unbalanced battles of Korea and Vietnam," he said shyly.

"Well Hell, between the monster with a flair for boobytraps and the historian who studied unbalanced warfare, we just might be okay!" Gordon chuckled.

The group continued their plans and began setting things in motion for booby traps and defensive positions to be set

210

up in key locations. It would be a couple more hours before the livestock was ready to herd out, and in the meantime there was work for everyone to do.

The field was finally quiet as the afternoon sun was just starting to hint at its golds and oranges that would later be painted across the evening sky. A final count of 38 Ranger Graves having been dug, a dozen of which had large rocks sitting next to the corners of the U-shaped embankments around them that indicated they weren't to be used by defenders.

The toe-poppers had proved somewhat difficult to set up without the proper end caps for the PVC pipes, but they had managed to rig something up. It would only take about six pounds of force to set them off, so they were set up where they were most likely to be stepped on. They had been paired with swinging door traps that would take slightly more, but would grab anyone coming to help the injured party. The final coup-de-grace would arrive from one of the truly horrible devices the men had rigged in the doorways of the buildings.

The barns had spiked balls made from chicken wire wrapped around large rocks, sharpened lengths of 2X2 boards stabbing out in all directions. They'd suspended them from a rafter on a length of rope that would hit an average sized man in the chest. They lifted them up with the bucket of the tractor and set their traps. They knew the balls were on a hair trigger as one had slipped loose and almost got Walton on his way out of the barn. He refused to go back in and help reset it.

The house had been set-up with shotguns that were tied off to the doorknobs, a single round of buckshot in the chamber and the safety off. These would make a horrible mess of the first and maybe even second man through the door, but would have almost no value if someone picked them up as they didn't have any other rounds in them.

If he'd had time Alex would have loved to set up more traps, even toying with the idea of fishing line and loose ammunition, but those wouldn't deliver the impact they needed right now. Instead, he spent his time going over the traps they *had* been able to set, looking for ways they could go wrong. He was glad Gordon had had the foresight to write down what was where so they could disarm things as needed afterwards.

Almost everyone had gathered to say their teary goodbyes to Donna, Jessica, Patti and the boys. Grady had chosen to walk out a ways into the field, where a lone tree stood. He'd climbed up and found a spot he could sit where he could look to the South and keep watch with a set of 15x binoculars that Max had received a year ago for Christmas. They'd gone from spotting for prey on deer and crane hunts to spotting for danger across a field of fighting positions and deadly traps.

Guille and Oscar were quietly standing out by the herd, trying to keep their distance rather than be forced to face their cowardice by the men and women they knew they'd never see again, one way or another. It simply wasn't in the cards though, as the large group walked over to them and exchanged hugs, well wishes and assurances of not blaming them at all. As all of the adults and the two young boys tried to hold it together, there was one clear holdout to the goodbyes. Patti was the only one that refused to cry or show sorrow.

Patti was enraged.

Alex walked over to where she stood, next to Geronimo who had been fitted with a <u>travois</u> to carry Jessica and the boys into town. Patti had refused to be loaded into it and had instead opted to walk next to the horse carrying her rifle and a backpack.

"You know how important your job is, right?" Alex asked her softly.

"I know I'm being sent away like a little kid," Patti shot back, venom hanging from her words.

"Miss Patti, what's coming is no place for a little girl, not even for a ferociously brave one like yourself," Alex told her.

Patti turned and faced the kneeling giant head on. She didn't waver, she wasn't whining or complaining or throwing a tantrum because she wasn't getting her way. Her resolve was absolute and she had no indications that she was misunderstanding what she was asking for.

"I want to help my family protect our land," Patti said frankly, "I know things are different now. If we don't hold onto this, we will have nothing."

The wisdom and resolve out of the brave little girl was almost enough to make Alex lose his balance. He closed his eyes and took a deep sigh, opening them to a steely gaze directly into his soul.

"Have you ever heard of a man named William Shakespeare?" Alex asked her.

"No," she replied, unsure of what he had to do with anything.

"He lived around 400 years ago, but he had a quote that I think was made for you," Alex smiled as he looked at her, "'*And though she be but little, she is fierce.*' You won't always be little, but remain fierce."

Patti turned the quote over in her young mind, trying to understand what that really had to do with anything that was going on at that time. So he was calling her little, great, just like everyone else. Patti turned and walked away from him, angrier now that he had called her little and didn't think she could handle herself or protect her family.

Alex stood slowly, smiling to her and hoping silently that she would remember the quote until she was old enough to understand it. She stood with her back to him, a .22 rifle slung over her back, bright pink Barbie backpack full of toys, bullets and a water bottle facing him as she pet the front shoulder of the horse.

"Good luck, fierce little one," he whispered as he turned and walked back to the group, if any one member of this group had a chance in this new world, it would be her.

They were just finishing up the rounds of goodbyes for the fourth or fifth time when the little pink radio on Todd's hip squawked to life. Everyone in the area froze, waiting to hear what Grady had to report as Todd reached down and turned the volume knob up on the little walkie talkie he'd found in his daughter's room.

"Todd, are you there?" Grady's came out, staticky but understandable.

"What's up, Grady?" he replied.

"I've got about two dozen men walking across the field out there," Grady answered, "can't tell how heavily armed they might be, but they are definitely out there about a mile away and headed towards us. There's also a couple on horseback."

"Thanks Grady, come back in before they get too close and you're out there all alone," Todd replied, turning his attention to the family. "Y'all need to get out of here, no more tears, no more goodbyes."

He quickly hugged his mother, kissed his wife and children on the foreheads, even the angry young Patti, and ordered Oscar and Guille to get them out of there. Donna mounted up on Geronimo as Jessica and the boys climbed onto the travois, Jessica pulling Patti on with them against her will. The priority was now getting out of there as soon as possible.

The two men on horseback started the makeshift drive into Coahoma. They only had about six miles total to go, and the Bulldog Boys were supposed to meet them about two and a half miles in, but it would take about half an hour to make it all the way into town. If they didn't put some major distance between themselves and the farm quickly, then the attackers might be able to track them.

Donna lead the herd out, Oscar taking up the rear and Guille using his experience to keep the edges together. They weren't cowboys of the old west by any means, but they were doing a fine job of getting things moving for the little experience they had. After they were almost out of sight, Grady arrived, huffing that he'd seen the men stop out in the middle of the field and huddle together.

"Well, it's time," Todd said as he picked up his AR15 and nodded to everyone else, "Max, Paul, y'all head home and pretend like you don't know us. You've got those walkies we found in the boy's room, listen close and call if you need us."

The two couples nodded and did quick handshakes before heading to their homes. Alex, Grady, Walton, Todd and Gordon would take up their positions. Grady and Alex in the field in the farthest out set of Ranger Graves, Walton in the next set back, and Gordon back in his barn loft, ready to handle anyone that came up on the sides. Todd was supposed to wait for them back by the house to try and talk before fighting. They were in position for a solid five minutes before they saw the men spread shoulder to shoulder coming at them.

Chapter 14

"Those are prisoners!" Grady shouted as the men came into view, "they <u>conscripted</u> prisoners!"

"Good, then they likely don't actually want to fight," Alex replied as he settled in behind the AR15 he'd been given from the prison stockpile.

Everyone was carrying a true-blue AR15 now, as well as a pistol and there were other weapons of various types positioned around the farms. They were not going to negotiate anything, but Todd had asked them to wait, wanting to try and talk to them first. Alex had tried to tell him it was a bad idea, but Todd insisted on at least trying before spilling blood.

As the conscripts lined up in the field Alex noticed that not all of them had firearms. Most of the ones that did were carrying shotguns or pistols, while others carried bats and other melee weapons. That was a good sign for the defenders, but it made him question the overall plan. Did Carver really think he was just going to ride up and walk into the farm from the south with no resistance?

A lone horseman started slowly riding forward, headed towards the house. A large part of Todd was now thankful they hadn't put any traps further out as it would have triggered confrontation before they could speak. He got up from his spot on the porch and started walking forward, carrying his rifle in the crook of his arm.

The rider continued to move at a slow pace, matching Todd's angle to arrive at the edge of the defensive positions. As he came closer he tilted his tan felt hat back and everyone could see that it was Deputy Carver on top of a white horse grinning down at them. Luckily Todd had chosen a spot that didn't give him a clear view of where the shooters were in the setting sun.

"Well, now..." Carver started, "I see my conversation with the Mexican inmate didn't die with him."

"No, *Ramirez* managed to tell someone else before he he was murdered," Todd shot back, emphasizing the name of the dead man.

"Well, appears I should've brought some more folks, but it doesn't matter. I'm not going to head all the way back and give you more time to build up," Carve said as he looked around the farm, "you're leaving with us, now. If you don't come quietly, I'm going to take in all of your family here, your mom and dad, and the inmates you've got working for you."

"I had heard that was your plan," Todd said, "but I'm not going anywhere. You've got your van back, I don't have anything else out here that belongs to you. Just go home, Orville, there's nothing out here for anyone but trouble."

"You think you get to tell me what to do? I may not have as many men as I probably should have brought, but I *know* I have more than you, and they've all been told they can stay in town and settle in if they help bring you in. You're coming with us, you and your family, especially Jessica."

"Jess isn't here," Todd said frankly, "nobody is."

"You expect me to believe you did all of this by yourself? Nobody else is here?" Carver sneered.

"Do you honestly believe a bunch of inmates would stick around to *protect* their former warden?" Todd chuckled back, "and when I found out you were coming for my family, you really think I would keep them here and let you? Damn... it's no wonder you never made Sheriff. I don't think you'd be able to figure out which end of that horse to feed if someone else didn't tell you first."

Alex, Grady, and Walton had to stifle a laugh as they heard Todd cut loose. Carver didn't find the remark nearly as funny. He adjusted himself in the saddle, looking down at Todd who simply smiled back up at him. He reached back on his belt and pulled out a set of cuffs, throwing them in the dirt in front of Todd.

"Put them on," he growled.

Todd took in a deep breath and sighed, "Orville, I got so damn bored waiting on you that after everyone left I dug a bunch of shallow holes to bury everyone you brought out. I clearly overestimated your popularity. Now get the hell off of my land or I'm going to start filling holes."

Todd turned his back on the deputy and started walking back to the house. He walked around one of the positions that had two large rocks on either corner.

"I don't have to take you alive!" Carver yelled after him.

"That's a good thing, because you won't," Todd yelled back over his shoulder, "and just so you know, that one there is for you!" he yelled as he pointed at the rocks.

Carver pulled his pistol from the holster on his hip and just as he brought it up to take aim at Todd a round split the air, narrowly missing his head. He had no idea where the bullet had come from, but it told him everything he needed to know about the situation he was in and he immediately whirled the horse around and headed back to his lines as fast as he could. Todd took off at a jog to get back to the house and bait them into running straight in.

The plan worked. Carver sent six men running straight towards the house, Gordon picked off one, and two others fell to Alex and Grady before they made the first row of fortifications.

The rest of the men began to fall back, even as Carver ordered them forward, not fully turning to run but showing no initiative to get closer to the bullets that were now flying through the air.

One of the runners carried a Glock of some type and sprinted quickly enough that he made it past the first row and dove headfirst into a slot where he intended to take cover and try to figure out where the rounds were coming from. Unfortunately for him, he chose a slot that had two medium sized rocks at the corners and landed head-first into a four-foot deep pit lined with sharpened stakes.

He screamed as the stakes pierced his body, his mouth being permanently fixed open as one went through his teeth and out his cheek. His arms desperately grabbed at the caliche on the sides of the pit but couldn't find traction to lift him off of the painful prongs that had impaled him. He slowly gave way to death spasms as his legs kicked a few times, the feet still sticking out and tapping against the rocks that had marked his bad luck.

Another runner actually ran directly past Walton, who immediately rolled on his back and used his pistol to shoot the shocked man upward through the chest, causing him to do a morbid pirouette on his way to the ground. Walton simply rolled back over and tried to ignore the terrified look the man had had on his face, and the fact that Walton remembered he had delivered letters to the inmate on more than one occasion in the past.

The final runner made it to the house and was met with a quick double-tap from Todd, who had resumed his position on the porch. He stepped forward, somewhat comfortable in his current position, leaned up against one of the uprights that held the roof over the wrap-around porch.

"You wanna keep sending them six at a time, that'll work for me!" he yelled confidently.

"I might just do that!" Carver yelled back across the field from about three hundred yards away.

Alex couldn't help but feel like this was too easy. Even for a sadist like Carver it didn't make sense to just send men to their death over one enemy, especially now that he knew that enemy wasn't actually alone. Alex did his best to scan the area, trying to figure out what he was missing. He noticed another man riding a horse turn to Carver and tell him something. Something that made the asshole smile.

Not a minute later a shot rang out from behind the defenders, one single explosion followed by a blood curdling scream, and then more screams shortly after, rising in crescendo of pain. Alex turned to look at Todd, who seemed far less confident in this moment, and then he jumped up and ran from his fighting position back to the porch.

A handful of rounds went off as the giant man ran across the field, not stopping to dive into any other positions, simply doing his best to change his pace and run irregularly until he got close enough he could yell to Todd.

"They're trying to flank us!" Alex yelled.

"We need to go see how many there are," Todd replied as he turned to go inside the house.

Alex had closed the remaining distance and grabbed him by the collar to pull him back at the last second. Apparently Todd had already forgotten about the nasty surprise that awaited whoever opened that door. The two men ran around the far side of the house as bullets popped and whizzed by them, slamming into the hundred plus year old clapboard siding.

The sun was starting to paint the sky and they would normally be coming in for a home cooked dinner at the hands of

Donna, Jessica and the others. There was no time to reminisce about what they had eaten before though, because as they came to the front corner of the house they saw six men wearing SWAT gear coming around the corner of the barn.

They appeared to set up a security point before two of them returned around the corner of the barn and dragged three more similarly clad bodies back out. They all seamed to be alive, although the trauma to their lower limbs was easy to spot, bleeding through the makeshift bandages they had used to cover them.

The toe-popper had been incredibly successful, two of the four rounds had gone off, blowing off the vast majority of the operator's left foot. When he'd gone down two others ran to help him and their feet hit the boards that covered the swinging fall traps, their body weight causing the ten-pound test zip ties to break loose and fall about a foot down.

While the three-inch long spikes at the bottom of the pit were no picnic, the natural reaction of pulling your foot back up would find nothing but more spikes, screws, and nails pointed at a downward angle on pieces of board that fell in around your leg. This was the fate of two more of the SWAT officers. It had taken their teammates a few minutes of causing them excruciating pain to realize what was going on. They had grabbed the injured men by their gear and tried to pull them straight out of the holes, only to find that they were driving the spikes deeper into their legs. The three injured men were propped up against the side of the barn as two more of the team stood at the door, preparing to open the door.

For a moment Todd wanted to warn them, to somehow stop them from being injured. Once upon a time, if they had been injured he would have snuck them a flask of bourbon in the hospital. If they had been killed he would have been at the funeral, and later at the bar listening to the stories of their lives. Now, he was not only silently watching as they were injured and more were about to be killed, but he had been the one to help set the traps.

As they threw the door in and made entry, repeating the movements they had practiced and executed a thousand times as a team, they planned for men to be inside. They planned for gunfire and having to find cover. They planned to get out of the <u>fatal funnel</u>, but they hadn't planned on a giant, rock-filled, spiked ball swinging from the rafters and striking them both, crushing them into the wall and impaling them.

They were down to only 4 able bodied men and 3 wounded ones. Todd saw the remaining men grab the injured ones and drag them into the barn. As this grizzly scene had unfolded before them more and more shots were going off behind them. It seemed that the team was calling in their dwindling numbers and Carver was trying another approach.

"We've cut their numbers in half and haven't had to do anything yet," Alex observed, "but those four that are left, they're coming for blood."

"Yeah, and I know those guys, they are good at what they do," Todd replied.

Alex moved back around the front of the house and watched as Carver pulled back another hundred yards, less than half of his people left from his attacks on the line. Alex could see bodies stacked on the wrong side of fighting positions and hear screams from men still impaled in the pits. He was relieved to see that Walton and Grady were still firing, although they had pulled back to the last two rows of fortification.

Alex pulled up his rifle and took aim at the arrogant deputy on the back of his horse. It would be a long shot, but he had a chair he could brace on, cover behind a corner of the house to take his time, Todd at his back to make sure he wasn't snuck up on. He could make the shot.

He settled in behind the chair and leaned against the house. He took a deep breath, exhaling as he settled the red dot about a foot over Carver's hat. He slowly squeezed the trigger back, waiting for the rifle to bark in his hands and split the sound barrier as it flew forward and split Carver's head.

Millimeters before Carter's life came to an end, gunshots broke out from behind Gordon's house, in the direction of Max and Paul's homes. Alex relaxed his finger, coming off the sights as Todd yelled that they had to go help them. Alex sighed quickly, knowing Todd was right, but wishing he had just finished the shot.

As they came around the back of the house bullets flew by them from the two SWAT officers still outside. The rest of the team was inside the barn, likely trying to bring some comfort to those who were injured. Todd immediately returned fire, striking the nearest one in the chest and sending him to a heap. As the other turned to grab his partner and drag him back he exposed his side where there was no armor and Alex fired, killing the officer instantly with rounds through the lungs and heart.

They closed the distance, knowing that the biggest value they could be was to try to take the highly trained, highly equipped warriors out of the game. As they ran up, Todd told Alex to cover the door and he ran over to the two injured men, confirming that the one Alex had shot was dead, then moving on to the man he had shot in the chest.

He was breathing, the rounds having stopped in his plate armor. Todd grabbed the moaning man by the arm and flipped him over, grabbing a set of cuffs from the officer's own belt and cuffing his hands together behind his back. It wouldn't take him out of the fight permanently, and anyone who came by could help free him, but it was a start, and kept Todd from having to kill him.

They were in the process of trying to take the flashbang grenades from the pouches of the two officers when they heard the feet on the gravel to their right. Alex and Todd froze. Even if Alex wanted to swing his rifle over and try to take a shot at the men that were screaming for him to freeze and drop it, he wouldn't have been fast enough. Todd's rifle was slung to his back as he dug through the pouches of the men on the ground. They were done.

They'd thought the last two able bodied fighters were in the barn, but apparently they had moved over to a small outcropping of trees and were supposed to be covering the doorway. They hadn't had an angle to see Alex and Todd coming, but when their teammates went down, they had a plan, and now they had the drop on them. They stood over them, getting ready to call in their victory on the radio when a bright light flashed from the side of the road.

The nearest officer's throat exploded in a crimson geyser, covering Alex's face and chest, the dying man collapsing on top of him. The other officer spun and emptied the entire 30 round magazine of his rifle into the side of the road, the rounds smacking the dirt all around a small pink backpack lying on the shoulder of the road.

There were around thirty men walking down the road as Paul pretended to tend the rest of the chickens that had been left behind. He was absently tossing feed as the men walked by, each one carrying a rifle and looking down the road at the sound of gunfire.

"Y'all going to go take care of all that racket?" Paul yelled to them as they walked by.

"Oh, we'll be taking care of it, Mister. Now get back in the house before you get too involved," one of them said.

"Isn't that a cop's house?" Paul asked.

"Not anymore, now get inside!" another man yelled.

Paul had heard enough. These were the men he had been waiting for, and he looked up at the window of the house where his wife was pretending to cook dinner. He nodded to her and she stepped away from the window back into the house. Paul wiped his hands on his pants and walked inside.

When he closed the door behind him his wife already had the two rifles and a small bag of magazines on the kitchen table. The small green walkie talkie had been liberated from the little boy's room and the toy now found itself next to actual weapons of war, waiting to fulfill its job of alerting the rest of the team that there was danger in the area. Paul picked it up and turned the little toy on, pressing the flimsy plastic button to make his call.

"Max, they came by, about 30 as best I can tell," Paul said.

"Okay, we'll head over there and wait for the call," came the reply.

As the sun continued to sink in the sky, the two older couples gathered in Paul's home. They looked over the weapons and made sure everyone remembered how to use them. They poured a glass of the whiskey they kept for special occasions. They pulled out the King James and said a prayer together. After saying Amen and giving Paul's wife a moment to wash the glasses and put them in the drying rack, they stepped outside into the last remnants of light left.

They would only have about twenty minutes to do their job, but if they were successful, they might save a lot of lives. Paul and Max would go forward, casually walking with the rifles slung over their back until they found where the men who had walked by were stopped. Their wives would be next to them, each holding their hand, pistols tucked into their bags next to the magazines they would need.

As they walked, they told stories of old times and brought up names most of them hadn't heard in years. They found the 30 or so men standing behind Gordon's house, looking for a way to flank the men who were firing in the field. They were gesturing to the barn, back to the house and then over to Todd's house. There really wasn't any time to debate, or anywhere to bother trying to get cover. The two old men simply gave one another a nod and brought their rifles around to the front.

An explosion of gunfire erupted from behind Gordon's barn, and almost as though it had been planned as a signal, the riders took off to the west leaving the four conscripts standing in the field. The men seemed confused, searching for what they were supposed to do before finally coming to the unspoken group consensus that their best bet would be to run away.

Grady desperately wanted to turn and see what was happening, but he noticed that the horsemen had turned north again, skirting the most distant edges of the fields, and he knew it was his job to keep the south side as secure as he could.

"You alright, Walton?" he yelled.

"Yup, you?" came the short reply.

"I guess as good as I can be," Grady grimaced as the groans and moans of the men in the pits or those who were gutshot in the field began to rise.

Maybe they had been there the entire time, maybe it was the ringing in his ears fading and he was just starting to hear them clearly. Maybe it was the adrenaline leaving his system and his mind being able to process more information. It didn't really matter, it was horrible. The sun was sinking quickly in the sky and it wouldn't be long before they couldn't fight anymore anyway.

"Bring it in, I'll cover!" Gordon yelled from the barn loft where he'd been taking precision shots from his hunting rifle.

He was frustrated that he didn't have a good shot on the men on horseback, but as the men on foot came in he could pick them off as needed. Grady came trotting up first with the older Walton following behind out of breath.

"I'll take care of this area. That should be Max and Paul shooting now," Gordon yelled down from his loft, "go help them out."

Grady simply nodded and worked his way to the front corner of the barn to get the lay of the land on what was going on. Walton shrugged and sighed heavily, shuffling as fast as he could behind his partner.

They turned the corner just in time to see Max take two bullets to the chest and go down, his wife diving on him and trying to shield him from any further wounds. Her efforts were rewarded with a half-dozen rounds slamming into her back. They would lay where they'd fallen, not so much as a breath from their bodies again.

Paul was on one knee trying to fire his rifle into the mass of confused men in front of them as his wife lay on the ground handing him magazine after magazine and shooting her own pistol into the crowd. It had been just over a minute since the two men had fired their first rounds into the backs of the unsuspecting force hiding behind the house, and the tide had clearly turned against the invaders.

Grady didn't have a great angle to help them, but he braced on the side of the barn and started picking off stragglers with shots as he could get them. He watched as Paul and his wife tried to do a kind of reverse crawl away, never turning their backs. It seemed to be working alright until Paul took a round to his shoulder, spinning him and throwing him to the ground. His wife lay down next to him and started trying to pull him backwards towards the side of the road.

Just as Walton arrived, Grady chose to run up to the corner of the house that the shooters couldn't see. Walton picked up the shooting from the corner of the barn and Grady started working his way around the house to shoot at the one protected corner the other side had. He heard men shouting behind him but knew he couldn't help them all.

He found a place to start shooting down the road-facing side of Gordon's house and started letting loose. He only had one more magazine in his pocket, but was going to be well worth the risk with the ease of the shots. He watched the men gathered at the corner fall and panic, unsure of where to run to. From their perspective it must have seemed like there were bullets coming from every angle.

Grady couldn't help but chuckle in his head as he saw the men scatter. This was the classic challenge of conscription: the conscripts didn't believe in the battle. They weren't fighting for something that mattered to them, they were fighting because they were being told to. These men had apparently decided that they were done fighting and were choosing to run.

Just as the tide looked to be turning, the horsemen came riding up and started to regroup the men that were left. The initial counter attack by the two couples had been well executed, and took them completely by surprise. It had cut the numbers of the attackers by around two-thirds within a minute and now Walton and Grady were thinning them even further.

As Carver came riding up he saw Walton at the corner and immediately turned and drew on the old man, leveling his pistol and squeezing multiple rapid rounds into the corner of the barn. Walton crumpled over against the corner of the barn and slid down to the floor. Grady lifted his rifle slightly and squeezed off three rounds in rapid order. The first pierced the ear of the horse, but before it could rear up in surprise and pain the second round struck Carver in the high chest, just above the coverage of his plate. The third round shortened his suffering considerably by striking just above his lip to the left of his nose.

As the horse reared up and turned to run, Carver's body started to topple off the back, one foot staying tangled in the stirrup as the horse bolted away and dragged the limp, lifeless body behind it.

Grady turned to take aim on the next rider, but was greeted with a shower of splintered wood as a round impacted the corner of the house next to his head. He felt the searing pain of the wood splinters as they peppered his cheek, neck and eye. He had to spin back around behind the building to take cover now that he could no longer see from his left eye.

The fighting was dying down as the two remaining horsemen turned back to the road and rode away. Grady was regaining his composure, watching the men chase after their leaders on horseback, begging for help. He cautiously walked down the side of the house, watching the dead and dying as he went. He made it to Paul and found his wife still alive, her right shoulder destroyed from two bullets that had impacted at the same time into the ball joint, but she would likely live.

Grady helped her to the barn where Gordon came down and helped patch her up. They pulled Walton's body inside as well, laying him down gently among the loose straw. Grady wanted to go back out and look for Todd and Alex, but Gordon made him sit. He assured Grady that the wounds to his face were far worse than he thought, and that he needed to sit down.

Gordon was dressing Grady's wounds when they heard the shouting that was soon overwhelmed by shooting.

The scream from the shoulder of the road by the pink bag could have caused the Devil's blood to run cold. It clearly wasn't a man's scream in any way, and it wasn't a woman's. Alex froze, he knew that bag.

The officer turned and dove at Todd, wrapping him up and trying to land blow after blow on the agonized father. Alex took off at a full sprint. He couldn't see Patti, but he knew she had to be near that bag. He ran over, not processing the rounds that were flying by him, oblivious to where they were coming from.

He slid to his knees at the side of the road to find Patti curled up, holding her shoulder, whimpering ever so softly. He scooped her up, using his body to shield her from the rounds that were still finding their way towards him. He could feel something, the occasional thud against his back, but he was focused. He lifted her gently with one giant arm, and carried her to the other side of the road, laying her down in a gully where the bullets couldn't find her.

As he laid her down in the dust she grimaced slightly. Alex opened her shirt and looked at her shoulder in the fading light, and exhaled heavily. It was a grazing wound. It would leave a nasty scar, but short of an infection she wasn't in any danger. He could feel the tears welling up in his eyes.

"You stay down Miss Patti," he said softly.

"I just wanted to help," Patti sobbed, "I ran away from Momma when she took her eyes off of me. I saw that man pointing a gun at you and Daddy and I had to help."

Epilogue

It was an absolute scorcher today. The West Texas sun was beating down mercilessly on the cattle in the field, and even though they bellowed in protest they simply chewed their cud and continued on with life. She looked out over the herd with her piercing blue eyes, brushing curly brown hair back behind her ear and tucking it under her hat.

She watched as her husband and a ranch hand from town circled the herd and cut a couple of cows out for breeding. They would bring them in and pen them up with the bull they'd traded for last month, hopefully bringing some fresh blood into the herd. Her son, Todd, was playing with some wooden toys his namesake grandfather had carved for him. She turned and gazed out to the corner of the field by Grandpa Gordon's old barn where they had buried her father last summer. The dirt was still slightly mounded and looked different from here.

Mom was to his left, resting peacefully where they had put her when she passed from a nasty fever four years ago. Dad hadn't been the same since she died, but he'd pressed on to see Todd born and built some core memories with him. As she reminisced, a beautiful, curly haired girl in her mid-teens came riding up on a deep brown horse.

"Brownie Too is getting better under the saddle, Mom," she said as the young horse fought to stand still.

The dark brown mare had energy to burn and chomped at her bit as she pawed the dirt and eyed the open fields wildly. She wanted nothing more than to run, and every shiver of tight muscle under her skin showed it.

"Good to hear, Alexandra," the woman replied with a smile, "go ahead, run it out of her."

The young girl smiled back, brushing curly brown hair back under her bandana and raking her spurs into the sides of the horse. Brownie Too's eyes got wide and she took off like a shot from a gun, kicking her heels together on her hind hooves and whinnying loudly as she streaked across the field.

The mother grinned and gave a loud whoop, followed by a cheer of "Get her, Alex!"

Patti rode over to the house slowly, dismounting her horse and turning back to the barn as she sipped water from a canteen she always carried. She could still see the mound that was her father's resting place, and she knew her mother's spot to his left, but the oldest grave there was the one on his right.

She remembered the day her father returned from work with the terrifying men. The silly Hispanics that talked funny and couldn't make up their minds whether or not they wanted to speak English or Spanish, the mulatto-skinned Grady who was blind in one eye that now lived in town and ran the trading post. He would sneak her children candy every time they came in to trade.

She also remembered The Rebel. The terrifying mountain of a man with long black hair and hard features. The one who had left the black and chrome Harley in their barn where it still sat to this day. He was gentle and smart every time he spoke with her, and even though he had only lived with them for a week or so, he had fought harder than anyone before or since to keep them safe. Her father had often talked about how smart Alex was, the deep meaning behind what he said and the esoteric references he would talk about. One week in their lives, and her father had visited his grave every single day of the rest of his life. He often referred to him as his best friend.

The wind blew across the yard, rustling her hair and rattling the dry leaves in the old live oak in front of her family home. She couldn't help but smile as she rubbed the scar on her arm and thought of Alex. How could one man love so much? She looked back at her young daughter, riding like lightning across a field that once housed traps and death.

She smiled, and whispered, "*And though she be but little, she is fierce.*"

Afterword and Acknowledgements

The American West has always held a wild and indomitable spirit. It was once associated with only the absolute toughest of people, many believing that only a fool or a mad man would venture there. Modern technology and travel have introduced highways, air conditioning, and food options that never existed in this rough land because they really weren't *meant* to. This land was only for the rugged, and after an event like what has happened in this series, it will return to that unique few.

I know. It's hard to say goodbye to someone we get to know and learn to care about. I hope you enjoyed Rebel's Redemption. I hope you laughed at Oscar's antics, and were angry when Ramirez died. Dear Reader, it's a sad fact that even the hardest, strongest, most prepared of us will not live forever, especially not in a world like this.

Alex was such a wonderful character to get to know, and I've enjoyed writing his story. In many ways he is a reflection of many people I've met in my travels. He wants nothing more than to do good, and even to *be* good, but his life's path simply isn't laid out like that. I hope his valor brought you peace as well.

Just know that not all of these stories from the edges of the Crown Acres world will end this way. These will not be a way for me to introduce and kill off beloved characters, but rather, a way to tell stories from the far corners of Clint's world, providing different struggles and different points of view.

I hope you enjoyed meeting Alex as much as I enjoyed introducing you to him. Stay tuned for the next installment of the Crown Acres series, *Hard Frost*.

Oscar's Prison Paella

It's no secret that those on the inside of the penal system have their own culture, and recipes are often a reflection of that culture. Here is a sample recipe of Oscar's Prison Paella, embracing the idea of doing the best you can with what you have.

Ingredients:

6-10 Slices of Pepperoni
1 package of Beef or Shrimp Ramen Noodles
1 package of Canned Squid
15-20 Saltines
1 Medium Potato (if available)
1 Medium Bell Pepper (if available)
1 Small Cooking Onion (if available)

Instructions:

Dice the pepperoni, potatoes, onions and peppers, then place in the water for the noodles, bring to a boil. Add the Ramen noodles, flavor packet, and squid pieces. Cook until all ingredients are soft. Crumble the Saltines into the liquid to create a paste. Enjoy?

Knowledge Center

After feedback from readers I've reorganized the Knowledge Center to be alphabetical. It can be difficult to track what you've learned from books like this. I hope that giving you a concise list of knowledge points from the book will help you to build your own capabilities and resources should you ever find yourself in this world. Don't forget to reference Books 1 and 2 for the <u>Knowledge Center</u> learnings from there!

A Poem: A reference to "Forgiveness" by George William A.E. Russell

Armadillo: While most readers will know what an armadillo is, it's a common misconception that they can't be eaten. Although they may look like an up-armored opossum (which you most certainly do NOT want to eat unless you absolutely MUST), armadillo is a delicacy in some regions of Mexico and the American Southwest.

B-Pillar: The area of a car behind the front driver and passenger doors that provides support to the roof.

Bight: a section of rope that is used for tying a knot. The are *in* the knot is a bite, but the ends that go in either direction are called "leads."

Blackjack: A Blackjack is a type of blunt, striking weapon that traces back as far as the Renaissance with Sand Clubs or the "slungshot" clubs of the Apache. The idea is to fill leather, cotton or another soft material with something heavy like birdshot from a shotgun round and then strike someone.

Booby Traps: There are a wide array of hasty booby traps and fighting positions that can be prepared with limited time. Some, like the punji pit or the toe popper, merely involve digging a small hole and placing a dangerous device inside like spikes or shotgun shells hovering over a nail. Others, like the Ranger Grave or the Fox Hole are for defenders, to be able to drive off an invading force while sustaining as little damage as possible.

Bow Up: When someone stands at maximum size, rolls their shoulders back and chest out and tries to appear as large and intimidating as possible.

Butt Stroke: A maneuver where the back end or "butt" of a rifle or shotgun is used as a club or blunt weapon to strike a person. It is not so much swung (like a bat) as it is shoved by the hand of the person who is holding it.

Caliche: (ke'leCHe) A naturally occurring type of soil that combines limestone and clay to result in a cement-like layer that is incredibly hard when dry and becomes slick on the surface when lightly wet and incredibly sticky mud when heavily saturated.

Cholo Shorts: "Cholo" is a style of dress and culture that is commonly associated with Latin Americans in the Southern/Southwestern part of the United States, often tied-into gang culture.

Chow Hall: A cafeteria where meals are eaten.

Clowning On: To joke around, tease or generally goof off. Clowning on someone usually involves good-natured insults or teasing.

Conscripts: An ancient practice of making prisoners fight battles for a leader, often motivated by promises of freedom and in extra glorious cases wealth.

Driller: A prison tattoo artist.

Fatal Funnel: A term used in room clearing and close quarters battle that indicates a doorway. This point of entry is considered especially dangerous and should be exited as soon as you are in the room.

Fragnet: Many motorcycle clubs use "road names" or nicknames when they ride. These are often awarded by other members of the club and have some type of story behind them.

GMRS: General Mobile Radio Service; 462 MHz and 467MHz channels for two-way communication, usually without use of repeaters. A pretty basic "walkie talkie" like you could buy at Walmart by Midland or Cobra.

Grade: Basically a "mutt" for horses. Nothing special, no specific breed or lineage, just a good, solid work horse.

Hangaround: A rank below prospect. You are not connected to and have no claim to the club, and the club has on connection to and offers no benefits/protection to you.

Hooch: Prison alcohol; an odd mix between wine and hard liquor it's usually made by fermenting fruits from the chow hall with yeast bought from the commissary. It's all cooked in a plastic bag in a plastic bucket for weeks and hidden under a bed or somewhere that can hide the smell of rotting fruit. When it was ready, it would be strained through a shirt into gatorade bottles for distribution.

Knuckleheads...: Different types of Harley Davidson motors. Harley changed their motors based on modern technology with the engines mentioned here ranging in production dates from 1936-1983.

Less-Lethal Rounds: OC Pepper is similar to pepper spray except that it creates a cloud instead of a concentrated stream. The rubber pellet rounds contain around 15-20 rubber pellets that spread and engage an area target or multiple targets at certain ranges. These two rounds are rarely lethal unless there is an allergic reaction to the OC or very specific strike from a small pellet. Sandbag rounds can be lethal if fired to the wrong area at too close of a range.

Long-Gun: General term for any non-pistol gun, often used when you can't tell if it's a shotgun or rifle.

Midnight: Remember that the moon acts much like the sun, and if you face due-south it will be midnight when it's at its highest point in the night sky.

PC: Protective Custody; a part of the prison system that is reserved for those who cannot be put in the general population for their own safety, often reserved for pedophiles and dirty cops.

"Petter": Slang term for pedophile, most common in prisons. Pedophiles are one of few categories of inmate that are despised by all others and are often in danger on a daily basis from the inmates themselves.

Phalanx: An infantry formation of personnel standing shoulder to shoulder in rank and file, covering one another with shields and armament.

Poacher's Knot: A very common knot that many have tied a thousand times without realizing what it was called. The end result of the knots that Alex has tied is a center loop that will not change in shape and two side loops that will tighten down easily.

Pro Se Defendants: To represent oneself in legal matters; according to Abraham Lincoln "The man who represents himself has a fool for a client." Lincoln believed that it was always better to have counsel than to go it alone in these matters.

Prospect: Prospects are not "full members" of the club and can be thought of as "probationary." Many times they are allowed to wear certain patches that attach them to the club but are not allowed full colors.

Raw Milk: While milk can be consumed directly from the animal the lack of pasteurization can result in certain food borne illnesses being transmitted. This includes bacterial issues that can lead to diarrhea, cramping, vomiting and even paralysis.

Rebels MC: Oftentimes what most people think of as a motorcycle gang or outlaw group is internally referred to as simply a motorcycle club as they try to claim legitimacy in the eyes of the law. This is meant to be a <u>FICTIONAL</u> organization, not to be confused with the <u>ACTUAL</u> Rebels in Australia.

Red Dot: A "red dot" is a common term for any non-magnified optic on rifles, shotguns and/or pistols. These optics help with target acquisition and are extremely effective at mid to short range. They can be paired with a magnifier if desired to extend their functionality.

ROE: Rules of Engagement; these are guidelines given to military personnel around how to treat locals, the circumstances under which they can engage combatants and how to maneuver within cities and areas that are sensitive in nature to the overall war effort. These are often viewed as highly restrictive by military personnel and have often been criticized as costing human lives on both sides.

Roving Patrols: The military would call these "walking teams" a roving patrol. Of all of the defensive tactics that can be employed by a group, a random roving patrol is one of the most effective for defense and problematic for attackers as you can never tell exactly when someone will walk up on you.

Sergeant At Arms: One of the leaders in a motorcycle club, under the President, Vice President, Treasurer, Secretary, and Road Captain. May also be known as an Enforcer, it's his job to keep the peace and make sure rules are followed at all costs.

Shank vs Shiv: A shank is a term for an improvised weapon primarily used to puncture or stab a target, whereas a shiv is a slashing weapon, designed to cut. Improvised examples could be filing down a toothbrush handle to sharpened point (shank) or heating it with a lighter and embedding a razor blade into the handle (shiv).

Shot Caller: Gang leaders.

Shovelhead: The name for the V-Twin engines used by Harley Davidson Motor Company between 1966 and 1984.

Solar Still: A solar still is a device that creates condensation in an almost completely sealed area, thus creating water out of thin air. It's a rather inefficient method and only creates a small amount (at best), but is passive in nature and once built requires no manual labor to utilize.

Solar Plexus: A bundle of nerves in the abdomen near the diaphragm. Easy target for sucker punches and powerful blows.

Tack: General term for the "stuff" used to ride horses. Tack can include saddles, blankets, scabbards, saddlebags, bridles, halters, reigns, bits, and a variety of other items.

The People's Elbow: A wrestling move made famous by Dwayne "The Rock" Johnson that involved swinging his arm full circle and dropping onto an unconscious opponent on the mat.

To Each According: This is the controversial quote that is often cited by Marxist fans about the distribution of goods. It's also the reason that many anti-Socialist and anti-Communist advocates (like myself!) say it will never work.

Travois: A method of moving people or goods on two joined poles that are attached to an animal to pull. One end of each pole rises to the animal's back as the other end is dragged along the ground. The two are joined in the middle by another piece of wood, animal skin, netting, or some other device to create a load bearing area.

Trustee: An inmate with an outstanding, positive record who is given a specific job that incurs certain privileges such as freedom of movement or less manual tasks.

Unbalanced Battles: While almost every battle is unbalanced in one way or another, significant differences in size, equipment, technology, and logistics often dictate the victor, but not always. These battles were a smaller, less equipped, less/equally technological group won over a larger one are often studied in depth by historians.

Well: The well is the large open area in front of the judge in a courtroom.

www.ingramcontent.com/pod-product-compliance
Lightning Source LLC
Chambersburg PA
CBHW060315260626

47160CB00007B/2623